Shifter's Moon

A Katie Bishop Novel

LUANNE BENNETT

For all the believers who kicked my ass along the way.

"Is there anything else I need to know about you?" I wondered if our entire relationship had been based on a lie. "CIA? Prison record? Please don't tell me you have a wife and a kid back in Atlanta." I gave him a sudden glance. "If you're even from Atlanta."

Jackson sank deeper into his chair and released the pent-up air he'd trapped in his lungs. We were about to have an unpleasant conversation, and honestly, I wasn't sure I was up for it. Until now our relationship had been easy. None of the drama I was used to with all the other men from my past. I wondered when that bubble of contentment would burst and if I'd cut and run like usual.

But then there was the part about me loving him.

He'd dropped a bombshell on me that afternoon that made me question his honesty. Lying was a deal breaker, even by omission. Apparently Jackson Hunter had a substantial roll of cash stuffed in his mattress, and now he had a dangerous pack of bikers heading to Savannah to get their hands on it. Not just any bikers—shifters.

"Why don't you start by telling me how you got the money. I'd kind of like to know if I'm sleeping with a thief."

He clutched his heart dramatically and then lifted out of his chair and headed for the kitchen. We'd gone our separate ways after having lunch at Lou's Diner that afternoon, and he was waiting on my doorstep when I got home from MagicInk, a bottle of tequila in his hand. He grabbed two glasses from the cabinet and headed for the patio door.

"Since when do you drink tequila?" I asked.

He smirked. "Something else you don't know about me."

"Great," I muttered, following him outside.

He poured two shots and handed me one. I downed it but decided to forego another when he reached for my empty glass.

"Uh-uh," I said, shaking my head. "I'll stay sober for this."

"When we met, you asked me what I did for a living," he began, sitting down in one of the metal chairs.

"Here we go," I groaned. Mr. Perfect was about to break my heart into tiny little pieces.

He downed his own drink and dropped the glass on the table, giving me a look that suggested I should shut up and listen. "Now why is it you assume I'm about to tell you I'm a thief?"

I flicked my eyes up to his but didn't respond. He was right. Assuming the worst was a bad habit of mine. The Sapanths were probably a perfectly respectable pack of feline shifters who just happened to ride motorcycles and every now and then killed people.

I bobbed my head thoughtfully. "You're right, Jackson. I should give you a chance to explain."

"The pack has a lot of different revenue streams. One of those 'streams' is to marry off their women to rich men." He glanced at me with a smirk. "You'd be surprised at how much a man will pay for his own personal cat woman."

"That's disgusting," I replied, imagining a father and mother marrying their daughter off to the highest bidder.

He looked at me curiously. "You think that's unusual?"

I couldn't argue with him. Arranged marriage was as old as time. It just seemed a little foreign in my own backyard.

"One of their most profitable streams of income is bounty hunting. Now that's where the real money comes from." He poured himself another shot and eased back into his chair, spreading his long legs wide as he sipped his tequila. "Nothing like tracking down some low-life piece of shit and getting paid for it."

"So you hunted down criminals and turned them in to the authorities?"

With a bitter laugh, he took another sip. "Not exactly. We hunted down whomever—or whatever—we were hired to and then turned them over to the person with the money."

An image of the Mafia popped into my head. "Please don't tell me you're running from the mob, Jackson." My dragon went into defensive mode, sending a wave of heat through me at the thought of a bunch of ruthless killers riding into town and storming my shop.

This time his laugh was sincere. "Kaleb would get a real hard-on from hearing that comparison, but I wouldn't call the Sapanths an organized group of Sicilian killers," he said, setting his glass on the table and leaning on his knees. "But they are killers, Katie."

Kaleb was the leader of the Sapanths, and Jackson was on his shit list. After a brief affair with Kaleb's daughter, Kara, he'd left Atlanta and come down to Savannah. Apparently Kaleb thought he could compel Jackson to rejoin the family. This time by marrying Kaleb's daughter and handing over his money as a bride-price.

"How much?" When he hesitated to say the figure, I said, "Come on, Jackson, I'm not a gold digger. I just want to know the scope of this clusterfuck you're in."

"Two million," he announced unceremoniously. "Give or take a little for living expenses."

"You've got two million dollars?" I'd known some pretty rich people back in New York City, and I guess in today's market that amount of money was chicken scratch. But you could live damn well on two million dollars. "Where is it?" I snorted. "Stuffed in your mattress?" Jackson's apartment was cramped and inconvenient, which was why we never went there. But suddenly that mattress of his was all I could think about. When he just sat there staring at me, I lost my cocky grin. "Tell me you're joking?"

"No, Katie," he replied, tilting his head. "I don't have two million dollars stuffed inside my mattress. But you don't just walk into a bank and hand the teller that much cash either." He let out a frustrated sigh and rubbed his eyes. "Knowing where the money is will put a target on your back. It's stashed somewhere safe. I earned it, and Kaleb's gonna have to go through me to get his hands on it."

Which brought up my next question. "Exactly how did you earn that much money?" Maybe I shouldn't have asked. That kind of cash usually came from illegal activities, like murder for hire, but I was willing to accept the consequences of his answer.

I *needed* to know.

He must have read my thoughts, because suddenly he looked a little offended. Betrayed by the one person he should have been able to confess all his secrets to without getting that kind of look.

"Jackson—" I began, realizing the accusations that must have been oozing from my eyes.

"She was a kid," he said before I could backtrack and wipe the judgment off my face. "Nine years old."

"Who?"

He got up and turned his back to me, staring out at the darkness. "They found her floating in the Chattahoochee River. She'd been—" His voice dropped to a muffled string of words that I couldn't make out. Then his shoulders expanded as he breathed

4

in and continued. "The cops called it molestation, but rape is rape."

Hearing the words "kid" and "rape" in the same conversation made me feel sick as I poured that second shot of tequila I'd refused earlier.

"Was she alive?" I asked without knowing who she was or what the story had to do with two million dollars.

He shook his head. "Stabbed seventeen times. They caught the animal who did it. His DNA was all over the girl."

I downed the booze and waited for him to continue.

"Escaped the death sentence due to some bullshit about his state of mind at the time of the murder. Got life instead, but that wasn't enough for her father. I happen to agree with that."

Me too, I thought.

"We were hired to get our hands on him before he reached the state prison in Reidsville."

"You and Kaleb?"

He nodded. "And Cairo. We were paid eight million to deliver him to the girl's father—alive. Kaleb took an extra chunk. Finder's fee, he called it. We split the rest."

The word "alive" was a small relief. For a moment I thought he was going to confess to murdering the man for money. Jackson wasn't a saint by any stretch of the imagination, and he'd admitted to killing someone in the past. *It was justified*, he'd said. I wondered if this was the justified murder he was referring to. Maybe it was Jackson's job to finish him off after his client took his pound of flesh from the monster.

"I guess you succeeded," I said. "That's a lot of money to deliver someone to a client—alive."

His brow arched. "Do you have any idea what it takes to hijack a prison transport bus?"

Not really. But now that he had me thinking about it, I imagined it probably involved a lot of guns.

"Never underestimate a grieving father, Katie. A very wealthy father. The man probably would have paid us twice as much if we'd asked for it. Hell, I would have done it pro bono to see that piece of shit put in the ground."

I stared at my formidable boyfriend standing at the edge of the patio. With his size and unusual strength, I understood why people would seek him out to pull off the impossible. Not to mention the fact that he used to ride with a club of dangerous shifters. I wondered how that worked, connecting potential clients with the Sapanths.

"Kaleb was the mastermind behind the guns-for-hire scheme," he told me before I could ask. "We stopped short of killing people for money. That was a line I wouldn't cross. It's also the reason I left."

I glared at him, remembering our conversation on this same patio months ago. "I thought you said you left because Kaleb killed your best friend for messing around with his daughter? You said he was about to kill you for the same reason."

"The part about Kaleb killing Pete is true, but it wasn't for sleeping with Kara. If that's all it took to trigger him, he'd be cleaning up a hell of a lot of bodies." He smirked and shook his head. "We barely knew each other when we had that conversation, Katie. What was I supposed to tell you?"

"So tell me the truth now, Jackson." It was an invitation to redeem himself. To help me understand who I was in love with.

"Pete had a little gambling problem. Owed someone a lot of money. When he couldn't pay it back, Kaleb was hired to kill him. Sent a pretty powerful message to anyone else considering skipping out on their financial obligations to that particular client." He took a deep breath, edgy and cautious as he turned around and surveyed the dark yard. "A leader who will kill his own for money is the most dangerous kind, and he's coming, Katie."

"That's the part I don't understand," I said. "He got his cut, right?"

Jackson nearly laughed. "Haven't you been listening to anything I've told you about him? Kaleb's nothing but a greedy criminal. Probably burned through his cut in the first month. Now he thinks he can come for mine."

"What about Cairo's money?" I asked.

"You saw Cairo's spread. Most of his money went toward that chunk of land and the house and barn he built on it. What's left isn't enough to whet Kaleb's interest, although since he'll be in town, I wouldn't put it past him to try to bleed Cairo dry too."

Jackson had taken me to Cairo's place on our second date for a barbeque. Cairo and his wife, Angela, had a sprawling ranch about thirty minutes outside the city, complete with a good bit of acreage and a herd of alpacas. Cairo and his clan were Dimensionals. Unlike your garden-variety shifters, Dimensionals had the ability to shift into objects, usually structures like walls or bridges. Just about anything that didn't eat or breathe. I'd seen it firsthand that afternoon when a pair of renegade bear shifters crashed the party and nearly destroyed the place. The second time was when Cairo and his clan saved me from a crumbling building, shifting into stone walls that kept me shielded from tons of debris while I was being dug out. That had settled any question I had about the usefulness of transforming into inanimate objects.

"Besides, Kaleb doesn't like loose ends," he said, turning back to me. "I'm a loose end. If I don't play his game and marry Kara, he'll try to take the money and kill me."

My dragon stirred, nearly catapulting me out of my chair. "I'll kill him before he touches you."

Jackson walked back to the table and grabbed my wrist to pull me to my feet. "You would, wouldn't you?" A smile edged up his face while his arms snaked around my waist. "How did I ever find you?" He gazed at my blue eyes, which were flashing with emerald green.

"You were damn lucky." I shot him a wicked grin.

A moment later, his light mood shifted. "Seriously, Katie."

"Seriously what?" I said, pulling away from him. "You're a grown man, Jackson, so I'll let you sort out this whole shotgun wedding crap. But don't expect me to sit back like some spectator when they show up."

"Just don't get too cocky," he warned. "Kaleb plays dirty when he doesn't get what he wants."

"Yeah? Well, screw him." My anger grew at the thought of Kaleb thinking he could waltz into town and take whatever he wanted. Even more infuriating was the image of his daughter waiting patiently at the altar for daddy to deliver Jackson, cowed and ready to be hitched.

"Just—" His lips tightened as he held his tongue.

"I'm not afraid of them, Jackson."

He drew a long breath and zeroed in on my eyes. "You should be."

2

———

MagicInk was eerily quiet when I walked inside. I rarely got there before eight a.m., but the news that Kaleb and his pack were on their way to Savannah had kept me up most of the night. I could handle an asshole shifter with a bone to pick with Jackson, but I feared what they'd do to the city. Not to mention the thought of coming face-to-face with Kara, with her deluded notion that she had some sort of claim to Jackson.

I headed for the computer at the front desk. Supplies were running low, and regardless of what was heading for town, the bills still needed to be paid. Nothing would get done if I waited until after we closed to do all the dirty work of running a business, and lately procrastination was my middle name.

Out of the corner of my eye, I caught a shadow move past the front window. Just for caution's sake, I kept my eyes on the spot for a few more seconds and then figured it was probably just a passerby.

"Jesus, Katie, get it together."

Heading toward the coffee machine, I heard a faint sound. I glanced around the empty room but saw nothing. I nervously started the machine and walked back toward the front desk. Something fell, and my eyes shot to the table between two of the workstations. A pencil rolled across the pine plank, coming to rest a few inches from where it had hit the floor.

I screamed, nearly climbing on the counter as a rat scurried across the room. The rodent ducked under a chair and ran along the baseboard toward the back door, which was closed unfortunately. Normally the sight of a rat wouldn't send me on top of furniture, but I took issue with one nearly cruising right over the top of my foot. And I was already jumpy. Next came the practical realization that I had rats in my shop.

"Jesus!" I blurted when the back door opened and Sea Bass walked in. "You scared the shit out of me!"

He followed my finger as I pointed to the creature running back and forth along the baseboard. Then it froze, trapped and terrified. A few seconds later it darted across the room toward him.

"I'll give you a Christmas bonus if you get that rat out of my shop."

He snorted, twisting his brow. "Jeez, Katie, that ain't no rat. Look at them tiny little ears." He turned back around and opened the door. "Ain't you ever seen a mouse before?" Then he stepped back and held it open wide. "Go on. Skedaddle before I wring your little neck," he said as it ran over the threshold and disappeared under my car.

"I don't care if it's a squirrel. I'm just glad it's out of here." My shoulders sagged with relief. "Last thing I need is a rodent infestation. Although I'm sure its relatives are in here somewhere."

"They're nocturnal. You probably scared the crap out of it when you turned on the lights."

"The mouse was scared?" I said in disbelief. "Well, I'll make a point of warning them before turning on the lights next time."

He cocked his head in thought. "Hey, maybe you should bring

Jet to work with you. Nothing deters rodents like a patrolling cat. Or I could bring Marvin to the shop." Marvin was his dog. More like a white wolf. Last time he brought Marvin to the shop, I tripped over the massive beast and nearly broke my elbow.

"Yeah, like that's gonna happen," I said, retrieving the pencil from the floor. "You need to pick up some traps. I just added that to your job description."

I suddenly realized I was witnessing a miracle. Sea Bass never got out of bed before the sun came up, and it was barely light outside. "What are you doing here this early?"

"Couldn't sleep." He headed for his station. "Got any coffee made?"

Still perplexed by the king of snoozing's sudden insomnia, I walked over to the coffee machine to pour myself a cup. "That's a first. What happened? You and Maggie have a fight?"

Sea Bass worshipped his girlfriend, and I couldn't think of anything that would upset him more than being on the outs with Maggie.

"No," he said, scratching his head and scrunching his brow. "We're fine. I've just been having these weird dreams for the past few nights. Hell, Maggie won't even stay over anymore. I keep waking her up. The other night she woke up and found me crawling around on the floor in my sleep. She said I—" He suddenly went mute and started fiddling with the supplies on his tray.

"Said what?" I prompted, curious about what had shut him up so quickly.

He stopped moving ink bottles around the tray and shook his head. "She said I pissed on the floor."

My mouth gaped, but I suppressed the snicker that was itching to come out. "You pissed on the floor?" I repeated, suddenly a little concerned.

He nodded, embarrassed to look me in the eye. "She said I

stood up and starting pissing in the corner. Didn't even bother to hold my pecker. Just let it dangle like a limp noodle!"

"That's a little more information than I needed to hear." I did my best to shake the visual.

"I mean, it's not like I haven't walked in my sleep before," he continued. "And it wouldn't be the first time I overshot the toilet after a night of heavy drinking." He made the comment with a little too much familiarity in his voice, and I recalled some pretty embarrassing things I'd done in my younger and stupider days. Then he shook his head and shuddered. "I don't know, Katie. Something ain't right. I might have to make me an appointment with Moses Greene. Maybe get one of them prostate cancer tests or something like that."

"Moses Greene is a cardiologist," I reminded him, referring to the Crossroads Society's resident physician. "I don't think there's anything wrong with your ticker. You didn't by any chance end up at Mojo's that night, did you?"

Mojo's was a local shithole known for its rough crowd. The liquor was cheap, and the fights that usually spilled out into the parking lot were legendary. I'd made the mistake of walking in there shortly after moving to Savannah, thinking I'd found the perfect neighborhood dive to frequent. Big mistake. If it hadn't been for my experience with similar establishments on the Lower East Side of Manhattan—and the dragon on my back—the encounter with the first guy who pinned me against the bar that night might have ended very differently.

Sea Bass walked over to the coffee machine and poured himself a cup. "Nope. Ain't had a drink in days." He patted his stomach. "Trying to take better care of the old temple."

"Maybe that's the problem," I muttered, knowing how withdrawal could do strange things to people. Not that Sea Bass was an alcoholic, but he did drink more than he should. He was surprisingly muscular and fit, having youth on his side. If he didn't rein in that drinking though, he'd end up with a beer belly and a pair of sticks for legs by the time he hit forty.

"What are you doing in here before the crack of dawn?" he asked. "I like this neighborhood, but you need to keep your eyes open between your car and the back door."

"I think I can take care of myself." I smirked.

"Oh yeah," he said. "The big bad dragon. What are you gonna do if someone sticks a knife in your side before the dragon has a chance to wake up?"

He had a point. Now that I was in control of the beast, it didn't just come out whenever it pleased. In fact, I hadn't really had the occasion to test my control over it.

"Don't worry," I said. "My head spins around in a continuous three sixty whenever I walk down a dark alley or when the hair on the back of my neck sticks up."

The look on his face was priceless.

"I'm kidding. But I do exercise a little extra caution these days. Especially now that a pack of killers is on its way to Savannah," I mumbled under my breath as I walked back to the front desk.

"What was that?" he asked. "Did I just hear you say something about killers?"

I sighed and squeezed my eyes shut for a second, regretting my loose lips. This was not a conversation I was in the mood for, especially when I hadn't yet figured out what to do about the situation. But since the Sapanths would probably show up at MagicInk eventually, I probably needed to prepare everyone sooner rather than later.

"You know that biker club Jackson used to ride with back in Atlanta?" I said. "Well, those bikers also happen to be shifters. Dangerous shifters."

He just stood there staring at me like he couldn't reconcile what I was telling him.

"You know," I said, trying to prompt his mind to work.

"Shifters. They turn into things. Cats, apparently. And not your average house cat like Jet."

"I know what a shifter is, Katie." He looked at me like I had two heads. "Hell, you know who raised me."

For a moment I was the one staring without any words. His grandmother, Davina McCabe, was a senior member of the Crossroads Society. She also came from a long line of Ozark folk. The kind you didn't mess with from what I'd been told. But I never imagined a connection to anything other than a little mountain magic. Then again, Davina was pretty skilled with the bones. "Are you telling me Davina is a shifter?"

"Hell no!" he said, rolling his eyes. Then he leaned in to whisper like we had an audience. "But we come from a long line of grannies, if you know what I mean. All kinds of shape-shifting shit goes on up on the mountain."

"Huh." I conjured images of Ozark granny-women sitting around cauldrons with a bunch of half-human wolves or bears. Whatever kinds of shifters lurked in the Ozarks.

"Turns out Jackson has a lot of money," I said, thinking it best not to go into too much detail about the amount or how he got it. "The guy who heads up the club in Atlanta wants to get his hands on it. His name is Kaleb. Now, I won't go into too much detail, but it's Jackson's money fair and square."

"Okay." He bobbed his head thoughtfully. "So what do we do about that?"

"Nothing. I only told you because I can guarantee they'll be showing up here eventually."

"At MagicInk?" His bravado waned a little, but then he puffed back up with confidence and let out a heavy sigh. "Might be wise to have Jackson stay away from the shop until everything blows over. I mean, it ain't your feud, Katie. If he cares about you, he'll be thinking the same thing."

I dropped my head in my hands and groaned. "There's more. Apparently Jackson had a thing with Kaleb's daughter. Kaleb thinks the fastest way to get his hands on the money is to formally welcome Jackson into the family."

"How so?" he asked, clueless. "Wait. You don't mean he wants Jackson to marry his daughter?"

I nodded my head slowly. "That's exactly what I mean. Her name is Kara, and I think she's coming to stake her claim on Jackson. So it's not just a matter of having Jackson stay away for a while. Kaleb's coming to the shop to scope out the competition for his daughter—if she doesn't show up herself."

"And that would be you," he said, pointing his finger at me.

I turned to look at the early-morning light that was starting to stream through the window, at the spot where I'd seen the shadow earlier. I was sure it was just a random pedestrian heading for work, but tomorrow it might be Kara coming to declare war.

Sea Bass tried to lighten the mood. "You ain't jealous, are you?"

I laughed under my breath, still staring at the same spot. "Of course I am. I love Jackson."

He flinched. "Wow! When did that happen?"

"Oh, about the first time he walked into the shop."

"Well, I seem to recall that encounter a little differently," he replied. "But I get it. I don't know what I'd do without Maggie."

"Speaking of Maggie," I said, trying to change the subject. "I'm sure the nightmares will pass. She'll be sleeping back at your place in no time."

Before I could explore Sea Bass's newfound sobriety, the back door opened and Abel came strolling in, carrying a box of donuts. Like any red-blooded Southern boy, Sea Bass made a beeline for it before Abel even had a chance to put it down on the counter.

"Now that's what I call a blessing in disguise," he announced, grabbing two of the bavarian creams.

I glanced at the heart-attack confections. "How's that?"

"Well, they may be deadly, but they sure as shit just cured my depression." He stuffed half a donut in his mouth and headed back toward his station.

"You want one?" Abel offered, holding the box out.

I helped myself to a jelly donut and then glanced back at Abel. "Why are you here so early?" There must have been an epidemic of insomnia.

"I was on my way home from Darla's place and saw the lights on. Figured I'd get a change of clothes before heading in but got a little curious when I saw both of your cars out back." He looked back and forth between me and Sea Bass. "Am I missing a staff meeting or something?"

I glanced at his jeans and T-shirt. "You wearing yesterday's underwear too?"

"Don't worry, boss. I keep spare essentials at Darla's place."

Darla was his new girlfriend. They'd met at a martini bar. "What's it been? A week?" I asked. "Kind of fast to be stocking her drawers with your stuff."

He set the box down and dropped into a chair, stretching his arms back to lace his fingers behind his head. "Yeah, I guess it is." He sighed. "But I think she might be the one, Katie."

I shook my head at him. "Just take it slow, Abel." He was just like the donut in my hand. Firm and crusty on the outside but soft and squishy when opened up. Barely divorced, he was already storing spare underwear at the home of a woman he hardly knew.

I don't care how good the sex is, you don't know someone until you *know* someone, and that takes more than a week. Even Jackson and I still had a long way to go. There was a whole lot of history he hadn't gotten around to telling me yet—such as what his parents were like and the fine details about the accident that triggered his powers when he fell through that freezing ice years ago. He'd never pushed me for details about my past, but now that we'd taken our relationship to the next level, we'd both be opening up about our family histories.

I took a bite of the donut and headed for the coffee machine to pour myself a second cup before getting back to the business of paying bills and ordering supplies.

Half an hour later, someone knocked on the front door. I looked up at the girl staring through the glass, her hands cupped over her brow to shield the glare obstructing her view inside.

"We're not open yet," I yelled across the room, pointing to the sign just below her chin that clearly stated the shop hours.

"What?" she mouthed through the glass.

"We're not—" I started to repeat myself but reconsidered. My focus was already shot to hell, and we needed all the paying customers we could get. Dropping my pen on the counter, I got up and walked over to the door.

She smiled as I opened it. "The sign says you open at nine, but I saw all you guys inside and thought…" She shrugged.

"Yeah, sure." I held the door open as she walked inside.

3

The shop wasn't open for another hour, but since I clearly wasn't going to get any bill paying done, I figured I might as well make a little money and procure a new client.

"Do you have something in mind?" I asked, leading her to a chair and hoping she'd brought her own sketch or at least knew what kind of tattoo she wanted. I wasn't feeling particularly creative at that moment.

She smiled slyly and flashed her brown eyes at Sea Bass. "Who's he?"

I glanced at Sea Bass while he tidied up his work area, then back at the woman who was suddenly making me uneasy. "Why? You want him to do your tattoo?"

She shook her head and forced her eyes back to mine. "I want him to do something to me, but not necessarily give me a tattoo."

I'd seen Sea Bass turn a shade of pink before, but never from a suggestion made by a hungry woman.

He fumbled with one of his instruments and then dropped it on the tray. "I-I'm gonna go across the street and get me some breakfast," he muttered with a slight stutter. The boy had an appetite like an ox. Then he scurried out of the shop.

"He's a little shy," I lied, giving her a firm look and wondering who the hell she was. "Now, why don't you tell me what you want?"

Her eyes locked onto mine. As dark as they were, her brown irises couldn't camouflage her slightly elongated pupils. Nor could they hide the intense green flashing through that doe-like facade. It took one to know one, and even though I'd never classified myself as a garden-variety shifter, we certainly had something in common. I'd say she was about my age with short brown hair and a tight body that suggested she worked hard to keep it that way. But it was that damn shit-eating grin on her face that captured my attention—in an alarming way.

She lifted the right sleeve of her T-shirt to expose a tattoo over the cuff of her shoulder. "I want a matching one on the other side."

I examined the elaborate tattoo that must have been applied by a skilled artist, estimating that it would take me until around noon to complete. As much as I wanted to hand her off to Sea Bass or Mouse, neither of them was present, so I was it. "Lucky for you I don't have any clients on the schedule until this afternoon."

"Yeah," she replied. "Lucky me."

After a few seconds of eye-to-eye combat, I motioned for her to sit down and pulled out my cell phone. "I'll just take a picture of it. For the stencil."

I took several and then walked over to the desk at the back of the room, out of earshot. Abel, who had been listening to the exchange and sensed my unease, followed me over and gave me a cautious look.

"What's going on, boss?" he whispered. "You look like you want to hand that chick her teeth."

"You're right about that," I replied. "Something's not right about her."

Since Abel didn't know about the Sapanths, it would have been awkward to explain why the woman sitting in my chair had the hair on the back of my neck standing on end. Of course, she might have just been some asshole creature off the street—like half of the fine citizens of Savannah—who for some reason wanted to mess with me, but I'd bet the shop that my instincts were right.

"You want me to show her the door?" he asked. "I'd be more than happy to get rid of her."

I shook my head. "That's all right, Abel. I think I'll use our time together to my advantage."

He cocked his brow at my strange response and went back to his business, staying close just in case.

I finished the stencil and walked back to my station. Without a word, I handed it to her. She eyed it carefully and passed it back, nodding her approval.

As I sat down to apply it, Mouse walked through the door. I guess none of my employees could sleep this morning.

I WIPED the last trace of ink off the woman's arm and motioned for her to check it out in the mirror on the wall. Through the entire session we barely spoke, filling the room with an awkward silence that was only broken by the occasional conversation between Mouse and her morning client. Sea Bass had taken his time returning to the shop, clearly as uncomfortable with the woman as I was.

"Looks good," she said, rolling her shoulder in front of the mirror. She turned around and surveyed the room before bringing her eyes back to mine. "How much do I owe you?"

As I was heading to the front desk to total up the work, Sugar came walking through the front door. We had a lunch date across the street at Lou's.

"Afternoon, babies," she said. She spotted Sea Bass at the back of the room and made a beeline for him, whipping off her sunglasses as she click-clacked across the floor in her sky-high heels. Her gold-and-brown-striped bell-bottoms swayed as she walked, drawing every eye in the room to her movement, including my new customer who hadn't even offered me her name.

"I'll be with you in a minute, Sugar," I said, handing the woman her bill.

"Take your time, Katie B," she replied. "I'm gonna have me a little visit with my boy."

Sea Bass grumbled as Sugar approached, hating the way she fawned over him.

Without asking for a name, I waited for the woman to pay.

She glanced at the computer. "Don't you want to add me to your client database?"

I ignored the question because she was baiting me.

Eventually she handed me cash. "Keep the rest," she said cattily. "Your tip."

"I own the place," I replied, handing her the change. "I don't accept tips." Which was a lie.

After our brief pissing contest, she turned to leave, giving Sea Bass a final hungry look.

As she was walking toward the door, I decided to play my card. "Tell Kaleb he's not welcome in my shop—or this town. Neither is his daughter." For a second, I wondered if the woman exiting my shop *was* Kara. But I doubted it. The woman I'd spent the past four hours with was nothing but a low-level spy sent to scout the enemy's territory before the Sapanths made their grand entrance.

She stiffened as she reached for the handle. Then she disappeared through the door without looking back.

"What the hell, Katie!" Sea Bass yelled from across the room. "Was that—"

"No," I said. "But she's one of them."

Sugar ran over to the window to get a look at the woman she'd barely given a glance to on her way in. "Did I miss something? Who the hell was that?" She looked back at Sea Bass. "And why was she looking at you like you was dinner?"

"A messenger," I replied, choosing to delay the details until we were across the street at Lou's. "I've got a client coming in after lunch, so give me a minute to straighten up my station."

Mouse was looking back and forth between me and Sea Bass, clearly confused by all the commotion over the stranger. "What's going on around here?"

"Good question," Abel added. "What *is* going on, boss?"

"Come on, baby," Sugar said, snapping her fingers to hurry me along, her stomach growling obscenely. "I got me a shitload of hunger trampling all over my stomach, and you got some explaining to do."

Sea Bass put his hand up to quell all the questions. "Uh... Katie?" he began, giving me a pointed look. "I think you need to prepare your employees. You want me to let everybody in on the news while you two head across the street?"

"Be my guest."

I grabbed my wallet and cell phone and headed for the door. Sugar followed, and we walked across the street to Lou's with her demanding stare burning a hole in the back of my head.

"You gonna tell me what the hell is going on?" she said before my ass even hit the booth. "Or do I have to remind you who the hell I am?"

"You're my best friend, Sugar," I replied with a mechanical grin. "Can I just have a bite of my sandwich first? I just spent the past four hours hunched over the skin of the enemy, and you're not the only one who's hungry."

She bobbed her head and picked up a french fry between her

middle finger and thumb, extending her pinky like she was drinking a dainty cup of tea. "Mm-hmm. I'll just have me a fry and wait then."

I bit into my chicken sandwich and ran the events of the morning through my head. Then I began to wonder if Jackson knew they were already here. Surely he would have warned me that morning before I left for the shop. "What the hell, Jackson," I muttered, dropping my sandwich on the plate and grabbing my phone to dial his number.

Sugar glanced at the phone in my hand and grabbed it. "Hell no! I'm next in line. You can make that call when you're done explaining this shit to me. Now, what in Hades is going on around here?"

I leaned my elbows on the table and pushed my plate to the side. "Remember when I told you about Jackson riding with those bikers in Atlanta?"

Sugar's demanding expression turned cautious, her head cocking slightly to the right as her wheels began to turn. "You mean them shifters who turn into lions or tigers or something catty like that?"

I nodded. "They're coming for Jackson."

"Well, what for?" Her eyes suddenly went wide. "Don't tell me he knocked up that woman you was telling me about. Kayla or—"

"It's for the money," I blurted. "Jackson has a shitload of money, and they want it." I rubbed my eyes and sank deeper into the booth. "I need to catch you up, Sugar."

She remained quiet—which was a feat for her—for the next fifteen minutes while I relayed all the information Jackson had given me the night before.

"You trying to tell me that woman in there was this Kara chick?" she asked after I finished enlightening her. "She didn't look all *that* to me."

"That wasn't Kara. She was one of Kaleb's acolytes though."

23

When I first met Jackson, he'd grilled me about who I really was. Said he thought I was one of Kaleb's "girls" sent down from Atlanta to tie up some loose ends, meaning him. I was pretty sure I'd just spent the morning with one of those girls.

Sugar took a sip of her sweet tea and gave me a questioning look. "Girl, you sure about this?"

"You bet," I said, replaying the morning in my head. "If that woman was Kara, she would have let me know. And I'm pretty sure my dragon would have too."

JACKSON'S APARTMENT was anything but cozy, which was why we never went there. The front door was barely tall enough to accommodate his size if he ducked. If it hadn't been for the unusually high ceilings, I'm sure he would have looked for a more suitable rental. Nothing like hitting your head on a daily basis to motivate you into moving. I used to think he'd chosen the place for financial reasons, what with the rent being so cheap, but with all this money he apparently had, I was beginning to wonder why he didn't live in a nicer neighborhood.

After lunch, I finished up my only scheduled client, which thankfully only required about an hour's worth of work. The whole time, I kept glancing at the front window, waiting for Kaleb or Kara to come walking through the door. But then again, that would be too ordinary. Something told me the Sapanths liked the spotlight. When they did finally show up, I had a feeling it would be memorable.

I told Sea Bass to hold down the fort while I headed over to Jackson's place to have a face-to-face chat with him about my morning visitor. I could have called him, but I wanted to see his face when I mentioned the possibility of Kara being in town. Call it jealousy, which I wasn't proud of.

The intercom button was broken when I pushed it.

"Figures," I muttered, reaching for the door handle to the building. It was already ajar. I pushed it open and headed for the second floor.

Jackson had the first apartment on the right, which at least gave him a decent view of the courtyard. He answered on the first knock, smiling faintly when he saw me standing on the other side of the door.

"Are you going to invite me in?" I asked when he didn't move aside.

Jackson didn't like surprises, and I never showed up unannounced. I guess I was lucky he was even home. He finally stepped back and motioned me in. The blinds were closed, which was odd. Jackson liked sunlight filling the apartment. It was the only thing that made the small space bearable.

I turned around to look at him as he silently stared back. "You're making me nervous. What's wrong?" Still not a word, so I just came out with it. "I'm pretty sure I had a visit from one of Kaleb's crew this morning. Which means Kara is probably in town."

He barely flinched, but I caught his eyes discreetly shift to the dark corner to his left. I slowly turned my head toward the figure in the shadow of the room. Then I looked back at Jackson, who was warning me with his eyes.

"Well," I said. "Looks like you already know that. I guess I should have called first."

Kara took her time standing up, strolling across the room into what little light was available. Then she walked over to the window and turned the lever on the blinds to let the sun in.

Jackson took a few steps closer to me and rested his hand on the small of my back.

"Look at that," Kara said, grinning snidely. "How sweet. He wants to protect you."

I took an involuntary step toward her, feeling the stir of the dragon, but Jackson gripped the back of my shirt to hold me in place. "Don't, Katie."

"That's right, Katie," she said, her grin fading as her eyes flashed. "Don't."

"Back off, Kara," he warned.

"It's okay, Jackson. We're just having a little girl chat." I yanked my shirt from his hand. "Was that one of your spies in my shop this morning?"

She started to move toward me with catlike grace, which I had to admit made me a little nervous. "Mira said you were pretty," she purred, absently twisting a strand of hair between her fingers as she eyed me thoroughly. "I agree." The growl coming from my throat stopped her, curiosity written all over her face. "But I'm prettier."

For some reason I expected her to be a brunette, dark like a panther. But Kara was a blonde. A very tall and sinewy blonde. Strawberry blonde really, with streaks of gold infused in her fucking gorgeous hair. Her eyes were the color of caramel. I hated to admit it, but she *was* beautiful.

"Hmm." She drew a deep breath through her nose. "Interesting smell. You have a secret, don't you? Jackson always did like his women on the wild side." Her grin got cockier as she looked me up and down. "What could you be?"

"Get out, Kara!" Jackson hissed.

"Come on, Jackson," she purred, feigning hurt. "I forgive you." She gazed at me lecherously and reached for a lock of my hair. "I'm tempted by her too."

"We've been over for a long time. That's not gonna change." He grabbed her by the wrist and squeezed until she dropped my hair, giving her a look that made me uneasy as I stood sandwiched between them.

A few days ago, the dragon would have already emerged, and Kara would have been a crispy bag of fur on the floor before I could stop it from happening. But I was in control now. No need to jump the gun and start a shifter war—yet.

Kara took a step back and yanked her wrist out of his tight grip. "I love you, baby, but you're going to regret that."

Without another word, she vanished through the front door. When I looked through the blinds, she was staring up at me from the courtyard like she knew I'd be running to the window. *Pathetic* was what the grin on her face said. Then she ran toward the street, only the tip of her leopard tail showing as she disappeared around the corner of the building.

4

Lillian Whitman's housekeeper showed me into the living room, quickly disappearing without even the courtesy of offering me coffee or tea. Ever since the night I barged my way past her and interrupted Blackthorn Grove's little ritual in the back room, she'd decided I was an annoying toothache that wouldn't go away.

I glanced nervously around the beautiful room, debating the most favorable way to tell the society what was about to invade the city. The Crossroads Society's primary mission was to protect the city from anything that threatened the peace—anything otherworldly, that is. Anything that the Chatham County PD couldn't handle. And there was always something trying to break through the crossroads, or in this case the county line.

The thought had crossed my mind to just pick up the phone and call Fin Cooper or Lillian Whitman, but it was better to deliver the news in person. That way I could plead Jackson's innocence before they tried to run him out of town for bringing a pack of vicious shifters to Savannah.

"Good morning, Miss Bishop." Lillian walked into the room

and glanced at the table in front of the sofa. She instantly lost her faint smile. "Vivian!" she yelled into the hall.

The housekeeper reappeared. "Yes, Mrs. Whitman?"

"Is there a reason why there is no coffee in this room?" she asked. "We have a guest."

I glanced at the housekeeper and watched as she withered slightly from the admonishment.

"Right away, Mrs. Whitman," she said as she practically curtsied her way back toward the kitchen.

Lillian shuddered out a long breath. "I don't know what's gotten into that woman, but I do apologize, Miss Bishop."

"It's fine, Lillian. It's just coffee."

She took a seat in the chair opposite the sofa and crossed her legs. Lillian reminded me of a movie star from another era. Lauren Bacall or Katharine Hepburn; one of those women who wore trousers and took shit from no one.

"Why are you here, Miss Bishop? Fin said it was urgent."

I glanced at the time on the mantel clock. Fin was usually prompt. "Where is Fin?"

Right about the time I said it, I heard the front door open. Fin walked into the room with Vivian right behind him carrying a tray. She set it down in the center of the table without looking at me and quickly left the room.

"Miss Bishop," Fin said. "Always a pleasure to see you. What's it been? A week?"

I snickered at his attempt at humor.

"We just can't seem to have a moment of normalcy these days, can we?" he said, referring to the calamity that usually accompanied me.

"Well now, Fin," I began. "You and the society are usually responsible for all the ruckus around this town. I just happen to get thrown into the mix, don't I?"

"That is true." He took a seat. "But not today."

Lillian reached for the tray and poured three cups. "I'll let y'all decorate your own coffee."

I added cream to my cup and took a sip of the strong brew, feeling fortified from the rush of caffeine as I prepared to tell them about the latest threat to the city. Fin knew that Jackson used to ride with a biker club back in Atlanta, but I'd intentionally left out the part about those bikers being shifters.

"Why don't you just tell us what's on your mind," Lillian suggested. "I have a busy day."

I looked at Fin. "That club that Jackson used to ride with in Atlanta," I began, steeling myself for the conversation. "They're coming to Savannah."

Fin's expression remained stoic as his cup landed on the table. He stood up and walked over to the window to look outside. "I guess you're not about to tell me that they're just another bunch of weekend warriors who enjoy the sport of riding motorcycles, are you?"

"They're shifters," I replied bluntly.

"Shifters?" Lillian repeated. "Good ones or bad ones?"

I saw no reason to draw it out. "Bad ones. Kind of like the Mongols or Hells Angels, but these turn into big cats."

"Well, fuck," Fin said, still gazing out the window like a sentinel. "You mind telling us what their business is in Savannah?"

Here we go.

"They're here for Jackson," I said. "But it's not what you think."

Fin turned around and headed back to his seat. "And that would be?"

"Jackson walked away from that life. He wants no part of them. They're after his money."

"Money?" Lillian said. "No offense, but Mr. Hunter doesn't exactly look like a man of means."

I glanced around the palatial room, knowing it would take a

lot more than what Jackson had to own a house like this. But it was still more money than most people would ever see in their bank accounts. I imagined that Lillian Whitman had never experienced an empty gas tank in her life, nor a meal consisting of only rice or boxed macaroni and cheese.

"He doesn't flash it around," I said. "The point is, they're coming for it."

"Why bring this to the society?" she asked. "This is a private matter between Mr. Hunter and these shifters."

The look I gave her must have touched a nerve, because her coffee cup froze at her lips for a moment before it landed back on the table.

"I don't think you're hearing what I'm saying, Lillian. These shifters aren't coming here to discreetly confront Jackson, steal his money, and then slip back out of town in the middle of the night. If what Jackson tells me is true, they're planning to make a little noise while they're here."

That got Fin's attention. "Then I guess the coven is going to have to make it very clear who's in charge in this town. Lay down the rules the second they set foot over the Chatham County line."

"They're already here, Fin. Well, some of them."

I had a feeling we would have already known if the entire club had arrived. The way Jackson described it after Kara disappeared the night before, they liked to announce their presence in a big way. Mark their territory. It was only a matter of days before everyone in the city knew they were here.

"They sent a welcoming crew," I continued. "One of them showed up at MagicInk yesterday morning." I considered mentioning Jackson's history with the leader's daughter and the fact that they might try to pull off an old-fashioned shotgun wedding right in the middle of one of Savannah's famous squares, but that would only add fuel to the growing flames. "My guess is the rest of them will be here any day now."

Fin stood up and automatically headed for the liquor cabinet

31

on the other side of the room. As if suddenly realizing it wasn't even noon, he stopped and turned back around. "Well, then." He sighed deeply. "I guess we better call a meeting."

"Better yet," Lillian countered, "I'll have the cook prepare something if Miss Bishop has no objections to a late dinner after that shop of hers closes."

"I eat when I can," I replied. "I suggest we do it soon though. When the rest of them get here, they won't waste any time trying to get everyone's attention."

"Agreed," Lillian said, getting up from her chair and heading down the hall. "Tonight then. You can show Miss Bishop out, Fin."

Fin walked me to the front door. "What does this club call themselves?"

"The Sapanths."

He rolled the name around in his head. "Odd name."

"Apparently it's a reference to humans and cats." I'd gathered that based on what Jackson had told me about them. "You know, Homo sapiens and panthers."

"I see," he said. "I don't suppose Cairo has any connection to all this? His clan being shifters." Fin knew Cairo from the night I was nearly buried alive under that building.

"That's a conversation for another day, Fin. But I can assure you that Cairo is on our side."

"Fair enough, Miss Bishop, but we will be having that conversation very soon."

He walked me to my car and stood on the cobblestone drive as I disappeared down the road. I was heading straight for Magic-Ink. If Kara or Kaleb showed up there, they'd have to go through my dragon to get past the front door.

By the time I walked into the shop, business was already in full swing. Mouse had a client in her chair, and another guy was waiting with his face buried in a magazine. She was pretty good about not double booking her schedule, so I started to feel uneasy as I walked over to the front desk to check if I'd accidentally forgotten about a new client of mine coming in.

Abel glanced at the man and followed me. "Where the hell is Sea Bass?" he whispered. "His client's been sitting there for twenty minutes."

"That's Sea Bass's client?" I asked, relieved that I hadn't gained and lost a new customer in the same day. Nothing like alienating new business by failing to show up. Then again, Sea Bass's clients *were* my clients.

"Yep. No sign of the boy wonder yet."

"Have you tried to call him?" It was obvious, but it seemed like the next logical question.

Abel cocked his head. "Now what do you think?"

I squeezed my eyes shut and tried to think of reasons not to kill Sea Bass when he eventually walked through the door. Dragging his ass in late wasn't a cardinal sin, but standing up a client was.

I got the man's name from the schedule and headed over to do damage control. "Mr. Clark?" I smiled sympathetically. With irritation written all over his face, he looked up at me. "I am so sorry for your wait. Sea Bass has had a little emergency this morning, so I'm afraid we might have to reschedule you for another day." I would have offered to work on the man myself, but I had another client due in an hour.

He stood up and dropped the magazine on the table. "Why don't I just get back to you on that?" He headed for the door, muttering something under his breath. I was pretty sure that call would never come, and some other tattoo shop in the city was about to gain a new customer.

As he opened the front door to leave, Maggie came barreling

though it and nearly sideswiped him. A statuesque personal trainer with fiery red hair that ran halfway down her back, Maggie Donovan left an impression on people. Mr. Clark did a double take as she passed him, and then he disappeared down the sidewalk.

"Is he here?" she demanded.

"I assume you mean Sea Bass," I countered, not too thrilled with her tone. But then I saw the look in her eyes. "What's going on, Maggie?"

She looked like she was about to break down. With a client in Mouse's chair, I thought it best to continue the conversation out back.

"Let's take it outside." I glanced at Mouse.

"It's cool," Mouse said. "Daryl don't mind a little drama."

Her client shrugged as she tried to apply ink to his pectoral muscle.

"Move like that again while I've got this needle against your skin and that eagle wing is gonna look more like a butterfly wing."

"You don't know where Sea Bass is?" I asked, deciding not to worry about Daryl's ears.

She shook her head frantically while her face seized up with emotion. "He never came over to my house last night like he was supposed to. He wouldn't answer his phone, so I drove over to his place. Nothing. He's just... gone." She looked like she was about to hyperventilate. "Hell, Katie, Marvin's bowl was empty and he'd peed all over the floor!"

Alarm bells went off in my head. Sea Bass worshipped the ground Maggie walked on. The one time she threatened to leave him, he nearly had a breakdown. And he loved that dog. He'd never let Marvin go hungry or neglect his nightly walk. Despite my concern, I did my best to hide it because seeing me worried would only escalate Maggie's fear.

Her eyes darted around the room. "He didn't show up for work, did he?"

"Okay, Maggie. Let's not assume the worst," I said, trying to de-escalate the situation, my mind racing. "He said he's been having nightmares and walking in his sleep. Maybe he's just walking around the neighborhood in a daze." It was a stretch but all I could think of to ease her mind.

"You don't get it, Katie. He never came home!" Her eyes were wild with fear as her imagination got the best of her. "Something happened to him!"

"Maybe he hooked up with some chick." Daryl snorted.

Mouse glared at him. "Shut up, Daryl."

Maggie looked at the man with horror and then back at me. "You don't think…"

"God, no!" I gave Daryl a warning look. "I'm sure he'll be walking through that door any minute now with a damn good explanation."

He better.

The truth was, I was worried. With the Sapanths showing up in town, none of us were safe. That's when I remembered the one who'd strolled into my shop the day before. "Mira," I muttered under my breath.

"Mira?" Maggie repeated, suddenly looking less petrified and more like a jealous girlfriend. "Who the hell is Mira?"

"No one," I said, shaking my head and realizing my callous mistake. "I was just thinking about my client coming in soon." The lie worked, and she pulled her she-wolf back inside.

Before I could ask my next question, Sugar walked through the front door.

"Hey, babies. Thought I'd stop by with a little treat." She headed over to the kitchenette and deposited a white paper bag on the counter. "Got y'all some donuts." She pulled out a bavarian cream—Sea Bass's favorite—and looked around the room. "Where's my boy?"

On that question, Maggie started to lose it again. Abel glanced at Sugar and gave her a visual order to shut up. I did the same, but that only fueled her curiosity.

She dropped the donut on the counter. "Someone gonna tell me what the hell is going on?"

"Sea Bass is missing," Mouse declared without looking up from her client's chest.

"Thanks, Mouse," I said, giving her a dirty look.

Sugar was about as fond of Sea Bass as I was, and based on the look on her face, I suspected Maggie wasn't the only one about to go off the rails.

"I-I don't understand," Sugar said, visibly shaken by the news that her "boy" was MIA. Then her eyes went wide, and she was probably thinking the same thing I was.

I shot her a look, pleading with her not to mention the Sapanths—or God forbid, Mira, who'd practically fucked Sea Bass with her eyes the day before. The last thing I needed was for Maggie to let that contained she-wolf back out and head for the door to hunt down her philandering boyfriend. No telling what would happen if she found him with Mira, but I was pretty sure Maggie was no match for a shifter.

"When he does show up, and he will," I told Maggie, trying to put her at ease and get her out of the shop, "he'll be heading straight for your place to smooth things over. The shop will be second on his list." That part was probably true.

She thought about it for a few seconds, sniffing back the tears as her suspicions grew. "I guess you're right. But if he does show up here, you give him a message for me. Tell him that if he didn't have a gun pointed at his head or he wasn't lying on the side of the road bleeding to death, he can dig his things out of my trash can!"

"I'll be sure to tell him that. But seriously, I'm sure there's a good reason for him not coming home last night." *Or picking up the phone to call her.* I shot her a weak smile. "Now you better go home. He might already be waiting for you."

She collected herself and walked out the door to go wait for her missing man.

"You don't believe that shit you just told her?" Sugar asked as soon as the door closed behind Maggie.

"I don't know what to believe anymore. For all I know, Daryl's right."

Mouse escorted her client to the front desk. "See what you started with that big mouth of yours, Daryl?" She yanked the money out of his hand. "Now get out of here before you say something else stupid." Most of her customers were regulars. Being a lifelong Savannahian, some of them went as far back as elementary school, which gave her the liberty of speaking her mind without fear of losing clientele.

After Daryl left the shop, Mouse headed back to her station to clean up. "You might want to ask around over at Mojo's," she muttered, her back to us.

"Mojo's," I said. "Why would you say that, Mouse?"

Sugar chimed in. "Yeah. What the hell would Sea Bass be doing in a bag-o'-shit dive like Mojo's? Them fools over there is nothing but penitentiary bait if you ask me."

"He used to hang out there sometimes," I said. "But I think Maggie put an end to that. Ever since they got all hot and heavy this past summer."

"Mm-hmm. Got to crack that whip with a fine specimen like Sea Bass," Sugar said. "Plenty of hoes up in that shithole."

"Not to mention the fact that he just told me he hasn't been drinking lately," I added. "Nobody's sober in that place."

Mouse snorted under her breath. "Bullshit he ain't drinking."

Sugar and I both eyed Mouse.

"What was that?" I asked.

She ignored the question, acting like she hadn't heard me. A minute went by before she finally relented to our silent stares.

"Look," she began, turning around but stopping short of meeting my eyes. "He's been going over there lately. Now that's all I'm gonna say. And you can't tell Maggie. She'll kick his ass out, and you know what'll happen then. The only reason I told you is because he's missing." She went back to cleaning her tray, muttering a few choice words to herself as she threw a handful of used gauze into the trash can with a little more force than necessary.

"He told you that?" I asked. They were as close as siblings, but I found it hard to believe he'd been leading a seedy double life at a place like Mojo's. I found it even harder to imagine him keeping that kind of secret from Maggie.

She shook her head. "I got friends who've seen him over there a few times."

"Your friends hang out at Mojo's? What else don't I know about you?"

She blew me off. "Look, you just need to trust me on this." Then she headed for the bathroom before I could continue with the inquisition.

"Girl, I think you and me needs to slide over to Mojo's tonight," Sugar said. "If he don't come home with his tail between his legs first."

Mojo's was one of those bars that didn't even open until nine o'clock, but they stayed open most of the night. And it being Saturday meant a rowdy crowd for sure. The mere thought of walking into that meat market made my skin crawl, and showing up with Sugar guaranteed trouble. The place was a magnet for rednecks and bigots.

"Yeah, we do," I reluctantly agreed. "Lillian's having a little dinner party tonight to come up with a strategy for handling our uninvited shifters. Jackson and I will be there, but we can go to Mojo's after that." Sugar and her mama were silent members of the Crossroads Society, but it was rare to see either of them actually attend a meeting. Not by choice anyway. "You want to join us for dinner? I can call Lillian. I'm sure she wouldn't mind one more guest."

Sugar gave me a deadpan stare but didn't answer.

"I guess that would be a no," I muttered, realizing the stupidity of the question. "I guess I'll call you when I get home then."

I hadn't even told Sugar about my introduction to Kara at Jackson's place, but that had to wait. Right now I had two problems I needed to focus on: making it through the day short one-third of my staff and coming up with a way to convince Jackson to go home after dinner. As long as Kara was in town, he'd be all over me. But walking into Mojo's with him at my side would eliminate any chance of seducing information out of the bartenders or any other assholes who might be linked to Sea Bass's disappearance.

"All right," she said, heading for the door. "I got to get out of here." Before leaving, she looked back at me. "Better get your skank on tonight, baby. We got to do whatever it takes to find that boy of ours."

5

B y the time I got home from MagicInk, it was a little after nine. Jet met me at the front door, swishing his tail until I bent down to greet him with a stroke along his arched back.

"What's wrong with you?" I asked. That tail action was usually a sign that he was irritated about something. "I'm here, aren't I?"

Some people wouldn't bother to go all the way home just to feed their cat and then turn around to leave again. I didn't think very highly of those people. You wouldn't let your kids go hungry, would you? And Jet was my baby.

Heading for the kitchen to get his food, I thought about Marvin sitting in that dark house, hungry and needing to relieve himself. The more I thought about it, the more I knew something was wrong. Sea Bass felt the same way about Marvin as I did about Jet. That dog came first.

Jackson tapped on the front door with his knuckles as he opened it. "You need to lock this thing, Katie."

"And you need to stop being so paranoid. I knew you were right behind me."

He walked inside, filling the entryway with his large frame. Jet stopped eating and ran across the room to greet him, rubbing against his legs.

"I think my cat is in love with you."

He reached down and lifted Jet off the floor to give him a good scratch behind the ears before depositing him back in front of his food. "Eat your Wheaties, little man." Then he gave me a kiss and lifted my chin to look me in the eye. "I'd feel a whole lot better if you locked your front door." Glancing at the sliding patio door, the one that opened with a simple lift of the handle from the outside, he let out a frustrated sigh. The metal rod was leaning against the wall. I'd forgotten to put it in the door track. Again.

"I'm buying you a new patio door in the morning," he announced. "I'll get it installed as soon as possible, but in the meantime you need to use that damn rod." Irritated by my carelessness, he picked the bar up and slid it into the track where it belonged.

"No, you're not," I replied. "That's my landlord's job."

I could argue about it all night, but it would be useless. Now that I knew how much money he was hiding, I expected to come home to a new patio door installed within the next few days, whether I approved or not.

"I'll just turn the dragon on anyone who breaks in," I said, trying to lighten his dark mood.

"You think this is a joke?" His face was humorless when he turned around. "You're impressive when you sprout those wings, but so is Kaleb and his crew when they show their claws. They're not furry little kittens. A pack of big cats just might be your match."

"Fine. I get it. I'll be more careful."

He checked the door to make sure the metal rod was doing its job, and then we headed out for the meeting. I walked toward my car while he headed for his bike. I needed him to go home after the meeting, so I figured if we drove separately it would be easier to convince him not to stay at my place for the night.

"What are you doing?" he asked.

"Getting in my car, Einstein." I tried to leverage humor to hide my nerves. I was a terrible liar. "I figured you could follow me so you won't have to drop me off after the meeting."

He eyed me suspiciously for a moment. "I wasn't planning to go home."

"Smothering," I said before he had a chance to insist on staying over. "You know how I feel about that." He knew better than to push me when I was feeling caged. The whole alpha-male thing turned me off and usually ignited an argument between us. "Just follow me."

The tone of my voice convinced him to leave it alone. He climbed on his bike and waited for me to start my car. Then we headed for Lillian's house so he could explain why a dangerous pack of shifters was heading for Savannah and why the Crossroads Society shouldn't try to run him out of town. The entire way over, my imagination ran wild, and I expected a leopard or a panther to come bouncing into the road in the beam of my headlights.

Fin was smoking a cigar at the top of the steps when we pulled up to the house. "Lovely evening for an inquisition," he said as we climbed the stairs. His eyes lingered on Jackson for a moment before shifting to me. "It's always a pleasure to see you twice in a single day, Miss Bishop."

We walked past him into the house where everybody was gathered in the living room. Jackson's eyes wandered around the massive hall, taking in the extravagance and grandeur of the place the way most people did the first time they set foot in Lillian's palatial house. He stopped to look at a painting hanging to his left, leaning in to examine the signature, huffing quietly as a smirk crossed his face.

"I understand you've created a little problem for the society," Lillian said, drawing his attention away from the painting.

He took a step toward her, looking down at the woman who barely cleared his chest. "Nice place," he said, ignoring her comment. "Is that an original?" He nodded toward the painting.

"Well, what do you think, Mr. Hunter?" she replied, glancing at his long black hair trailing down the front of his leather jacket.

I guess we were both underdressed for dinner in a house like this. Fortunately, neither of us cared. We were here for business, not to socialize.

A loud clap rang through the cavernous space as Fin got everyone's attention. "All right now. I believe everyone's here."

That was Lillian's cue to lead everyone into the dining room. As I followed the procession, a hand wrapped around my forearm. It was Emmaline initiating contact, which was rare. Her hazel eyes flashed as I looked at her.

"I think it's exciting," she whispered. "Shifters coming to town."

Her boldness surprised me. Emmaline usually preferred to blend in with the walls and drapes, without opinion and completely at the mercy of those at the society who made most of her decisions for her. But here she was, discreetly revealing her excitement at a dangerous threat that could alter her very way of life. It made me wonder if I really knew the demure ghost of a girl at all.

The last time I was here for dinner, Lillian had strategically orchestrated the seating arrangements, but tonight we picked our own places. Jackson took a seat on the other side of the table, a passive-aggressive move due to my earlier comment about smothering, I assumed. Emmaline took the seat next to mine. Davina McCabe, Moses Greene, Fin, and several other members took their seats. The majority of Blackthorn Grove was conspicuously missing, but I figured it was difficult to arrange dinner for such an extensive group of guests on such short notice. I also assumed our dinner gathering was really just a vetting party to see what the town was up against. Bring in the cavalry later. I was surprised, though, not to see Fiona there, considering she was Lillian's granddaughter and actually lived in the house.

"Where is everyone?" I asked.

Lillian took her place at the head of the table after we were all seated. "We thought it might be best to find out exactly what we're dealing with before involving the entire group. No need to cause panic yet."

"Goddamn right," Davina said. "Bunch of alarmists in this coven."

I wondered if Davina knew her grandson was missing. If she did, she was doing a stand-up job of hiding her concern. Then it occurred to me that he might have shown up at her house the night before. Maybe there was trouble in paradise. Sea Bass was a little unstable whenever he was on the outs with his queen, and that would explain his careless disregard for his job. Maybe Maggie wasn't telling me the whole story.

"Davina—" I nearly blurted the news across the table, but I caught myself and decided it wasn't the time or place.

She shook her napkin into her lap and leaned her right elbow on the table. "Well, what?" she asked, annoyed by my sudden mute stare.

"I just had something to ask you," I said. "Never mind. It can wait until after dinner."

One of Lillian's staff pushed a cart into the room. He placed two large platters in the center of the table, followed by several smaller ones containing side dishes. Claire—Lillian's much nicer housekeeper—followed him in with the wine.

"Thank you," Lillian said as the two departed the room. "Help yourselves, folks. We're informal tonight."

My idea of informal was a piece of cold pizza straight from the refrigerator or a bag of french fries on my lap while I drove home from work.

As soon as everyone filled their plates, Lillian opened the conservation by asking Jackson a blunt question. "Mr. Hunter, what the hell are you doing in our town?"

Jackson's fork landed back on his plate as he thought about the question. "Right now I'm getting ready to take a bite of this fine food. Then I'm planning to wash it down with some of this expensive wine."

Someone cleared their throat nervously as the sound of clicking utensils picked up around the table.

"Don't be flip, Mr. Hunter." Lillian lost her condescending smile. "I asked you a question."

In all fairness to Jackson, she was being a bitch.

He leaned back in his chair and looked around the table. Most of the guests were too uncomfortable to meet his eyes as he challenged the grande dame of Savannah. "No offense, Lillian," he continued. "I'm just not used to being talked down to. At least not when I'm a guest in someone's house." He pushed his chair back from the table and stood up, placing his napkin next to his plate. "Excuse me."

"Jackson?" I got up from my chair as he walked away.

"I don't mean to be rude," Lillian finally conceded. "But you have to understand something. Savannah is my home, and I will do whatever it takes to protect this town."

Fin held his hands up to referee. "Now, everyone in this room needs to shut up!"

Lillian glared at him.

"Especially you, woman."

"Preach, Fin," Davina said as she continued to eat her pork loin without looking up from her plate.

Jackson sat back down and answered the question. "I'm here because I needed to get out of Atlanta. I'm staying because of Katie." He glanced across the table and locked eyes with me. "I've got some money hidden away that somebody wants to get their hands on. I'm not gonna let them."

"The shifters Miss Bishop was telling us about?" Lillian asked. Jackson nodded.

"Well then, the question is, how do we get rid of them?"

"We don't," he said, giving her an irritated look. "I don't think you understand what I'm telling you, Lillian. The Sapanths aren't a group of unintelligent thugs who like to steal from people for fun. They're killers."

Alma Turner nearly choked on a brussels sprout.

"Cough it up," Davina said, smacking her on the back with the flat of her hand before looking at Jackson. "Why don't we just get to the point. What's their weakness?"

He cocked his brow at Davina. "You're assuming they have one."

"Everybody has a weakness. Even that dragon sitting across the table," she said, nodding at me.

My weakness used to be my inability to control the beast, but now that I had a tight rein on the dragon's will, I wasn't sure I had an Achilles' heel anymore.

"Sounds to me like we need to just let them come," Moses said with a firm nod. "Pardon me if I don't agree with your passive attitude, Mr. Hunter. I say we ambush them with some magic when they cross the city line. Show them what a real coven of witches can do."

"Now that's the stupidest thing I've ever heard come out of your mouth." Davina sneered. "You ever gone up against a shifter? Hell no!" she said before he could answer. "Well, I have. The Ozarks are full of shape-shifters, and they can be mighty nasty. No offense, Katie." She glanced at me.

"None… taken," I awkwardly replied, a little uncomfortable with being lumped in with shape-shifters.

Jackson looked around the table. "I'm afraid this is something the society can't fix. It's me they're coming for, so I'll be the one getting rid of them." He turned to Fin. "I'd appreciate you

46

keeping me in the loop if your contacts downtown notice anything strange going on."

Fin nodded. "That goes without saying."

Emmaline started to speak but hesitated. "I might be able to help," she eventually said, barely above a whisper. She had some pretty fierce powers; telekinesis for one. I'd witnessed it firsthand.

Lillian abruptly stood up from the table. "No!"

"For God's sake, Lillian, calm down," Fin said.

She shot him a look that upped the tension in the room. "I will not have that child anywhere near a pack of murderous… male shifters!"

"Emmaline is not a child!" he replied just as sharply.

Jackson interrupted the quarrel. "It doesn't matter. We won't see them coming. It's part of their strategy. Emmaline might be useful to us if we can back them into a corner, but until that happens, I'll handle this my way."

Suddenly realizing that everyone at the table was looking at me, I followed their eyes down to my hands. My fork was gripped between a set of sharp talons protruding from the tips of my fingers.

"Shit," I whispered, closing my eyes and taking a deep breath, trying to let the nervous energy I'd absorbed from the tense room seep back out of me. Unfortunately, the claws were still there when I opened my eyes.

Jackson appeared calm, but I knew what was running through his head. Everyone in the room knew what I was, but he was the only person who knew about the deadly ritual I'd gone through that supposedly made me master over the dragon, the one my aunt facilitated that nearly killed me. This wasn't supposed to happen anymore, so why was I spontaneously sprouting talons in the middle of a dinner party?

"Katie?" Jackson was staring at me intently.

Fin glanced back and forth between us, picking up on our

silent conversation. "Something you're not telling us, Miss Bishop?"

"Everything's fine, Fin." I wiggled my fingers as my claws receded. "See? Show's over, folks." I resumed my meal. Obviously I was still trying to master my new skills as the dragon's commander in chief. A minor glitch.

I stuffed a forkful of salad into my mouth as we got back on topic.

"Agreed, Mr. Hunter," Lillian said. "But I expect you to let the society know when the pack arrives."

Jackson smirked. "Don't worry, Lillian. You'll know."

We spent the rest of the night enjoying the delicious meal Lillian's cook had prepared for us and drinking copious amounts of overpriced wine to settle the nerves that had afflicted everyone at the table. Even Emmaline had a glass.

Jackson took a final bite of his food and deliberately laid his fork and knife side by side at the four-o'clock position on his plate, a signal for Lillian's staff to clear it from the table.

Lillian watched as the man left with the plate. "Something tells me you're no stranger to eating off fine china, Mr. Hunter. Now where does a man like you learn that kind of table etiquette?"

Jackson suddenly seemed uncomfortable. "Thanks for the meal," he said to Lillian as he stood up, igniting a unified murmur around the table as he left the room.

I glared at Lillian for a second before following him down the hallway and out the front door. "Wait, Jackson!" I yelled as he climbed on his bike. When I caught up to him, the look in his eyes made me freeze for a second. "What the hell was that all about?"

"I guess I should be asking you the same thing," he replied, glancing down at my hands.

Lillian had pushed a button somewhere deep inside him, and

I deserved to know what it was. "Don't change the subject. What was Lillian talking about back there?"

"Let it go, Katie," he said, evading the question. He held my gaze as if he wanted to say something but then started the engine. "Am I coming home with you?"

"I think I'd like to sleep alone tonight." It was a lie, but I had somewhere to be. "Lunch tomorrow?"

He reached for me and cupped the side of my face, saying nothing. Then he backed away on his bike and took off down the road.

6

Sugar was meeting me at my house around midnight. Mojo's would be in full swing by then, and for reasons that weren't quite clear, my little Jackson problem had taken care of itself. Though I did feel like shit for letting him drive off like that. Something Lillian said had triggered him, and as soon as this night was over, I intended to find out what that was.

On my way home, I kept expecting to see Jackson's bike in my rearview mirror, following me from a discreet distance. But he never showed up. I guess he was abiding my request for some space. In the morning I'd tell him the real reason for making him back off.

Sugar's Eldorado was parked in my driveway when I pulled up to the house, the music blasting some obnoxious beat all over the neighborhood. I pulled up behind it since there wasn't room to park next to that boat.

"Jesus, Sugar," I said, walking up to the car. "I'm surprised my neighbors haven't called the police yet."

She gyrated in her seat for a few more seconds, singing to a seventies classic. Then she killed the music and glanced in the mirror. "Girl, you got to move that thing so I can back out."

I looked at her like she was crazy. "We're taking my car, Sugar."

She was about to argue with me until I made my next point. "You're going to stand out like a disco ball at a funeral when we walk inside that bar. Do you really want to make it worse by driving up in this thing?"

"Hey, I like that idea, having a big ol' shiny disco ball at my wake. Maybe you can hang it over my urn and play some Sylvester or Rick James."

Shaking my head, I walk up the driveway to my front door. Jet was lounging on the kitchen counter when I walked inside.

"Off!" I yelled. "You know better than to jump up there."

"Girl, you in a mood tonight," Sugar said, glancing at Jet sympathetically.

I reached down to pet him. "Sorry, baby. Mommy's just a little bit on edge tonight because she's about to walk into a hell-hole to look for Uncle Sea Bass."

Sugar sat at the island and glanced around the kitchen. "Got anything to drink?"

"Let's not get trashed before we even get to Mojo's."

She was wearing a pair of skintight jeans and a tank top with a Rolling Stones logo, both allowing her private parts to telegraph through. "Fine."

"You look… trashy," I said, thankful that her vintage leather jacket would cover some of it up.

"When in Rome, baby." She eyed my outfit distastefully. "I hope you're planning to change them clothes you got on." She hopped off the stool and walked over to me, placing her index finger at the neck-line of my T-shirt and pulling it down toward my cleavage. "You need to show them girls tonight, Katie B. Ain't gonna get shit out of them boys over at Mojo's without giving them a little peek at the boobies."

51

I swatted her hand away and headed for the bedroom. Before I had a chance to kick my shoes off, she was rooting through the top drawer of my dresser. She dug through my shirts like a dog digging up dirt, tossing the rejects on the floor as she hunted for the perfect one.

"Now this one will get you some free drinks." She held up a T-shirt I'd never actually worn before—at least not in public. It was about two sizes too small and had the word JAILBAIT written across the front. It had been given to me as a joke years ago and needed to be thrown in the trash where it belonged.

"You've got to be kidding me, Sugar."

She gave me a mock look of surprise. "Do you see a smile on my face? Now let's find you some tight jeans."

We compromised. I wore those tight jeans she pulled out of my drawer, but I insisted on a plain white tank top that hugged the "girls" nicely. I also agreed on a pair of stiletto boots that I seldom wore on account of how my feet screamed every time I put them on.

After a few minutes of back-and-forth, she finally conceded to riding in the Honda. As we drove, I told her about the conversation at Lillian's.

"Davina was there, of course."

She looked startled. "I didn't even think about Davina. Did you tell her about Sea Bass?"

After Jackson had taken off, I'd gone back inside to question Davina. "I pulled her aside and asked if she'd seen him recently. She claimed she hadn't seen him in days, so I had to tell her he didn't come home last night or show up for work."

"Well? Did she go ballistic?"

My brow twisted as I recalled Davina's strange reaction. "Not really. She looked a little surprised at first, but then it was more like she wasn't shocked at all. She told me not to worry about it. Said he was probably just off on a bender."

I could tell by the look on Sugar's face that she wasn't buying it. Neither was I, which was why we were headed for a dive that you couldn't otherwise pay me to set foot in after my accidental introduction to the place a while back.

My stomach sank as we pulled into the parking lot of Mojo's, which was filled to capacity. The motorcycles lined up along the front of the place were an indicator of the fun we were about to have the second we walked inside. I found a spot near the entrance where a car was leaving. A truck trying to sneak in from the other side nearly cut me off.

Sugar was about to stick her head out the window to yell a few choice words, but I grabbed her by the arm before she had a chance to start something with the regulars. "Jesus, Sugar. Can we at least get inside before you start a fight?"

"Sorry-ass, backwoods rednecks!" she spat out as she settled back into her seat and adjusted her blond wig.

I turned the car off and took a deep, therapeutic breath. "Sea Bass is going to owe me one," I muttered as I reached for the door handle. "You ready?"

She looked in the mirror and puckered her lips. "Ready as I'm ever gonna be."

We stepped out of the car and headed for the front door. There had to be at least a dozen guys hanging out in front of the entrance, the designated welcome wagon for the women walking the gauntlet to get inside. But I figured any woman who came to Mojo's on a regular basis was expecting the attention. My sympathies went out to first timers who had no idea what they were walking into.

"Hey little kitty," one of them called out to me, pushing away from the wall he was leaning against so he could pump his hips back and forth. "Wanna hop on and have a little ride on my pipe?" He was clearly drunk.

Sugar stepped forward and planted her long legs wide, bracing her hands on her hips as she towered over him. "You wanna ride mine, baby?" Her skintight jeans left nothing to the imagination as his eyes wandered downward.

The guy lost his cocky grin when laughter erupted around him.

"Yeah, man," one of his buddies blurted out. "Why don't you go around back and fuck that."

I grabbed Sugar by the arm and got her inside before one of them took her up on her offer. "I appreciate the backup, Sugar. But *please* don't do that again."

Stevie Ray Vaughan was coming through the speakers as we walked through the crowd, searching for standing room near the bar. I figured the bartender was a good place to start. At least the music wasn't deafening, so we could actually hear each other speak. I grabbed Sugar again and made a beeline for an opening when one of the waitresses picked up a tray full of drinks and headed back into the crowd.

"Damn, girl!" Sugar yelled, rubbing her arm. "You got the Jaws of Life at the end of them arms?"

Ignoring her remark, I looked for the bartender. "You want a drink?"

"Yeah. Get me one of them strawberry daiquiris."

I glanced at her awkwardly. "I don't think they serve those here, Sugar."

"Fine. Get me a martini then."

A few minutes later the bartender finally appeared. "What can I get you, baby?" he asked, giving me that age-old leer as he glanced down at my cleavage. Then his eyes shifted to Sugar as she squeezed in next to me and planted her tits on top of the bar. They were impressive.

"You got any Stoli back there?" she asked. "'Cuz I'd like me a vodka martini with three olives. Please."

He popped a toothpick in his mouth, eyeing Sugar like she'd just asked for a glass of Dom Pérignon.

"We'll just have a couple of beers," I said, trying to mitigate the damage. Rule number one when walking into a bar like Mojo's—don't piss off the bartender.

For a terrifying moment, I thought Sugar was going to give him some attitude about that martini. But by the grace of God, her sour expression lit up as he slammed two bottles of Budweiser down on the bar followed by a couple of drinks.

"Well, what do we have here?" She flashed him a smile.

He nodded to the other end of the bar. "Courtesy of Mr. Steele." The man who'd bought the drinks was staring at us— staring at Sugar actually. The bartender removed the toothpick from his mouth and leaned closer to Sugar. "Now you be nice to Mr. Steele," he said with a little too much amusement. "He likes ladies like you."

Sugar lit up even more and waved across the bar. "He is kind of attractive." As the bartender walked away, she turned on her heel like she was going to personally thank our drink benefactor.

"Wait, wait, wait!" I said. "Where do you think you're going?"

"Girl, I ain't going into the bathroom with the man. I'm just going over there to thank him for these nice drinks." Before I could argue, she took off across the room toward Mr. Steele.

I waved for the bartender. "What's your name?" I asked when he came back over. Never hurt to establish a little rapport. He leaned into the bar and shifted the toothpick around his mouth with his tongue, catching on to that little trick right away. I guess I sounded like a bar groupie trying to wrangle more free drinks.

"Just tell me your name," I demanded, irritated at the whole situation.

"Tom," he replied. "What's yours?"

"Linda." I don't know why I lied. After tonight I'd never see him again.

He read my bullshit and scoffed. "Whatever."

"It's Katie. Okay? I'm looking for someone."

He snorted and straightened back up. "Everyone in this place is looking for someone."

"You know a guy named Sea Bass?"

His face sobered as he took a step back and started wiping down the bar.

"I'll take that as a yes."

"Is he your boyfriend?" he asked, and I laughed under my breath. "Your husband?"

"Just a friend. He's missing. Someone told me he's been coming in here lately. All I want to know is if he was here last night."

He dropped back down on his elbows and got dangerously close. "What do I get for talking?"

I'd seen that look so many times that it made my skin crawl. I leaned into his space and zeroed in on his eyes, allowing my beast to surface for a split second. "You get to make it home tonight," I said as the dragon's emerald eyes leered back at him.

He stumbled back against the rear wall, nearly taking out a row of liquor bottles lined up on the shelf. "What the hell are you?"

The people standing at the bar looked at me, but all they saw was an ordinary woman with black hair and blue eyes, startled by the strange behavior of the bartender. He pulled himself together and ran his hand over the top of his head before obliging me with an answer. "Yeah, he was here. Stayed for a couple of hours."

"By himself?"

"Fuck this," he said, walking away without answering my question.

"Answer the question, Tom. You don't want me to come back here after closing when you're walking to your car, do you?" It was a threat I planned to make good on if he didn't answer me. Sea Bass was like family, and this asshole knew something.

"Look," he said, coming closer. "He used to come in here every now and then for a few beers. But for the past week he's

56

been showing up around three a.m. every morning. Orders the same thing."

"Oh yeah? What's that?" I tried to sound cool and calm when what I really wanted to say was *what the fuck!*

"The only thing left in the kitchen after it closes—chicken livers. Sits over there at a table and chases chicken livers with tequila."

I pulled out my cell phone and showed him a picture of Sea Bass. "You sure it's this guy?"

"Yeah, that's him. Told me his name when he started coming in here over the summer. I don't know many guys named Sea Bass, do you?" He stared at me for a few seconds, waiting to be dismissed or something. But I just kept running his words through my head, trying to make sense of them. How was Sea Bass sneaking out of the house every night with Maggie sleeping right next to him? And why? Then I remembered him telling me she wasn't spending the night lately because of his wild dreams.

When I looked back up, the bartender was still standing there, waiting for me to tell him he could leave. "We're done," I said, but he just stood there. "Don't worry, you cooperated. I'm not coming back for you."

Relieved, he headed for the guy two stools down who was waving his empty beer bottle in the air. He slid a fresh one in front of the guy and started to walk away.

"Hey, Tom," I called out. "You got a ladies' room in here?" It was a stretch, but as long as it had a toilet and a door, I'd manage.

He nodded toward a hallway on the left side of the room.

"Don't let anyone take my spot," I warned with another flash of my dragon eyes. As least something worked on command.

I ducked into the small alcove and spotted two doors without a sign on either. "Shit." I wished I'd used my brain and peed before we left the house. Following my first instinct, I pushed open the door on the left, making a mental note to wash that hand before I went into the stall.

The first thing I saw when I stepped inside was a row of four stalls without any doors. Then I spotted a mountain of blond hair cascading over the edge of the sink on the other side of the room. The woman was jerking rhythmically against the porcelain edge as the guy behind her thrust himself against her naked ass.

My eyes went from the sagging jeans circling his thighs, back up to his eyes which were now focused on me as he got down to business and finished the act. I found it nearly impossible to look away. When he finally pulled out of her and yanked his pants back up, he ran his hands over his shaved head and then washed them in the sink where she was still slumped over and oblivious to my presence. Or she just didn't give a shit.

I backed out of the bathroom when he headed straight for me, his eyes piercing mine as he squeezed past, forcing me back against the wall in the narrow hall. He stopped and planted his hand against the wall next to my head, raising his brow in question.

"In your dreams," I said, sliding to my right and into the other bathroom, praying it had doors on the stalls.

My spot was still available when I got back to the bar.

Good boy, Tom.

"What are you drinking?" someone asked.

I turned around and leaned my back against the bar to see who'd just offered to buy me a drink. I hadn't even touched the one Mr. Steele had sent over, and knowing now what I was in for if I had to use that bathroom again was incentive enough to keep my bladder empty. Besides, it was best to stay sober in a place like this.

"Well, look who it is," I said to the guy who'd showed me his dick a few minutes earlier. "Mr. Clean." Then I slowly shook my head to let him know he was wasting his time.

He was good-looking. Too bad he was such an asshole. Tall, ripped, eyes the color of amber. I had a feeling he was one of those guys who wouldn't look half as good with a headful of hair.

And I had a thing for bald men. Funny how I'd ended up with a guy sporting a black mane that fell halfway down his back.

I spotted Sugar at the other end of the bar, still talking to Mr. Steele. She pointed to herself and then at me with a question on her face. I shook my head to let her know I was fine because the two seemed to be hitting it off.

"Come on," he said with an overconfident grin. "It's just a drink, not an invitation to go back into that bathroom." His grin darkened. "But if you'd like to?"

I knew guys like him from the biker bars on the Lower East Side back in Manhattan. Refusing a free drink was tantamount to saying *fuck you*, guaranteeing a bruised ego and possibly a parking lot confrontation on your way out. On the other hand, accepting that drink might give him ideas.

"Sure," I said, choosing my battle. "But that's as far as it goes. I have a boyfriend. And I already have a drink I haven't even touched yet," I added, nodding to the bar behind me.

He glanced around the room and brought his eyes back to mine. "If you were my woman, I wouldn't leave you alone for a second. A lot of dogs in this place."

"That's kind of antiquated," I said. "If my boyfriend tried to pull that shit with me, he wouldn't be my boyfriend for long."

"Is that right?"

"That's right." I turned back to the bar to retrieve my untouched beer. When I turned back to face him, he was dangerously close. So close I could smell him. "You might want to take a step back," I said, gently warning him. No need to start a war with a guy who probably had a pretty high success rate with a face like that in a place like this. I just needed to show him some boundaries.

I tried to step to the side, but his arm braced against the bar, stopping me.

"Dude," I heard Tom say from behind the bar. "You might want to rethink that."

By the time I looked across the room, Sugar was already on her way over.

"Move your arm," I asked nicely, offering him a chance to redeem his bad manners before I went all dragon on him. He moved closer, and I could feel his crotch press against me.

"You *fucking* guy," I gritted out, grabbing his wrist as my fingers began to split where my claws were emerging. "I didn't want to do this."

As the blood began to run down his arm from my talons puncturing his skin, his pupils thinned and his irises stretched to cover the whites of his eyes. He wrapped his hand around my neck in a painful grip and pulled me against him, running his tongue down the side of my face.

"Baby, you taste different. I wonder what the rest of you tastes like," he hissed into my ear. Then he shoved his other hand between my legs and gripped my neck so tight I couldn't breathe. "What the hell are you?" he asked. "I like to know what I'm about to fuck."

What little air I had left in my lungs came rushing out as my feet lifted off the ground. He took several steps back, suspending me like a rag doll for the whole bar to get a good look at. Then he scanned the faces of the people in the room before bringing his eyes back around to mine. I was losing consciousness. "I like my whores pretty. And fucking quiet!" He sneered as they scattered. "Now, you gonna shut up?"

The black spots floating around my inner eyelids suddenly burst into green, and my eyes began to burn. I took a strangled breath and his hand went limp. I suspected it was the uncomfortable heat from my skin. He let go of my neck, dropping me to my feet. Then I slammed backward, hitting the bar as I sent him flying through the room with a flick of my fist. The place went up in a collective scream as people crashed into each other, scrambling to get out of the line of fire, knocking over tables and chairs as they fled for the exits.

Sugar came to a halt just before she slid into the middle of it. "Jesus, Katie!"

With my other arm, I sent her in the opposite direction, trying not to slam her into the wall. The alternative was worse. She landed near the entrance with a sickening thud, but I was thankful to see her crawl out the door on her hands and knees.

When I looked back at my target, he was on his feet again, tracking toward me with a grin on his face.

He stopped a few yards away and spit blood on the floor, wiping the rest from the corners of his mouth with the back of his hand. "Well, that was fun," he sneered. "You're like a leopard in heat. But you've got some real fire, baby."

I gasped as he turned around and headed for the giant window at the front of the bar, smashing the glass with his bare fist. As he stepped through the frame, I could clearly make out the tattoo written in bold black letters across the back of his head.

SAPANTHS.

7

Sugar lay in my bed, convalescing from the concussion I'd nearly given her the night before. I'd called Jackson from Mojo's after realizing Sugar was down, and as soon as we got her back to my place he took my car to fetch May—Sugar's mama.

May took one look at her child and shook her head, spouted off some gibberish that I was pretty sure was actually some sort of powerful conjure magic, and then stuffed a small pouch inside Sugar's mouth—to her displeasure.

Don't let her spit it out till the first bird sounds off in the morning, she'd said.

I slept in the chair next to the bed, waiting until I heard a bird chirp past the window that morning. Then I walked over to the bed and told Sugar she could spit it out.

"'Bout time that damn bird showed up," she said, dropping the saliva-soaked pouch into my palm.

I walked over to the window where I'd seen the bird fly by and opened it to drop the pouch on the ground, which was the second half of May's instructions. "What was in that?"

"I don't know, but it tasted like ass." She threw the comforter off her legs and then quickly pulled it back over them. "Where the hell are my pants? I ain't got nothing on under here."

I headed for the folded pile of clothes on the dresser and tossed the laundered jeans and underwear to her. "You had a little accident last night. Scared the shit out of you—literally."

Don't laugh.

Her eyes flashed wide as she scrambled to remember what happened, humiliation crawling all over her face.

"Don't worry about it, Sugar. I almost shit my own pants when he lifted me off the ground."

"Yeah, but you didn't, did you? Don't tell me Jackson stripped me naked."

I tried not to snicker at her expense. "No, your mama did."

Sugar had passed out with that thing in her mouth, and May took care of all the dirty work before Jackson drove her back home.

"Feel good enough to get up?" I asked. "Jackson's making breakfast."

Sugar's nose went up, catching the smell of bacon floating through the air. "Damn, that boy can cook too?"

"I guess we're about to find out," I said. He'd never cooked for me before, so I wasn't sure what to expect. But who couldn't fry up a pan of bacon? "Get dressed. We'll be in the kitchen."

The sight of bacon, eggs, and biscuits spread over the kitchen island triggered an explosion of endorphins in my brain. I was starving. "Where's Julia Child?" I said, glancing around the room.

He took a bite of bacon and laughed. "You're a lucky woman. I can cook."

"I can see that," Sugar said as she appeared in the hallway. She walked into the kitchen and poured herself a cup of coffee. Then she grabbed the plates from the cabinet and handed me one.

We sat around the island and ate. Jackson had been particularly patient with the questions I knew were burning a hole in his head. All I'd told him when he picked us up at Mojo's was that someone had attacked us at the bar, but I knew he was just waiting for me to start talking.

"You remember how you got all moody last night during dinner and decided to hop on your bike and take off?" I figured I'd leave out the part about Sugar and me actually planning that trip to Mojo's prior to dinner.

Jackson lifted his eyes from his plate and swallowed his mouthful of food. "You mean after you told me you preferred to sleep alone?"

I set my fork down. "Well, why didn't you just say something if you wanted to come over that bad?"

"Will you two shut the hell up!" Sugar blurted out. "Katie went all dragon on some guy last night when he lost his manners. But that wasn't no normal guy," she added under her breath.

Jackson shot me a demanding look, so I just put it out there. "The Sapanths have arrived. I met one last night."

"You met one?" His cocked brow suddenly furrowed. "What did he look like?"

"Tall, brown eyes, ripped like a… lion. He was pretty good-looking." I shrugged.

"And what makes you think he was a Sapanth?"

I shoved another forkful of eggs in my mouth because I knew breakfast was about to abruptly end and I was still ravenous. Then I washed it all down with a swig of coffee before confirming the sighting. "Because he had SAPANTHS tattooed across the back of his bald head. Kinda gave him away."

Jackson looked like he'd just been punched in the gut. He stood up and went for his leather jacket hanging over the back of the couch, returning with this phone. "Is this him?"

I looked at the guy in the picture straddling a Harley. He had a full head of hair, but it was the same guy from Mojo's who'd charmingly informed me about how he liked his whores. "Yeah, that's him." But something told me I wasn't looking at one of Kaleb's men. "That's Kaleb, isn't it?"

The look on Jackson's face was murderous. "Yeah, that's him. I'm gonna kill him for coming near you."

"Let's just slow down, Jackson," I said, raising my hands. "Everyone's okay, and the last thing we need in this town is a war."

He stood up and put his plate in the sink. When he turned back around, he gave me an accusatory look that I didn't particularly appreciate.

"Don't look at me like that."

"You still haven't told me what you two were doing at Mojo's last night." He glanced at Sugar as she buried her face in her breakfast to avoid his glare.

I didn't have that option.

When he showed up at the bar to pick us up the night before, I put him off because I had more important things to worry about, like Sugar possibly having a concussion. "It's Sea Bass," I said. "He's missing. Mouse said he's been going over to Mojo's. We went over there to ask around to see if anyone had seen him."

"And you didn't think it was a good idea to bring me along? To a biker bar?" he practically growled. "Damn irresponsible woman."

I knew he was just shaken by the fact that Kaleb had shown up at Mojo's, but he was starting to piss me off. "Jesus, Jackson," I said, irritated by his Neanderthal temper. "How much information do you think I would have gotten if I'd walked in there with you? The pissing contest would have started before we made it through the front door. And by the way, it's not a biker bar," I added with an angry rise in my voice. "It's a shithole dive that I'm perfectly capable of maneuvering without an escort." I stood up and nearly knocked over my stool. "Have you seen these before?" I held my hands out and flashed my talons.

"Damn, girl!" Sugar blurted, stumbling off her stool. "Put them things away!"

"I'm sorry, I'm sorry." I shoved my hands behind my back.

Jackson stepped around the island and pulled me against him. He reached for my right hand and kissed my palm, calming me and banishing my claws. "I'm trying not to be the type of guy that you hate, Katie. But if we're partners, you have to let me be that guy when shit like this happens. Just tell me before you do something stupid like that again."

I pulled away to give him a pointed look, taking exception to being told I'd done something stupid. "Does that mean you would have let me walk into Mojo's by myself last night?"

"It's a free country. I probably would have argued against it and camped out at the diner across the street, but I wouldn't have tried to stop you."

"What do you mean by yourself?" Sugar said. "Baby, I was right next to you. Got you past that dickhead outside, didn't I?"

I laughed at the thought of that guy's face. "Yeah, Sugar. You were fierce."

"Did you at least find out anything about Sea Bass?" Jackson asked.

"The bartender confirmed that he's been in there every night this week." I still couldn't believe that the Sea Bass I knew, who worshipped Maggie and was one of my closest friends, was leading a double life in a dive like Mojo's. It made me wonder what else he was hiding. "Apparently he shows up around three every morning and sits at a table eating chicken livers."

"Chicken livers?" Sugar said with a sour expression. "Them things is nasty."

Jackson shrugged. "Not bad if you bread them and cook them right."

"Did anyone call Maggie this morning to see if he came home last night?" Sugar asked.

"Still MIA." I sighed.

Maggie had left me a message on my phone early that morning to let me know she was ready to call the police if he didn't show up by noon. I had to agree with her. The police wouldn't have thought much about a guy like Sea Bass vanishing for twenty-four hours, but after two days they'd have to listen.

Jackson glanced at my hands as I nervously twisted my napkin. "What are you not telling us, Katie?"

"It's Mira," I said, looking at Sugar. "You know, that shifter who was in the shop the other day eyeing Sea Bass like he was a T-bone steak."

"Mm-hmm," she replied. "Does that mean you know for a fact that this Mira chick is one of them Sapanths?"

"Kara confirmed it when I ran into her at Jackson's apartment."

The shock on Sugar's face reminded me that I hadn't told her about that yet. There hadn't been time.

"And when was you planning to tell me about this?" she asked, bobbing her head. "You know, me being your best friend and all."

"How about right now? I decided to pay Jackson an unannounced visit the other day, and guess who was there?" I said with a saccharine smile.

Jackson went mute when Sugar glared at him.

"He did tell her to get out though."

"Is she at least ugly," Sugar asked.

"On the contrary," I said. "She's... gorgeous. Tall, with strawberry-blond hair and doe-like eyes."

Jackson stood up and grabbed his jacket. "I can't listen to this. Want me to drop you off at the shop?"

I could tell he was just itching to stick to me like glue, but he didn't dare push his luck. And after last night, it was pretty clear I was Kaleb's match.

"I'll drive myself," I said. "But you can follow me if it makes you feel better."

I DID a double take when I walked through the back door. Unless I was hallucinating, Sea Bass McCabe was sitting at the desk at the back of the shop, hunched over a drawing he was working on. I glanced at the clock on the wall. It was ten a.m.

Abel gave me a funny look when I noticed him on the phone at the front desk, and Mouse was just sitting at her station, her mouth gaping the way it always did when she was deeply entranced by something interesting.

I started to say something, but Abel slowly shook his head and pointed to Sea Bass, who had his back to me.

"Sea Bass?" I said, quietly approaching him to look over his shoulder.

He had a red pen in his hand and was drawing circles, filling them in with the dark red ink until the paper was so thin that he was actually drawing on the wood of the desk.

"I'll take that now." I stilled his hand and pried the pen from his fingers. He let go of it but kept moving his hand like the pen was still there.

Mouse glanced at me when I walked past her on my way to Abel, but then her eyes went back to Sea Bass, her mouth still gaping as she watched him.

Abel was the first to say it. "I think he's lost his mind, boss."

"How long has he been doing that?"

He shrugged. "I came in about a half hour ago, and he was sitting just like that. Mouse said he was here when she got in around nine."

I took a steady breath and walked back over to the desk. "Sea Bass, honey," I began, but quickly realized I had no idea what to do next. Then I reached under his arm and coaxed him to stand up.

A shred of recognition crossed his face as he looked at me. "Katie?"

"It's okay, Sea Bass. You and I are going over to Lou's to have a nice cup of coffee. Then you're going to tell me where you've been all this time. Okay?"

He nodded his head and followed me toward the front door.

"We'll be across the street, Abel. Can you do me a favor and cancel his appointments?"

Abel glanced at the phone in his hand. "Already did that. How about you, boss? Want me to cancel yours too?"

"My schedule's open this morning. Just take care of business till I get back."

We walked across the street, and I deposited him in one of the window booths. Sunday mornings were usually pretty busy at Lou's, but the diner was relatively quiet today.

"You hungry, Sea Bass?"

He lifted his head and swallowed hard. "I'm so hungry, Katie," he said, looking at me like a vampire thirsting for blood. "Get me a number four, please." The number four was the biggest breakfast meal on the menu. He reached for his wallet, but his pocket was empty.

"Don't worry about it," I said. "It's on me. Be right back."

At the counter, I placed the order and then went back to the booth to wait for Lou to call out my name. We sat silently for a few minutes, with me trying to give him some time to come clean. But all he did was sit there staring at the table. I finally got a little impatient with the mute act and decided to dive in. "Where've you been for the past two days?"

He swallowed again and looked around the table at everything but me, reminding me of a dog that had been caught chewing up an expensive pair of shoes, remorseful and horrified by his actions.

Before I could push him harder, Lou walked up to the booth and personally delivered our food. He glanced at Sea Bass curiously and then gave me a knowing look. "Let me know if you need anything else, Katie."

"Thanks, Lou. I think food might help."

As soon as Lou turned to head back to the kitchen, Sea Bass grabbed his plate of eggs and sausage and inhaled half of it like an animal that had been starved.

"Slow down before you rupture something." Even a ravenous dog couldn't eat that fast without puking it all back up a few minutes later.

He eventually closed his eyes and pushed the plate away, washing it down with a glass of milk before sinking back into the booth.

"All right," I said, losing my patience. "Maggie and the rest of us have been through the wringer for the past two days. And now that you've got a nice full belly, you're going to explain what the hell's going on with you."

Hearing Maggie's name seemed to shake him up. "Maggie?" he repeated. "Is she okay?"

"Well, that depends on whether you mean mentally or physically. She's been out of her mind with worry."

His eyes locked on mine for the first time. "But she's okay? Physically?"

"You're starting to scare me. Why wouldn't she be?" It did occur to me that I hadn't actually talked to Maggie since yesterday morning, and it had been hours since she left me that message on my phone. "And where's your car or your bike? Neither one is parked behind the shop."

He just sat there, ignoring my questions and staring out the window at the shop across the street. I'd never seen such a vacant look on his face.

"Stop ragging me around. You haven't been home in two days. You haven't shown up for work. The bartender at Mojo's said you've been coming in there every morning to wolf down a plate of chicken livers at three a.m. Now why don't you tell me why I shouldn't fire you?"

"You've been over to Mojo's? Jesus, Katie. That ain't no place for you."

"Yeah, no shit." My sympathy for whatever had turned him into a ghost for the past two days was wearing pretty damn thin. "Now, I'll ask you one more time before I walk out that door and put a Help Wanted sign in my window. Where have you been for the past two days?"

"I don't know," he said with the most fearful expression I'd ever seen on his face. "You got to believe me, Katie. I don't know where I've been for the past two days."

I gave up and climbed out of the booth, waiting for him to follow. We walked back to the shop in silence, and he headed for the same seat at the desk where I'd found him when I came in that morning.

"Abel," I said before going over to make sure Sea Bass didn't start doodling all over the desk again. "Do me a favor and call Davina McCabe. Her number is in the database. Tell her we found her grandson, and she needs to get over here now."

He looked at me oddly. "Shouldn't we call Maggie first?"

"I'll call Maggie in a few minutes." My instincts were screaming that this was a family matter—a blood matter. "Right now he needs Davina."

8

Davina McCabe walked into the shop and scanned the room. She looked at every face before her eyes stopped on her grandson.

"He's been like this all morning," I said. "He doesn't seem to remember much about the past two days. Not even where he's been."

She gave Sea Bass a long look, and I could see him visually relax for the first time since I'd found him hunched over that desk.

I walked over to him and picked up the red drawing he'd been obsessed with and handed it to her. "It's just a bunch of red ink, but he's been scribbling it all morning." I nodded toward the desk. "It went right through to the wood."

"He stinks too," Mouse added.

Normally Sea Bass would have bantered back and forth with her, but he didn't even flinch. She was right. He did stink. Probably hadn't bathed since he disappeared a couple of days earlier. And I could tell by the way the comment rolled off her tongue that it wasn't meant as an insult. She was just being Mouse, stating the obvious in case the rest of us hadn't noticed.

"There, there, Sebastian," Davina crooned in a consoling voice, calling him by his given name. "Grams is going to take you home now. We'll get you all cleaned up." She cupped the side of his face and looked him in the eye for an extended moment. Then she nodded, and he seemed to understand that it was time to go.

She led him toward the front door and looked back at me. "Does Maggie know he's home?"

"No," I said. "I thought I should call you first. I was planning to call Maggie next."

Davina smiled at me, her wisecracking tenacity conspicuously absent. "Why don't you let me talk to Maggie," she said. "I'll give her a call when we get to my place." Before the door closed behind them, she turned to say one more thing. "I wouldn't count on him coming back to work for a few days, Katie. I hope it's not too much of an inconvenience. I'll compensate you for any lost revenue while he's recovering."

I shook my head vigorously. "That's nice of you to offer, Davina, but not necessary." I glanced at Abel. "Abel can fill in for him."

Something crashed against the floor a second later, and Abel bent down to pick up the broken coffee mug he'd dropped. Having been an apprentice for less than a year, he wasn't officially ready to work on clients yet. But he had more talent than some of the seasoned tattoo artists I knew, and I intended to supervise his work until I was satisfied with it. I figured if the clients were willing to be his guinea pigs, there was no time like the present to pop his cherry on actual skin.

"Well, you let me know if you need anything," she said.

"Just keep me updated."

Sea Bass looked like a lost child towering over Davina while she loaded him into her car. As I stood there watching them disappear down the road, one of Sea Bass's regular clients walked through the front door.

"Is Sea Bass off today?" he asked, looking around the room.

"He's taking a few vacation days," I replied. "Do you have an appointment, Mike?" Abel was supposed to have canceled all of Sea Bass's appointments.

"Nah. I figured I'd stop in and see if he had time to give me a small one here." He pointed to the only bare spot on his forearm. "Need to put something here to fill my arm up, but I can come back in a couple of days. When did you say he's back from vacation?"

I glanced at Abel. "Probably Tuesday or Wednesday, but Abel's available if you don't mind being his very first client."

Poor Abel. He looked faint. I'd almost let him work on me a few weeks earlier, but I changed my mind at the last minute. Not about him, about the tattoo.

Mike looked skeptical at first.

"I'll be right here watching," I said. "And it's half price. It's up to you."

He shrugged and headed over to Abel. "Just don't screw it up, dude."

I'D NEVER BEEN SO happy to close the shop. If we didn't already close early on Sundays, I probably would have locked up at six anyway. The day had been stressful, supervising Abel through his first three tattoos—which turned out amazing—and keeping an eye on the door just in case Kaleb or Kara decided to pay me a visit.

"You two mind locking up?" I asked Abel and Mouse. Abel swept the floor around his work area and nodded. I think he was relieved he hadn't misspelled anyone's tattoo. I'd caught him in the back making a stencil for his second client, sounding out the word he was about to tattoo on the guy's leg and double-checking it at an online dictionary. We'd all done that before.

I was cooking Jackson dinner at my place. Things had been so crazy that morning that I'd forgotten about our lunch date. When he showed up at the shop, he ended up running over to the deli to get everyone sandwiches. We'd all be eating in until Sea Bass came back to work.

Jackson's bike was parked in my driveway when I pulled up to the house. The smell of something heavenly hit my nose the minute I opened the front door, and I realized he'd taken the liberty of cooking me dinner.

"I thought I was cooking tonight," I said, tossing my bag on the table next to the door.

Before I even made it to the kitchen, he wrapped his arms around my waist and lifted me off the ground, setting me on the island and pressing his weight against me as he worked his mouth down my neck.

"It's been a couple of days," he reminded me as he lingered over my lips.

"Damn it, Jackson," I whispered, my voice breathy. "You know what that does to me." I was a boneless mess when he used his mouth like that, but I was also thoroughly exhausted and in need of a shower. "I don't have the energy tonight, and I think you'd prefer my active participation."

He pulled back and gave me a brief kiss, inhaling deeply as he walked back to the stove. "I made pasta," he said. "Threw in a little basil and tomatoes."

I hopped off the island and joined him. "That's two meals in one day, Jackson. I might have to marry you." As soon as I said it, I felt awkward. I'd just told him I loved him a week earlier, and now I was making marriage jokes?

He must have sensed my discomfort, but he just let his eyes linger on mine for a minute as if he wanted it to continue. He had no intention of letting me off the hook for that one, which made me even more uneasy.

I quickly changed the subject. "You know, you still haven't told me what upset you so much at dinner last night."

He pulled two bowls from the cabinet and filled them with pasta. "Grab a couple of forks," he said as he turned to put dinner on the island. "We need to get you a dining room table."

"And put it where?" I barely had room for the couch in the living room, so the kitchen island had to serve double duty as work space and table.

I decided to drop the dinner incident. Jackson and I rarely felt awkward around each other, but the sudden cold vibe in the room was making me uncomfortable.

"We should probably have some wine," I suggested a few minutes into the silent treatment. I also decided to grab the scotch from the cabinet while I was up. I set both bottles in front of him. "Wine is fine, but booze is even better."

He poured two glasses of scotch and handed one to me. Then he pushed his bowl of pasta away and started to talk. "I'm not hiding anything," he began. Which was good, because after he'd shared the other night that he had a couple million dollars stuffed in a cubbyhole somewhere in the state of Georgia, I wasn't sure our relationship could survive another big secret. "It's nothing. Just something I'm not proud of." He pulled his bowl back with his index finger and started to eat again as if the subject was dead.

"Oh no," I said. "You don't get to do that."

He laid his fork down and stared at the table while he chewed and swallowed his mouthful of food. "It's my parents," he eventually said. "They're not what you'd expect."

Since he avoided the subject of his parents like the plague, how would he know what I was expecting? The only time he'd ever mentioned them was when he told me about falling through a frozen lake when he was sixteen, the day he died and then miraculously came back to life an hour later with sudden Superman strength. I doubted he would have even told me about his strength if I hadn't witnessed it with my own two eyes at

Cairo's barbeque a while back, when he tossed a guy who'd shifted into a rowdy bear across the yard. Even then he'd barely mentioned his mother and father. I'd asked him a couple of times to tell me about them, but he always shrugged it off and changed the subject, something I could certainly understand considering my own warped pedigree.

"Don't tell me their names are Jonathan and Martha Kent and they live in Kansas," I said.

That coaxed a chuckle out of him. "Not exactly. But Ma did make my first superhero outfit."

"All right, I'll let it go," I said, standing up and grabbing my bowl. "But don't think for a second that this relationship is going any further without you trusting me enough to tell me who your damn parents are!" I tossed the rest of my pasta in the trash, suddenly realizing the man I'd professed my love to didn't think enough of me to tell me about his own family, let alone let me meet them someday.

He caught my arm as I started to walk past him to leave the kitchen. "Will you please sit back down," he calmly said. "Better yet." He grabbed the bottle of scotch and the glasses and headed for the patio.

I followed him because I had a feeling he was about to finally let me in on his big family secret.

He handed me my untouched drink and poured himself another.

"I thought you were drinking tequila these days," I commented.

"Why? You got any?"

"You finished the bottle the last time you gave me surprising news, remember? But I'll be sure to stock up if you plan to keep bringing tequila-worthy revelations into my house." I made a note to pick up a bottle the next day.

I welcomed the cool metal against my skin when I sat in the chair. Pretty soon I'd be dreading that cold sensation as fall set in and dropped the temperature into the arctic high sixties at night.

"I haven't always looked like this," he said.

I wanted to make some snarky remark about his lame opening to the conversation, but I was afraid of scaring him back into silence, and that door might never open again.

"Should have seen me ten years ago." I snickered. "I was a real nerd in high school."

He got his wallet out and reached into the side pocket to pull out a worn snapshot. "I don't usually carry pictures in my wallet." After staring at it for a second, he handed it to me. "Something told me we'd be having this conversation, so I dug it up."

After examining it for a minute, I looked at him. "This can't be you." I furrowed my brow. The boy in the picture had fair skin like Jackson's, but his hair was light brown. He looked sullen and small next to the man standing behind him who was gripping his shoulders. The resemblance was striking, so I assumed it was his father. I looked at the picture again, and I finally saw a glimpse of Jackson in the boy's green eyes hidden behind a pair of dark-rimmed glasses. "You look pretty angry in this picture."

He took the snapshot from my hand. "I wasn't angry," he said. "I was in pain. My father's hands were digging into my shoulders like a vise. He beat the shit out of me about twenty minutes before he made me stand in front of that camera. Kept photographic documentation of my corporal punishment because he got off on humiliating me." He laughed, and for a second I thought he was going to crumple the photo in his hand. Instead, he held it up. "I keep this picture as a reminder."

I was at a loss for words as I listened to him tell me about the man who raised him. Jackson was decent and kind. I couldn't imagine someone with his qualities being brought up by a man like that. "A reminder of what?"

"A reminder to stay clear of Louisiana," he replied with a raised brow. "New Orleans is Randall Hunter territory, and that state isn't big enough to keep us from going at each other." The look on his face was one of relief. It must have felt good to purge his secrets, but I had a feeling this one would take some time to fully unravel. "Mean as a snake. Damn rich too. Founded one of the biggest law firms in Louisiana and thinks everyone in the state owes him a debt because he did a little pro bono work after Katrina." He shoved the picture back in his wallet. "The only reason he did it was to make a name for his firm. He didn't give a shit about those people. But the real money comes from his side businesses. He owns a couple of clubs in the French Quarter. Washes money for his clients through them."

"Wow. I don't know what to say." I saw the uncomfortable look in his eyes and realized he took my reaction the wrong way. "I'm glad you told me about your father, Jackson," I quickly added. "I know you, and I hope you didn't think I would ever judge you because of your family."

He shook his head. "I never wanted to open that door, Katie. And you need to understand that you're never gonna meet him. The son of a bitch is poison."

"What about your mother?" I tentatively asked, hoping she wasn't just as bad. Maybe I should have left it alone, but I had to know the extent of his miserable childhood. We're all a reflection of our parents in one way or another. Sometimes it's as subtle as the way we talk, other times as obvious as our prejudices. But we all carry something forward, and I prayed his mother was a bright light to balance out the darkness of his father.

His mood lifted as he thought about her. "My mom was the opposite of my father. She died when I was seventeen. About six months after my accident. Had a stroke in her sleep." He glanced at me with a puzzled look on his face. "She wasn't even forty. The doctors didn't have much of an explanation, but I think it was the stress of living with the king of assholes for so many years. I'm sure keeping my secret from him took a toll on her mentally."

"You mean your powers?" I asked, incredulous at the thought that his father had no idea how special he was.

He nodded and clarified further why his father was such a colossal dick. "Dear old dad would have found a way to capitalize on my new skills if he'd known what I could do. We were living in New Orleans after all. All kinds of interesting streams of revenue from the strange and unusual in that part of the world. My mother made sure I kept my mouth shut, and so did she. I left home the day after her funeral. Haven't seen him since."

I was floored by everything he'd just told me, and it made me love him even more. "Well, don't worry about me wanting to meet your father. I'd probably sprout claws and try to kill the bastard if he said the wrong thing."

He got up and walked to the edge of the patio, surveying the darkness. I used to think he was looking for Kaleb in the shadows, but now I wondered if he was watching for the devil he'd been running away from since he was seventeen.

"That remark that Lillian made about my etiquette," he said, finally explaining what set him off the night before. "It spooked the shit out of me. Last thing I needed was to explain how I grew up eating beluga caviar off fine china. I was trained since I was old enough to hold silver in my hand how to choose the right fork at a fancy dinner party and how to *properly* position them on my plate when I was done with my meal. My father demanded that his wife and son look the part of the perfect privileged family." He snickered and muttered something under his breath that I couldn't make out. "If I embarrassed him in public by picking up my salad fork to eat my entrée, I'd pay for that little mistake when we got home. You don't just pull that etiquette shit out of your ass, Katie. And you don't just unlearn it either."

We sat under the night sky for a few more minutes, letting the dark but enlightening conversation sink in. A lump formed at the back of my throat as the images of that little boy suffering at the hands of his own father ran rampant in my head. Made me want to take a trip to Louisiana to show the bastard what it felt like to get his ass kicked.

My phone rang, breaking the silence we'd fallen into. When I saw Fin's name appear on the screen, my heart sank.

"What's wrong, Fin," I blurted without a proper greeting.

"Are you watching the news?" he asked.

Jackson and I went back inside and turned on the television. With the phone still in my hand, I watched numbly as the news captured an invasion taking place in Forsyth Park. The fountain at the north end was surrounded by bikers revving their engines and circling a group of reporters to the point where I couldn't hear what they were saying. One female reporter dropped her mic and screamed as one of the bikers rode past her and swept her off her feet. The others fled as the bikes began to circle them too. Through the chaos, the fountain in the background continued with its spectacular display of waterworks. But instead of the crystal-clear sprays that usually burst from its sides, the water ran red.

9

Jackson made a phone call and then we rode to Forsyth Park to meet Fin a few blocks south of where all hell was breaking loose.

"These are your people," Fin said to Jackson the moment we arrived. "How do we approach them without getting ourselves killed?"

"They're not my people," Jackson said. "You got that?"

Fin nodded, lighting a cigarette as he grumbled a few choice words. "I guess we need to go in there and find out what it's going to take to get them to spare our lovely landmark."

"You think you can bargain with them?" I said, incredulous at Fin's overconfidence.

"Well, Miss Bishop," he began, exhaling the smoke from his mouth. "I don't know a whole lot about their kind, but I do know when someone is trying to get my attention. That usually means they want something."

"Of course they want something," I said. "But it's Jackson's attention they want, and this is them pissing in the corner to let him know it."

"They're getting everyone's attention," Jackson said.

"Maybe I should fly over the party and get *their* attention with a little fire," I suggested. "Scorch the bastards."

I thought Fin was going to choke. "And destroy Forsyth Park? Like hell you will."

"As tempting as that sounds, it won't work," Jackson said. "I guarantee you they already know we're here. You won't make it past the tree line before they throw up a wall to block you."

"Thank God," Fin muttered, seeming more concerned for his precious park than the people standing around him.

"What kind of wall?" I scoffed.

Before Jackson could answer, we heard motorcycles in the distance.

"The Dimensional kind," he replied. "That would be Cairo arriving."

Before we left the house, he'd called Cairo and told him to meet us at the park.

Seeing the confusion on our faces, he clarified. "Most of Cairo's people followed him when he left the club, but a handful stayed with Kaleb. Unfortunately, that's all it takes to throw a pretty big wrench in our plan."

Fin chimed in. "We have a plan?"

A procession of bikes came roaring down the street and parked next to Jackson's Harley. Cairo climbed off the first one and removed his helmet, running his hand over his rust-colored hair, which matched his beard.

"Hey, you ugly motherfucker," he said to Jackson as he approached, greeting him with a firm hug and a pat on the back. Then he turned to me and did the same, reminding me that he didn't do handshakes. He turned to Fin next. "Well shit, Fin, I'd hug you too, but something tells me you'd try to kick my ass."

Fin held out his hand. "Cairo."

The two had only met once, but their acquaintance was still pretty fresh.

Cairo's wife, Angela, climbed off her bike and released a mane of long black hair from under her helmet. She was a real beauty, tall and lean with an air of confidence that made me wonder how she got together with an unpolished stone like Cairo.

She shot me a cocky grin as she walked up to us. "I guess you two are official. Lucky you, Jackson. I figured Katie would have ghosted you by now, but since she's prepared to walk into the lion's den with us, she must be into you for the long haul."

Jackson looked at me and held my gaze, letting me know that he agreed with her. He'd finally purged the secrets that I hoped were the last barriers between us, and he was also in for the long haul.

"I hate to break up this little lovefest," Cairo said, glancing toward the park, "but we got rats to get rid of. You ready to go in there and see what those fuckers want?"

"We both know what they want," Jackson replied.

"Yeah, well, I want to be a six-foot-four supermodel," Cairo snorted. "But that ain't gonna happen."

Jackson turned to Fin. "I don't think you want to go in there with us," he said, offering him an easy way out. "It's me they want."

"On the contrary, Jackson," Fin replied. "This is my town they're destroying, so I'd be delighted to go in there to have a little talk. As long as you folks are going in first," he quickly added. "I'm not entirely off my rocker."

Cairo shrugged and headed for the street. "Suit yourself." He motioned for the others to follow, and the band of malevolent-looking bikers climbed off their rides and headed toward the park. Jackson and I did the same with Fin behind us.

"Just do me a favor," Fin said to Jackson. "If I don't walk out of this park alive tonight, make sure those bastards don't either."

We crossed over the park boundary and headed for the fountain where Kaleb and his crew seemed to be having so much fun terrorizing the locals. The first thing I saw when we reached it were three bodies floating in the water, lifeless and turning the fountain the bright red color we'd seen on the news.

"Jesus," I whispered, wincing.

Fin seemed almost indifferent to the sight, but I knew him well enough to recognize the quiet rage festering under his skin.

One of the motorcycles circling the fountain came to an abrupt stop when we advanced closer to the scene. I recognized Kaleb as he kicked the stand down and climbed off the back of his bike, cocking his head at me in a curious way.

I took an involuntary step back, remembering how quickly he'd been able to get his hands around my neck at Mojo's the night before.

"Well, isn't this a small world," he said, grinning at me.

Jackson stepped between us when Kaleb looked like he was about to walk in my direction.

Kaleb jerked his head back and studied Jackson's protective stance. "She yours?" he asked, flipping his thumb at me.

Jackson didn't answer but gave him a warning look.

"Well, Jackson," Kaleb went on. "Your woman tastes like fire."

I gripped Jackson's arm as he took a step toward Kaleb. "Don't," I whispered. "That's what he wants you to do."

The pissing contest had begun, the two of them staring each other down like a couple of dogs getting ready to rip the other's throat out—or cats, in Kaleb's case.

Kaleb broke the stalemate, laughing as he looked at the defensive line of Dimensionals. "What's the matter, Jackson? Don't like to share your women anymore?"

My brow went up, but that was a conversation for another day.

I glanced around the area, looking for the face of the woman I'd met at Jackson's apartment a few days earlier. If Kara was in the park, she was doing a damn good job of hiding. I suspected she was a drama queen, so she'd probably decided to skip her daddy's grand entrance, not wanting to be overshadowed when she made her debut to the rest of Savannah.

Someone started to whistle. I glanced to my right and realized it was coming from Cairo. Every eye turned to look at him as he continued with his rendition of "You've Got Another Thing Coming." He strolled toward the fountain and reached over the edge to fish for one of the floating bodies, flipping it over to expose a face frozen in a surprised stare. It was the female reporter I'd seen on TV earlier that night. The one who'd screamed as one of the Sapanths grabbed her.

"Hey, is this that reporter from channel—" He snapped his fingers, trying to recall her name, a puzzled look on his face. "Annette, or... Anita something."

Before any of us had time to figure out what he was up to, his arm flicked toward the sky, releasing a series of concrete blocks from the tips of his outstretched fingers. They cascaded up through the air like a row of dominos, each one multiplying into the next as they flew over the fountain. He gave his wife a single nod, and Angela dove past me, hitting the ground and rolling toward the other side. The blocks came back down, crashing into Angela's body as she seemed to absorb them. I looked back at Cairo, but the only thing I saw was a concrete structure stretching into the sky. The two of them had formed a bridge over the fountain.

Jackson hooked me around the waist and pulled me out of the way as the edges of the bridge expanded, quickly fanning out into a dome that slammed down to the ground around the perimeter of the fountain, shaking the park as it trapped the Sapanths inside.

"Where's Fin?" I yelled, fearing he'd gotten himself trapped in that thing, which meant he was a dead man.

Jackson nodded behind me. Fin was on the ground about ten feet back, shaken up but safe.

The rest of Cairo's clan were standing at the edge of the

dome, their hands on each other's shoulders, forming a human chain.

"What are they doing, Jackson?"

"Holding the wall and throwing up some interference," he said. "Kaleb's Dimensionals are trying to breach the dome from the inside, which will happen if they can get past that mountain of energy the clan is raising."

"Where're Cairo and Angela?"

He looked at me like I'd asked a stupid question. "Where do you think?"

That's when I realized that they *were* the wall, which also explained why it was so critical for the clan to hold it up. If Kaleb's shifters raised enough power to demolish that dome, they'd destroy Cairo and Angela along with it.

"What the hell are they trying to do?" Fin asked, climbing back to his feet.

Jackson shook his head, seeming surprised by the simple genius of the plan. "They're gonna bring that wall crashing down once they've built up enough energy. It'll crush everything inside."

Fin looked horrified. "You mean the fountain?"

Assuming he was either in shock or he'd lost his mind, I ignored Fin's comment and gawked at the giant dome. "They're going to sacrifice Cairo and Angela to kill the Sapanths? And you're just going to stand back and watch?"

Maybe it was noble to sacrifice a few for the greater good, but the thought made me sick. I really liked those two, and Cairo was one of Jackson's best friends.

"Not if they bring it down themselves," he said with a sly grin. "They'll just shift into the rubble."

A sound came from the center of the dome. It started as a low rumble and built steadily until the ground started to tremble. A light radiated from inside, and the line of clansmen holding the wall took a step back.

"We weren't fast enough!" one of them yelled. "They're building their own dome inside!"

The look on Jackson's face confirmed my next question. Cairo's former clansmen, the Dimensionals inside that dome, had found the strength to fight back. They were throwing up a second dome inside that would protect them from the one threatening to come crashing down, basically calling it a draw.

"Now what?" I asked.

Jackson shrugged. "We wait for Cairo and Angela to take it down, and then we get the hell out of here." He turned to Fin, who was looking a little vulnerable. "I suggest you leave before that wall comes down. We have enough dead bodies to deal with."

Fin didn't argue, but before heading out of the park, he made it very clear that the Sapanths had just started a war. "The grove will be gathering soon," he said, glancing up at the nearly full moon. "Maybe we'll come up with a way to send them straight back to hell where they came from."

"Get in line," Jackson said. "If it was that easy to kill them, someone would have done it by now. This isn't Grove business, Fin."

"Well, we'll see about that." He turned to take Jackson's sage advice. "Call me when the park is clear," he said without looking back. "I have some bodies to clean up."

The comment made me shiver. I'd seen Fin in action when ugly things needed fixing. He'd saved my ass earlier that summer when I killed the man I was sleeping with—in self-defense—after a deranged god possessed him and nearly sucked the life right out of me. Fin had arranged to have Christopher Sullivan's body "cleaned up" so I wouldn't spend the rest of my life rotting in prison. It was a debt I could never repay. I owed him.

By the time we turned back around, Cairo and Angela had already shifted back and were lying on the ground.

As they regained their energy, one of Cairo's men came

running up to Jackson. "We need a diversion to get Cairo and Angela out of here."

Cairo managed to get up, but Angela was still struggling to climb to her feet. Building that dome had taken everything out of them.

"Get them out of here," Jackson said, looking back at the wavering smaller dome the Sapanths had erected. "You too," he said to me.

"I'm not leaving, Jackson."

He opened his mouth to argue, but there was no time. Cairo scooped Angela off the ground, shooting Jackson a look that showed his reluctance to leave. Jackson signaled for him to get going.

Without wasting another second, he told me to shield my eyes. As the smaller dome began to disintegrate, Jackson headed for it and dropped to his right knee. He brought his fist down so hard that the large pavers circling the fountain shattered into a hurricane of rocks and pebbles, causing the lampposts around the park to flicker and go out. I shut my eyes as it all exploded in front of me, slowly reopening them as the debris settled into a cloud of dust and the tremor reached the edge of the fountain. Initially the walls held. A few seconds later, a giant crack appeared on one side, quickly spreading around the entire structure. Then the dam burst, sending blood and water spilling out to the surrounding grass, followed by the bodies of the reporters who'd had the misfortune of showing up to cover the story of the renegade bikers tearing up Forsyth Park.

I knew Jackson was strong, but I'd had no idea he was capable of leveling the giant fountain. Fin would go ballistic when he found out.

The diversion worked. Cairo and Angela had made it out, but now we were alone with the Sapanths, who seemed unfazed by the explosion.

"Shit, Jackson!" Kaleb said, brushing the dust from his arms and looking at his Harley lying sideways on the ground. "You've been holding out on me."

The grin on his face was enough to make me want to stalk up to him and knock his teeth out, but before I could satisfy that urge, Jackson turned around and clocked him in the jaw. Kaleb stumbled back a few feet but caught his balance, shaking off the sting before sporting that shit-eating grin again.

Jackson reared back for a second blow but stopped. "Everywhere you go, people start dropping like flies. You're a goddamn death magnet, Kaleb."

"I'll take that as a compliment," he sneered. "But just remember something. You used to be right there next to me when they fell."

Jackson flinched as the comment hit home. I could smell the rage coming off him, making me itch to spread my wings and show Kaleb what he was up against. Jackson shot me a warning look when he heard the growl escape the back of my throat. This was his fight, and he was doing just fine. Good thing, because I was having a little trouble sprouting those wings.

What the hell?

"What?" Kaleb continued. "You think your shit doesn't stink anymore because you walked away and now you're fucking that sweet little creature over there?" He glanced at me and winked, sending Jackson into a second round of fury. Kaleb's crew tried to jump in, but he called them off, throwing his arms wide as he offered himself as a punching bag. Not that they could have stopped Jackson if they'd tried.

For the next ten minutes, Kaleb just stood there, letting Jackson turn him into a bloody side of meat. But shifters healed fast.

Jackson finally stopped, glancing at me with a weary look in his eyes. He'd won the battle today, but it was an empty victory.

"Come on, Katie," he said. "We're done with this piece of shit."

Kaleb laughed as we started to walk away, his eyes swollen half shut and blood saturating his clothes. "Hell, we're just getting started, Jackson. And there's still a lot of unfinished business between you and Kara."

He was baiting both of us. I squeezed Jackson's arm and smiled faintly to let him know it didn't bother me—which it did. Then we headed out of the park. There'd be plenty of time tomorrow for a feud, but right now we needed to get out of there to let Fin clean up the mess.

"One more thing, Jackson," Kaleb yelled out. "That's a fine woman you have there. When you rejoin the family, I expect you to share."

Jackson didn't flinch this time, having taken that bait one time too many tonight. Without turning around, he flipped Kaleb the bird and kept walking.

"Had to get one more in, didn't you?" I said.

I had no intention of telling him what actually happened at Mojo's the night before. All he knew was that I'd had a brief run-in with Kaleb, which was disturbing enough. The details would just eat at him until he did something really stupid.

We climbed on his bike and headed back to my place, with me dreading the thought that Kaleb probably knew where I lived. But I could take care of myself. In fact, I kind of welcomed the idea of him trying something when Jackson wasn't around. I owed that son of a bitch a good choking and a kick in the balls in return for that groping he'd given me.

Bring it on, Kaleb. Bring it on.

10

I slipped out of bed while Jackson slept. His night had been full of restless dreams, and I had a feeling Kaleb and his father were the stars of those nightmares. It was Monday, so the shop was closed, giving me some time to have a cup of coffee in peace while I replayed the incident in the park and braced myself for what was coming.

My peace didn't last very long.

Someone knocked on my door before I even had time to start the coffee maker. Most of my friends just jimmied the patio door to let themselves in, so a knock this early was not a good sign. Sugar was standing on my doorstep when I opened it.

"You knocked?" I said, surprised. "What's the matter? Forget your key? Oh, that's right. You don't have one."

She breezed past me, dropping her bag and newspaper on the counter as she headed into the kitchen. "I need me some coffee."

"I was just about to make some." I would have asked what she was doing in my kitchen at eight a.m. on my day off, but her early-morning visits were becoming a regular thing.

The interrogation began as she took the liberty of starting the coffee. "What the hell was that all about in Forsyth Park last night?"

"How do you know about that?"

"Shit, the whole damn town knows about it." She confirmed my worst fear by pointing to the newspaper.

I grabbed it and read the headline on the front page: FORSYTH PARK FOUNTAIN DESTROYED. THREE PEOPLE DEAD.

"So much for Fin taking care of those bodies," I muttered.

"What was that?" she asked. "Baby, you better get to talkin'."

I took a seat at the kitchen island as the shit started to rain down on me. The Sapanths, Sea Bass, Jackson's recent revelations; it was all a little too much to consider without caffeine. "Hurry up with that coffee, Sugar."

She poured a couple of cups from the half-brewed pot and handed one to me. "Now that's some high-octane stuff right there," she said, puckering her face as she took a sip and sat down on the other side of the island. "Okay, I'm ready to talk now."

"The Sapanths finally made their grand entrance last night," I said, sipping the rocket fuel in my cup. "Jackson called Cairo, and we all took a little ride over to Forsyth Park where they were leaving their calling card."

"You was down there when all that ruckus was going on?" She got up to get the creamer from the refrigerator. "I don't know why that surprises me. You always in the middle of it, girl."

"Thanks, Sugar. You're a real pal."

"Well," she said, whipping around to look at me. "It's true, ain't it?"

"Yes, Sugar, it is. But don't forget who's usually right next to me."

She gave me an appalled look. "I can't help it if you drag me into all your messes."

"Good thing Cairo and his clan decided to join us. Things got a little out of hand, and if it wasn't for them, I don't know if

Jackson would be back there asleep in my bed right now. Lord knows I was useless," I mumbled, sipping my coffee. "I don't think they were trying to kill us though. Kaleb was just getting everyone's attention. He's playing some kind of game with Jackson."

"I hate to ask," she said, "but who killed them reporters? Lord Jesus, don't tell me it was you."

I winced at the thought of how useless I'd been the night before. Jackson and Fin had convinced me not to fly over the park with guns blazing, but something else was grounding me. Something wasn't right. My dragon still had a pretty vicious set of claws, but something was holding it back. I'd had that feeling since a week earlier at the ritual that supposedly made me the master over the beast. From unpredictable and half-cocked to a tethered pit bull with a mean bite, I'd gone from one extreme to another. I hadn't flown once since setting myself on fire in my Aunt Marianna's backyard, and I was beginning to wonder if that ritual had gone too far and clipped the dragon's wings permanently.

"Of course I didn't kill those reporters." I scoffed, eyeing her like she'd lost her mind. "They were dead by the time we got there. Fin said he was going to clean it up, but I guess it's kind of hard to hide the bodies when the murders are streamed on live TV."

"The newspaper said them reporters was covering a pack of outlaw bikers tearing the place up," Sugar said. "A bunch of witnesses said they got the hell out of the park when they saw all that crazy shit going down." She suddenly cocked her head and squinted her eyes at me. "And why didn't you just go all dragon on them bastards? That would've ended it." She took another sip of her coffee, a disturbing thought seeming to cross her mind as she frowned. "Don't tell me you was scared of them shifters."

I mulled over the question for a few seconds. "Something's wrong with me."

Her cup went still at her lips. "What do you mean, something's wrong with you?"

"I don't know, Sugar. It's like the dragon is sedated or something."

She gave me a funny look. "What the hell you talking about? I seen what you did at Mojo's Saturday night. That dragon looked wide awake to me. Felt like it too."

My brow twisted. "It's like it's at the edge of a cliff just itching to break free and fly. But then it can't... burst past the surface of my skin."

"Well, I don't know about all that business," she muttered over the rim of her coffee mug. "But them claws of yours sure as hell came out, and that backhand you gave me was no joke."

"But you didn't see any wings, did you? I'm telling you, Sugar, I'm grounded."

Jackson walked into the kitchen wearing only his jeans and grabbed an apple from the bowl next to the refrigerator. He took a bite and glanced at Sugar. "Morning," he said with a cool tone before heading back to the bedroom.

He liked Sugar, but I could tell he was getting a little irritated by her regular morning visits. I couldn't fault him for wanting a little privacy. To be able to coax me back to bed every now and then.

She watched him disappear down the hall. "What the hell's wrong with him?"

"I think he's just tired after last night."

He came back out a few minutes later, fully dressed with his jacket on.

"Are you going somewhere?" I asked. We had a lot to discuss, and I had a feeling he was heading out to find Kaleb, cocked and ready to start a war.

"I'm driving out to Cairo's place. Then I'm gonna find out where Kaleb's hiding."

"I don't think he's hiding, Jackson. I think he's just waiting to finish that little pissing contest you two started last night."

The look on his face shut me up. If I didn't know better, I'd swear he was embarrassed for losing his cool in the park and feeding right into Kaleb's sick little game. Probably fueled his need for revenge even more, so maybe it was good that he was going to see Cairo, the voice of reason.

"This is my fault!" I suddenly blurted out, feeling guilty for not being able to do what I was born to do—incinerate those bastards. Or if my dragon had managed to take Kaleb out at Mojo's Saturday night, the rest of them probably would have hightailed it out of town by now and those reporters would still be alive.

"Fuck," Jackson hissed, shoving his keys back in his pocket before walking over to me. He took a deep breath before raising my chin to look me in the eye. "None of this is your fault, Katie."

"Damn right," Sugar chimed in. "It ain't your fault you couldn't sprout them wings and fry that SOB when he put his nasty hands all over you at Mojo's the other night."

Jackson stiffened. Then he dropped my chin and took a step back as Sugar's words sank in.

"Shit, Sugar." I winced and shut my eyes, sighing before reopening them to see the sheer hatred on Jackson's face. Whatever chance I had of keeping him levelheaded before he walked out that door had just been blown to hell by Sugar's big mouth.

"Don't do this, Jackson," I said, following him out the door.

Ignoring me, he climbed on his bike. "Try not to get yourself killed before I hunt him down," he said, starting the engine.

After he disappeared down the street, I went back inside and gave Sugar a venomous look. "You have got to put a filter on that mouth of yours."

She pursed her lips and stood up, grabbing her bag but leaving the newspaper on the counter. I thought she was about to storm out like Jackson had, offended by my harsh but true words. Instead, she looked back at me. "Come on. Let's go."

"Go where?"

WE PULLED up to May's house a half hour later, Sugar giving me the silent treatment the entire way over. She shifted the Eldorado into park and turned off the ignition.

I reached for the door handle to exit the car.

"Hold on," she barked, compelling me to let go of the handle. "I'm gonna forgive you for talking to me like you did back there," she said a few seconds later, her lips stretched tight across her face. "Do it again, and we gonna have us a problem." Then she opened her door, grumbling under her breath about my being lucky to have a friend like her, which was true.

"I'm sorry," I said. "But dammit, Sugar, you just cocked Jackson's trigger so tight there's no telling what he's going to do when he finds Kaleb."

"That's why we need to get that dragon back up to speed, baby. Find out what's got you all plugged up."

"I'm not constipated, Sugar."

"The hell you ain't," she replied, heading for the steps. "Got you some psychic constipation going on up in that head of yours."

Since she hadn't called May to let her know we were coming, Sugar knocked on the door instead of just walking in. Pearl May Mobley didn't take kindly to unannounced visitors, something we'd learned the hard way the last time we made an unexpected trip to see her and ended up with a shotgun in our faces.

"It's just me, Mama," Sugar yelled through the door.

We heard something crash. Sugar burst inside to find May sprawled on the floor near the entrance to the kitchen. "Mama, you been messing with them kudzu queens again?" She propped May into a sitting position, swatting a cloud of green particles away as she lifted her mother to her feet.

"What's a kudzu queen?" I asked, staring at the stuff floating all over the kitchen.

"Trouble, that's what they is. Mama's been trying to conjure up a good kudzu spell for years, but every time she messes with them nasty little demons, she ends up blowing out a window or knocking herself on her ass. Ain't that right, Mama?" she said with a chastising nod.

"I'm fine, Ray," she shot back. "Now back up, boy. Let me breathe."

Sugar walked into the kitchen and lifted a heavy pot off the floor. There was more of that green stuff hanging from the hazel tree branch bolted against the ceiling. May used it to dry herbs.

May finished brushing the debris from her arms and apron, shedding the confetti-like substance into the air where it disappeared before it hit the ground. "How you doing, Katie?" she asked, brightening up as if she'd just noticed I was in the room.

"She ain't too good, Mama," Sugar answered before I had a chance to reply. "She's a little stuck."

May's bright expression suddenly deflated as she cocked her head and studied me for a minute. "I can see." Her thin eyebrows pulled together. "Fire's gone out."

"We got us a real mess back in town, Mama," Sugar continued. She put the pot back on the stove and headed for the refrigerator. "You got any ginger beer?"

"Ain't made a batch yet, but I got some sweet tea in there." She looked back at me and grinned. "Bring Katie a glass too. She looks thirsty."

We headed into the living room where I took a seat on the sofa. Sugar and May sat down in the two chairs on the other side of the coffee table and stared at me.

"Why are you two looking at me like that?" I asked, uncomfortable with their intent scrutiny.

Sugar cleared her throat. "Now, I don't want you to panic or nothing, but girl, your eyes are red as fire."

I blinked. "I didn't get much sleep last night."

She took a sip of her tea and smacked her lips. "I think you'd have to stay up for a whole month to look like that." Reaching inside her bag, she pulled out her compact and handed it to me. "Take a look, baby."

I gasped when I peered into the small mirror. The whites of my eyes were the color of blood. "What's happening to me?" I whispered to myself. I was grounded, and now I looked like a demon.

May stood up and walked over to the sofa, bending down to take a closer look. After she'd examined me for a minute, she went into the kitchen and returned with a small jar. Then she told me to close my eyes.

"Why? What's in that jar?" I'd seen the things that lived in the mason jars in Pearl May Mobley's kitchen, and I thought it wise not to blindly consent—no pun intended—to whatever she planned to do with the contents of that jar.

"It's best not to question Mama," Sugar advised. "Unless you want to look like a zombie."

I trusted both of them with my life, but I wasn't sure I trusted anyone with my eyes. "Oh God," I whispered, reluctantly complying with the conjure woman. I could feel her breath against my skin as she got closer to my face.

"You can open your eyes now," she said.

My lids popped back open, and May blew the powder that was resting in the palm of her hand into my eyes. I gasped and almost struck her involuntarily as I bolted off the sofa and tried to clear the powder away from my face. "Jesus, May! What the hell!"

Sugar leaned forward in her chair to get a closer look. "Did it work, Mama?"

"Did what work?" I asked, still trying to clear my eyes and comprehend what May had done to me.

May handed me a napkin so I could wipe the irritating

power away. "You right, Ray," she declared. "She's blocked. That dragon can't feel a thing. Shoulda seen some fireworks come out of them eyes." She shook her head and squinted at me. "But nothing."

I glanced back and forth between them. "Will one of you please tell me what you're talking about."

"Ain't got no juice," May said. "Like it's got a lead weight around its neck. Can't hardly move."

Sugar suddenly looked as confused as I was. "Now Mama, I ain't trying to argue with you, but I know it can move. I got me that concussion Saturday night to prove it."

"Yeah," I said. "In fact, my claws have been coming out a lot lately."

May took a steady breath and thought about it for a second, still seeming to look past my eyes and into my soul. "Well, even an ailing beast is nothing to mess with." Her eyes went wide as a grin spread across her face. "You still channeling its parts, but the dragon can't get past the flesh."

"What does that mean?" I asked.

"Means you got to be patient. Ain't nothin' can keep a beast like that down for long. Medicine's coming, Katie. I can feel it."

My mouth opened, but Sugar shook her head and warned me with her eyes not to push it. "Mama don't always know all the details when she gets the wisdom."

If I'd learned one thing about Pearl May Mobley, it was that her words always imparted wisdom, even if it took a while to get to the crux of that wisdom. The key was patience. I just hoped that wisdom manifested before the Sapanths started a war. I needed my dragon fit and strong.

I glanced at the white powder sprinkled all over the coffee table. "What was that stuff you blew into my eyes?"

She picked up the jar, dipping her finger into the white powder before sticking the tip into her mouth. "Powdered sugar," she said, grinning widely. "Goes up like a torch when you throw it into a fire. If that dragon wasn't so weak, your eyes would have burst into flames."

I licked my lips where some of the residual powder was still stuck. "Powdered sugar," I muttered, shaking my head. If I wasn't immune to the devastation of fire—being half dragon—that might have scared me a little.

"Now," she continued, getting back to business. "About these shifters been tearing up town."

"You know about them?" I don't know why it surprised me. May was as clairvoyant as anyone I'd ever met. The thought of a marauding band of shifters invading her territory without her sensing it was absurd.

She nodded her head once. "You got to take the witches to them. Got to fight evil with good."

"The grove has agreed to back off and let Jackson handle the problem," I said. "They're too dangerous. If anyone can get them out of town with minimal casualties, he can."

The look on May's face surprised me. She knew just about everything, but I quickly realized that she didn't know Jackson's connection to the Sapanths. "They're here for Jackson," I informed her. "He has something they want."

She gave me a sympathetic look, knowing what he meant to me and perhaps foreseeing things to come. Then she grunted something under her breath as she headed back toward the kitchen. "Go on, now," she said without looking back. "I got me some queens to deal with."

We climbed back in the car and just sat there for a few minutes, trying to decide what to do next. The whole purpose in coming out here today was to figure out what was wrong with me. May had zeroed in on my problem, but all she said was to be patient and wait for some mysterious "medicine" to show up. But we didn't have time for patience.

I needed to pay a visit to the person who'd gotten me into this mess.

11

My aunt was leaving Savannah soon, having accomplished her mission. She'd been following me for years, eventually introducing herself and offering me a choice about how I wanted to live the rest of my life, the same choice she'd been given when she turned twenty-five. If it hadn't been for her, I'd be with my father at Mount Triglav, soaring over the Slovenian Alps as a full-blooded zmaj dragon. On my twenty-fifth birthday, she'd guided me through a dangerous ritual that changed the course of my destiny and made me master of the beast.

Supposedly.

"Katie!" Sugar yelled, bringing me back from my distracted thoughts. "Where the hell you at, girl?"

"Take me to my aunt's house."

Instead of taking the turn back to town, Sugar took a left and headed for Aunt Marianna's remote property where she'd stood watch over me during that fateful ritual. She was probably thinking the same thing I was, that the one person who could help me get my dragon back was the person who'd helped me wrestle it into submission.

"You better call that woman and let her know we're coming," she said. "Tell her to lock that dog up. I don't want that big ol' wolf trying to hump my leg when we get there."

I snickered at the memory of my aunt's Great Dane taking a liking to Sugar.

Aunt Marianna answered on the first ring when I dialed her number.

"It's Katie," I said. "I need your help." After briefly explaining that I was having issues with my dragon, I hung up and sank back in the seat while Sugar drove.

The remote road my aunt lived on looked benign in the daytime without the dark, eerie shadows that the giant live oaks cast at night. Built on a deep slope, Marianna's house seemed deceptively small from the outside. Inside, it was a cavernous midcentury with a high ceiling that reached a second-story loft. She'd been renting it, but now that I'd made it past my milestone birthday, her work was done and it was time for her to go home.

She was waiting for us at the front door when we pulled up.

"That dog ain't gonna come flying out of that house, is he?" Sugar asked.

Aunt Marianna laughed. "Wolfgang isn't here, Sugar. You're safe."

We went inside the house, and I took a seat in the living room. The last time I was here, I'd set myself on fire in the terrifying ritual that freed me. At the time, the dragon had come out and flapped around the vaulted space in a confused stupor and nearly destroyed everything in the room. Jackson had shown up and managed to talk me down. We thought that was the end of it and the dragon had become my servant. I never imagined it would become a shadow of the beast that it once was. The thought made me sad.

I glanced at the boxes around the room in various stages of being filled. "You're packing."

She nodded and exhaled. "My job here is done, Katie. Wolfgang is already back home in his own bed. But I guess we still have some minor tweaking to do before I join him, yes?"

I'd barely gotten to know her, and now she was leaving. She'd given up her home for years, following me from New York City to Savannah while she waited to approach me with the uncomfortable truth about my fate. Was it selfish of me to want her to stay?

"Good thing you ain't left yet," Sugar said, nosing around the room and picking up a carved figurine from the bookcase. "You planning to have one of them moving sales?"

Aunt Marianna glanced at the figurine in Sugar's hand. "You can have that if you'd like."

Sugar's eyes lit up. "Well, that's awful nice of you, but it looks kinda expensive."

"It is, but I'd like you to have it. My gift for your being such a good friend to Katie."

Without another word, Sugar stuffed the figurine inside her bag. "I'll treasure it," she said, taking a seat on the sofa next to me. "Go ahead and tell her what Mama said, Katie."

Aunt Marianna shifted her eyes from Sugar to me, her curious look suddenly turning cautious. "Don't tell me that dragon is throwing its weight around again? I've heard of that happening, but it's extraordinarily rare once a beast has been... broken."

Broken. The word sent a sharp pain through my chest. Is that what we did to it? Broke it like a wild horse?

"Not exactly," I said, trying to find the words to describe its new demeanor. "It's like it crashes into me when I try to let it out, but then it hits a wall."

Her brow tightened. "A wall?"

Unable to stay quiet, Sugar cut to the chase. "Damn thing is acting crazy. Them claws of hers come out and her eyes get all snakelike, but that's it."

Aunt Marianna looked bewildered. Her lips parted slightly, but she was having difficulty finding words.

"No. Uh-uh," I said, shaking my head. "You don't get to look at me like that. You're the one who got me into this mess. If you're stumped, I'm screwed."

She snapped back to attention and took a seat. "Why don't we start over. You say the dragon refuses to come out?"

"I was attacked by a shifter the other night. My talons came out and I had no problem flashing him the dragon's eyes, but that's it. No wings. No scales. I was able to fight him off, but I have a feeling he would have won if he'd decided to play a little rougher."

"Looked like you was kicking his ass," Sugar muttered.

My aunt looked horrified. "A shifter attacked you?"

"It's a long story," I said, not wanting to rehash all the details. It would probably send her into protective mode and have her unpacking. It was bad enough that Jackson wanted to move in with me. "There's a pack of them in town. I ran into one at a bar Saturday night and he got a little presumptuous with his hands."

She went into thinking mode, cocking her head as her wheels began to turn. "What we need is an intervention."

"Intervention?" Sugar said.

"Hold on." Aunt Marianna got up and headed for the kitchen. "I think I have everything we need." A few minutes later, she came back into the room with a cup.

"It's time to have a conversation with the dragon," she said, handing me the drink. "See for yourself what the problem is."

I glanced at the liquid. "Have a conversation? With the dragon?"

"Why not? It's your dragon. That drink will get you inside your own head."

Sugar's face scrunched up like she'd eaten something bitter. "You mean a trance?"

"Something like that."

"I don't know about all this, Katie," Sugar said, still looking like she'd eaten something nasty. "Sounds a little crazy to me."

I deadpanned, "Really? Your mother's a conjure woman." She claimed to be one too, although I'd never actually seen her do anything magical like May. I figured she considered herself a conjure woman through her lineage. Kind of like a hereditary witch.

Hesitant, I sniffed the cup. "Is this stuff safe?"

Stupid question.

"In small doses," my aunt replied.

"What uh… exactly is it going to do to me?"

"It'll put you face-to-face with the dragon so it won't be able to hide. I'm sure the two of you can come to a meeting of the minds. Now drink up. The effects will only last for a few minutes, so you'll have to work fast." Her eyes lingered on mine for a moment, making me second-guess putting that potion in my mouth. "This is your only opportunity, Katie. Do you want the dragon back?"

I stood and raised the cup of liquid that looked like human bile. "Bottoms up," I said, shuddering from the taste. "Like licking the inside of a toilet bowl."

"I ain't even gonna ask how you know that," Sugar said.

A half-baked laugh came out of my mouth as the room began to spin and fade the second I set the cup down on the table. Talk about a fast-acting drug. My eyes had closed somewhere between the time I fell toward the sofa and the moment I found myself lying on a cold stone floor. When I opened them, I had to adjust to the darkness around me. All I could see was a barely lit corridor with a wide gaping hole in front of me. A tunnel.

In the distance I heard something shuffling or swaying back and forth across the floor. A brushing stroke. "Where are you?" I whispered, only loud enough for my own ears to hear. I was spooked. Terrified of what waited at the end of that dark tunnel. It was impossible to gauge how deep it stretched, which made me wonder if the dragon was a mile away or if it was close enough to hear me breathe. That shuffling sound came again. This time it sounded farther away. The dragon was on the move.

With a ceiling that appeared to reach as high as the tunnel was long, the space I was standing in seemed to have no boundaries. If it weren't for the solid floor under my feet, I would have sworn I was floating.

I never imagined my mind was so desolate.

With only a strange glow radiating from my skin to illuminate the way, I followed the corridor into the darkness. The only sound I could hear now was my heart nearly beating out of my chest, thumping frantically against my rib cage.

I'm inside my own head, I kept telling myself, but the fear wouldn't let up.

As I walked down the tunnel, I heard the shuffling sound again. This time it was right next to me. A wave of heat hit me, and an odd clicking sound filled my right ear. I slowly turned my head. The dragon's eyes met mine as its massive head swung around, coming within inches of my face. My lungs filled sharply and I froze, the dragon so close I thought it would crush me against the wall I was suddenly pressed against.

"I'm in control, I'm in control, I'm in control," I kept repeating in a whisper. But was I?

"S-stop," I stammered, praying it would obey. The dragon moved back a few feet and opened it jaws, flashing its sharp, glistening teeth. And then the epiphany came. I was looking at myself. I'd seen those eyes in my own reflection. Those teeth. The shimmering scales that covered the dragon's face.

I reached out and it met me halfway, grazing its armor across my palm as I touched its face. "We'll figure this out," I whispered.

Suddenly the dragon reared back, stumbling in the darkness like a wounded animal. The cavern shook from the impact of its wings pummeling the walls, coming within inches of me as they flailed around the dark space. I tried to move back, but there was nowhere to go. My heart pounded as the massive beast teetered sideways. It swayed back and forth, trying to stay upright, sending a quake through the cavern when it finally hit the ground and rolled on its side. A second later, it lifted its head and swung around, sending a river of fire straight toward me. The flames hit the glowing aura around my body and diverted to the wall behind me, traveling up toward the invisible ceiling where they burst into an explosion of blue light.

The dragon let its head fall back to the ground, limp and exhausted.

Ain't got no juice. Like it's got a lead weight around its neck. Can't hardly move.

May's words came roaring into my head. The dragon was drained. Had no juice left. Maybe that ritual had done it in. Maybe there wasn't enough "juice" for both of us anymore.

"Damn it," I hissed as the light from the outside world peeked into the darkness. The potion was wearing off.

The light intensified, and I closed my eyes to shield them from the stinging brightness piercing the veil. When they reopened, I was back on the sofa with my aunt and Sugar looking down at me.

"Well?" Sugar said. "Did you see it? You was making all kinds of strange noises."

A flood of emotions hit me as I looked at my aunt.

"Yes," she said, reading my face. "She saw the dragon."

Sugar continued to fish for details. "Did you talk to it?"

"May was right," I said. "The dragon is weak."

The expression on my aunt's face didn't offer me any comfort. I got the distinct feeling that I was losing a significant part of myself and I'd suffer from phantom-limb syndrome for the rest of my life.

"I think we made a terrible mistake," I said, looking at my aunt. "I think it's dying."

She shook her head. "We did nothing to strip its power. In fact, I think it's getting stronger."

"What the hell you talking about?" Sugar said, her confusion echoing mine.

Aunt Marianna thought about it for a minute before answering. "It's getting stronger, which means it needs more fuel to sustain it. Better fuel."

"I hope you're going to tell me you know what that fuel is."

She let out a weary sigh. "I have no idea, darling. But have faith. It may be weak, but it takes a lot more than a little lethargy to kill a dragon. We just need to find the right chicken soup."

"Well," Sugar added, "Mama did say the medicine was on the way."

Marianna smiled at Sugar. "Interesting. I'd like to meet your mother someday. She sounds like a wise woman."

"Mama's wise all right. If it comes out of her mouth, you can bank on it."

"For now," my aunt continued, "let's keep you from getting yourself killed. Go home, Katie. Let Jackson play the hero until we find out what the dragon needs."

"He's gonna love that," Sugar muttered. "That man's been dying to move in with you, girl. But we need to set us some ground rules," she quickly added. "Ain't no man worth the headache if he don't know the rules, like me coming over whenever the hell I please."

"No one's moving in," I said. "Just because I can't fully shift doesn't mean I can't bite. I think I proved that at Mojo's the other night."

"Just promise me you'll be careful," my aunt pleaded. "And stay out of that bar."

I snorted a laugh. "No problem." Then I glanced at the boxes and changed the subject. "When are you leaving?"

"When my job is done, darling."

I got up and gave her a hug before heading for the door, deciding to hold my tongue and not mention that her job *was* done. She couldn't help me anymore. Finding the dragon's cure was my job now. "Don't you dare leave without calling to say goodbye," I said as I walked out of her house for what I assumed would be the last time.

Sugar and I climbed into the Eldorado and headed back to town. My phone rang as we pulled away from the house. It was Fin informing me that we had a new problem on our hands. A big one that rivaled the catastrophe at Forsyth Park.

"Who was that?" Sugar asked after I hung up the phone.

"Fin. He wants me to stop by Lillian's this evening. With Jackson," I added to keep her from freaking out about me going out without a chaperone.

This babysitting bullshit was for the birds.

She glanced at me out of the corner of her eye. "Something you ain't telling me?"

"Nope. Fin just wants to talk strategy."

It was a justifiable lie. Until we could confirm that the Sapanths were responsible for the latest bodies that Fin had just told me about on the phone—the ones found mauled to death near the river by what appeared to be a large animal—there was no need to worry Sugar any more than she already was.

The inevitable truth could wait until morning.

12

Jet was calm when I walked into the house. That was always a good indicator that there was no one inside, but I checked every room just in case. It was becoming a joke how often I forgot to secure the patio door with that metal rod in the track. I figured if someone really wanted to get in, all they had to do was break a window. Fortunately, there were more enticing houses on the street to burglarize.

Maybe I was subconsciously daring some asshole to enter my house.

"One of these days someone's going to break in and realize there's nothing in here worth stealing," I said to my cat. Jet meowed and paced around his empty food bowl. "I know you're hungry. Give me a minute."

Before I could dial Jackson's number, I heard his bike pull into the driveway. I met him at the door and noticed the concerned look on his face. "Are they okay?" I asked, referring to Cairo and Angela.

"They'll live," he said, walking past me toward the kitchen. "Have you eaten? Because I'm starving."

"I'm not hungry," I said. "There's leftover pizza in the fridge."

I thought I'd let him get some food in his stomach before I broke the news about the other murders and the fact that we needed to head over to Lillian's house as soon as he finished eating.

He heated his pizza in the microwave while I fed Jet. Then I joined him at the kitchen island and watched him inhale his food.

"You really are hungry," I said, trying to start a little small talk before broaching the subject that was on both of our minds. "Did you find out where Kaleb is hiding?"

"Not yet," he said, glancing at Jet eating on the floor. "He's done a damn good job of disappearing. Cats do that."

"Do what?"

"Hide. Crawl into small spaces. Kaleb doesn't want to be found."

The old adage about keeping your friends close and your enemies closer was particularly relevant when your enemies were dangerous shifters. But Kaleb and the Sapanths were lying too low to keep an eye on.

"Maybe I should go back to Mojo's," I said, only half joking. "He seemed to like the place. Fit right in with all the other scumbags." Joking or not, it was a valid suggestion. I'd have backup, and despite the dragon's lethargy I could still sprout a set of deadly talons. "I could be the bait and try to draw him out."

As he finished chewing his last bite of pizza, he gave me a look that made me regret the suggestion. "I don't think you understand who we're dealing with." His voice was deceptively calm. "Kaleb has taken an unhealthy interest in you, Katie. If you bait him, he'll bite. And if he finds a way to get you out of that bar, and there's a good chance he would, he won't think twice about using you in some pretty creative ways to get to me. Do you understand what I'm telling you?"

So much for telling him about my little dragon problem.

"Does that mean you won't be going with me to Mojo's

then?" It was a smart-ass response that just kinda rolled off my tongue.

He grabbed his plate and put it in the sink, his anger growing.

"Come on, Jackson," I pleaded. "It was a joke." We'd been arguing a lot lately, and it was beginning to wear on me. One of the reasons I loved being with him was the ease of it. Not letting every little thing erupt into an argument or the silent treatment, unlike what was happening now. "I've had a shitty day too, so I'd appreciate it if you'd lighten up a little."

Choosing to take the high road and end the argument, I got up and grabbed my keys. "We're meeting Fin at Lillian's," I said, heading for the door. "A couple of bodies were found near the river. Fin said it looks like an animal attack."

WHEN WE ARRIVED at Lillian's house, her housekeeper escorted us to the library. Fin was sitting at the desk with his feet propped up on the edge when we walked into the room. He had a document in his hand.

"Get those damn shoes off my desk," Lillian said as she entered right behind us and shot Fin a warning look. "Why do men always do that?" She looked at Jackson. "But something tells me you've been taught better than that, Mr. Hunter."

She headed for the table near the window and motioned for us to sit. Fin swung his feet off the desk and joined us, tossing the document on the table. It slid and came to rest in front of Jackson.

He glanced at it and then back at Fin. "I guess you want me to read it?"

"Your friends are overstaying their welcome," Fin said, nodding toward the report. "My connections down at the coroner's office were kind enough to provide me with a copy of that before the media gets ahold of it."

Jackson flipped the cover of the report and revealed a couple of pictures stapled to the first page. He examined them without reaction and then looked at Fin. "Where was the body found?"

"Near the river," Fin replied. "About a dozen yards from the tourist district. In fact, it was a couple of tourists who found it. I don't think they'll be coming back to Savannah anytime soon after seeing that."

"Time of death?" Jackson asked.

"It's all in that report."

I leaned in to get a better look at the pictures, suddenly wishing I hadn't. The body was eviscerated. Well, what was left of it. "Jesus." I averted my eyes.

Fin glanced at me as I shied away from the pictures, seemingly annoyed by my sensitive reaction. "It gets worse, Miss Bishop. If you're having trouble stomaching those pictures, you might want to sit this one out. Although based on your past work with the society, I am surprised."

I'd seen some pretty disturbing things during my short tenure with the Crossroads Society, but the brutality of this particular crime took things to a whole new level of depravity. "Don't worry about it, Fin," I said with a brief snort. "I just need a minute to let the nausea pass."

"I have a second report if you'd like to see the other victim," Fin said to Jackson. "More of the same though. As I'm sure you can imagine, the police are having some difficulty identifying the bodies."

Feeling a little braver, I took a second look at the gruesome images. "I'll just play devil's advocate here," I said, no longer repulsed but fascinated, making me wonder what kind of person I really was. "What makes you think this wasn't just some random animal attack?"

Fin stared at me for a few seconds, probably considering how to respond to such a naïve suggestion. "Well"—he headed back to the desk and fetched a cigar from the top drawer where Lillian kept them—"to my knowledge, Miss Bishop, there are no lions or tigers indigenous to Georgia."

"Don't be such a smart-ass, Fin," I shot back at him. "I just thought maybe a pack of dogs—"

"He's right," Jackson interjected. "This was no dog attack." He flipped through the report until he found what he was looking for. "Says the estimated time of death was between two and four a.m."

"Is that significant?" Fin asked.

Jackson shrugged. "Could be. It proves that it was after the incident in the park, and it lines up with when they like to feed."

I shot Jackson a wild look. "Feed?"

"Take a good look at those pictures," Fin said. "Do you see any legs? The head is missing too. Those bodies have been partially eaten. The police are officially calling it a wild animal attack, which I suppose is technically correct."

My eyes went back to Jackson for confirmation that it was true. The Sapanths weren't just killing people in town. They were eating them too.

Jackson closed the report and shoved it across the table toward Fin. "They usually stick to animals. Deer or cattle. Keeps them under the radar, and they want to blend in. When they feed, they rarely leave evidence." He quietly seethed for a moment before continuing. "This was a message. They'll keep killing until they get what they want."

"Which is you, Mr. Hunter," Lillian interjected. "You and your money are the reason these animals have invaded our town. Logic would suggest that if you leave, they'll follow."

I stood up so fast my chair nearly tipped over. "If you're trying to blame Jackson for this, Lillian, you're off your rocker." Glancing around the grand room that only someone of signifi- cant wealth could afford, I brought my eyes back to hers. "They

115

could just as easily try to extort you for money, seeing how you have so damn much of it."

"She's right, Katie," Jackson said, grasping my arm to try to pull me back down into my chair. "Kaleb's here for money, but he wants *my* money. My guess is he'll try to take what he can get from Cairo too."

I sat back down and felt my heart sink at what I feared he'd say next.

"But it's not really about the money at all," he continued. "It's about control."

When Jackson first told me about the Sapanths, he'd said he had a bounty on his head. Said he walked away with their secrets. Kaleb was fine with disclosing those secrets as long as you remained a lifetime member of his club. But Jackson committed the ultimate sin. He walked away when they weren't looking and started a new life.

"They'll take my money, and then they'll try to take me back." I could tell by the way he looked at me and squeezed my hand that he was trying to prepare me for something I didn't want to hear. "Lillian's right."

I shrank back and pulled my hand out of his, reconciling what he was suggesting. "What are you saying?"

"If I leave, they'll follow me." He turned to look Lillian in the eye, and I thought I saw a rare touch of fear flash over her face as she must have recognized the power underneath his cool exterior. I'd seen it the first time he walked into my shop. "The problem is," he said to her, "they'll be back. For Cairo. You might be able to run me out of town, Lillian, but Cairo and his clan won't leave Savannah just because you ask them nicely. You're just trading one problem for another."

She composed herself and steadied her gaze on his. "Then what do you suggest we do?"

Jackson let out a bitter laugh. "I suggest you and the society back off before one of you gets killed. Just a little free advice. Trust me on this. Blackthorn Grove has met its match."

"Thank you for that sage advice, Mr. Hunter," she replied with smug politeness. "But I think we can handle a few renegade shifters. I'm only suggesting that the solution might be as simple as removing a key variable."

I had to give him credit for tolerating her arrogance. Then again, maybe not.

"I don't give a shit if you slap a side of beef outside your front door and ring the dinner bell," he sneered. "But don't ever suggest that you have the power to run me out of this town."

Lillian seemed a little stunned by his unwillingness to back down. But she didn't know Jackson Hunter very well.

"All right now," Fin said, trying to mediate. "Let's all just simmer down and let Jackson tell us what he has in mind. You do have something in mind, don't you?"

"I'll give them the money," Jackson said. "Then I'm gonna kill Kaleb."

Fin stared at Jackson blandly. "Well, shit," he eventually said with a little too much passive-aggressive sarcasm. "Why didn't I think of that? You mind expanding on that?"

Jackson looked my way and gave me a faint grin before answering the question. "At dinner the other night, Davina McCabe asked me what their weakness was. I didn't think they had one, but I've been considering that question for a few days. In fact, I'm starting to think it's been right in front of me the whole time. Their weakness is the consequence of their power."

Lillian sighed dramatically, losing her patience. "How's that?"

"Sleep," he replied. "After a night of shifting, they sleep like the dead. Their bodies weaken and require a long catnap."

I envisioned a bunch of vampires sleeping it off after the sun came up "Are you saying they all fall into a dead sleep at the same time, leaving themselves vulnerable?"

Jackson smirked because I'd nailed it. "When I rode with

them, one of my jobs was to keep watch while they slept. The biggest challenge will be finding the lair. Like I said, cats tend to slip into small spaces. It won't be easy to find them."

"Well, I guess those sons of bitches picked the right town," Fin said with disdain. "Savannah is full of nooks and crannies. There are tunnels running under our very feet."

"I'll find them," Jackson said. "Then I'll give them the damn money. Cooperating will make them think they've got me running scared. Then I'm gonna wait until Kaleb is deep into one of his catnaps." The look of satisfaction on his face was chilling. He was going to enjoy killing Kaleb, and I found that a little unsettling.

He must have sensed my unease, because the satisfaction on his face suddenly disappeared. But I knew he had the taste of blood in his mouth—Kaleb's blood. As much as that disturbed me, I understood it. Between his father and Kaleb, he'd been someone's victim too damn long, and I was the last person who would judge him for taking great pleasure in ending that cycle.

"Whatever you have to do to fix this problem, do it fast." Lillian stared at him. "If it's not too much trouble," she quickly added. "A few more days, Mr. Hunter. That's all you get. But if those animals so much as break another window in this town or leave another body down by that river, I'll bring Blackthorn Grove down on them so hard they'll think it's raining shit."

13

Jackson took me home after having one final tugging match with the grande dame of Savannah over Blackthorn Grove throwing their cards into the game. Lillian had about reached her breaking point, and I was pretty sure she was already preparing the coven for a battle even if she had agreed to give Jackson a few more days.

We'd driven my car to Lillian's house that night, and he was unusually quiet on the ride home. He stared out the window for most of the drive. I thought it was just the lingering tension from the confrontation, but the quieter he got, the more I knew something different was going on.

"I have to go to Atlanta tonight," he informed me the second we walked inside the house. Before I could respond, he was already checking every room. He came back into the kitchen where I was pouring myself a glass of scotch. Then he gave me that look.

"Forget it," I said, taking a sip of the whiskey. "I'm not going with you."

"Did I ask?"

"Not yet, but you were about to." I grabbed the bottle off the counter when his hand went for it. "Uh-uh. You have to go to Atlanta, remember? I don't want to get a call from the state patrol telling me your bike has been obliterated on the highway with you right alongside it."

He was smart enough not to argue with me and took a seat.

After a few minutes of silence, I finally broke. "Why are you going to Atlanta?"

"To get the money."

I cocked my head and gave him a questioning look. "You're kidding me, right?" When he slowly shook his head but didn't expand, I asked, "Why on earth would you leave all that money a couple hundred miles away? And right in Kaleb's backyard?"

"Because he won't look for it there. He probably thinks I have it buried in *my* backyard."

"You don't have a backyard."

He glanced over my shoulder toward the patio door.

"But I do," I said, completing his thought before he said it. "So you're telling me Kaleb's planning to dig up my yard? My neighbors will love that." I snorted, finishing off my drink.

A quiet laugh escaped him. "Kaleb's not going to dig up your yard, Katie. He's too lazy for that. He'd rather wait for me to dig it up and then steal it from me."

I leaned into him and looked him square in the eye. "He better not dig up my yard."

He let out a deep sigh. "You know I'm gonna worry like hell until I get back. You should come with me. We'll be back by morning."

Glancing at Jet on the floor, I squashed any ideas he had about that happening. "I have a client at ten a.m., and I'm not putting a needle to someone's skin without any sleep."

He fixed his eyes on mine for a moment, and then he kissed me like it might be the last time. "You be careful," he whispered against my lips before kissing me again. The look in his eyes when he pulled back was so... final.

"I wish you wouldn't do that," I said. "It scares me."

He seemed genuinely perplexed, and I doubted he even realized how suggestive his eyes were when he had something on his mind. "Do what?"

"Look at me like it might be the last time."

He gave me a thorough embrace, taking his time before letting go. Then he walked over to the patio door and dropped the metal rod into the track, surveying the darkness behind my house one more time before heading for the front door.

"Jackson," I said as he opened it. "Is this going to work?" I think he thought I meant us. "Your plan to kill Kaleb while he sleeps?"

His shoulders rose from the deep breath inflating his chest. "It has to."

I DIDN'T THINK I could sleep knowing that Jackson was heading back to Sapanth country. Kaleb and Kara, along with a handful of their crew, might have already taken up residence in Savannah, but Jackson had told me there were others still back in Atlanta. My fear was that they'd smell him out the second he crossed the city line. I prayed he'd be able to grab the money and get out of town before that happened.

Absently, I wondered how big a bag was necessary to transport two million dollars on the back of his bike.

A few minutes after mercifully dozing off around three a.m., the sound of cubes dropping from the ice maker woke me up. Reading in bed was a pretty effective tranquilizer for me, so I sat up and grabbed a book from the nightstand. Atlanta was a three to four-hour drive from Savannah, depending on how strictly you followed the speed limit, so Jackson had probably already arrived. I selfishly hoped he'd grabbed the money and was already on his way back. On second thought, I hoped he was smart enough to get a couple of hours of sleep first. I needed him alive.

Jet jumped off the bed but stopped in his tracks as soon as he hit the ground. A low growl came from his throat, like a dog smelling a possum on the patio in the middle of the night.

"What's wrong with you?" I said as the hair on my arms stood on end. A shiver raced up my spine as a sound came from one of the other rooms. A flapping sound so quiet I could barely hear it.

But I did hear it.

Jet growled again, louder this time as he ducked under the bed. I put the book quietly back on the nightstand and swung my legs over the side of the mattress. Just in case that sound wasn't the floor expanding from the oppressive humidity making the wood bloat, I grabbed a pair of yoga pants and quickly pulled them on. This old bungalow was always making noises. No need to panic yet.

I crept down the hallway toward the kitchen. I had a clear view into the living room, which was empty, but as I moved closer to the end of the hall, the sound got louder. It was coming from around the corner to my right, maybe half a dozen feet away.

The dragon began to stir on my back as I felt my talons ready to break through the tips of my fingers. I forced them back inside with sheer will until I knew what was on the other side of that wall.

Jet brushed past my leg, nearly making me yelp. He crept toward the living room, his growl growing deeper as he suddenly screeched and darted under the couch.

My heart beating painfully against my chest, I stepped around the corner and confronted my empty kitchen. I sagged against the island as the pages of the newspaper Sugar had left on the counter fluttered. The fan was blowing against it, forcing the pages to fly up and snap every time the oscillating blades passed back and forth.

"You are one hell of a watchdog, Jet," I said, laughing nervously as I reached over and turned the fan off. "You can come out now, you little chickenshit."

The paper settled on the counter, displaying the headline about the damage to the park and the three bodies left behind. A frightening thought occurred to me. What if they were out there right now, killing more people? What if they started killing kids? Something told me Kaleb didn't have an ounce of morals, and to him eating children would be no different than dining on their parents.

I poured myself a glass of water and walked over to the patio door, glancing down at the metal rod in the track. Yeah, my house was a real Fort Knox. When I looked back up at the yard, I spotted something move in the darkness. I nearly dropped my drink on the floor before realizing it was Jet's reflection in the glass door. He'd finally run out from under the couch and was heading back down the hall toward the bedroom.

"Little monster," I muttered.

I glanced at the clock on the stove. I had to be up in about four hours, and I'd meant what I'd said to Jackson about not putting a tattoo on a client's skin without any sleep.

As I put the glass in the sink, I glanced up at the ceiling fan, triggering a nagging feeling in the back of my mind. I never actually used that countertop fan in the kitchen, seeing how I had a much better one mounted over my head. I'd gotten it for the patio, for those nights when even a hot breeze was better than nothing. I'd brought it inside a few days ago when the forecast had called for rain.

Trying not to give away the adrenaline that was suddenly

crawling up the back of my throat, I headed out of the kitchen with my eyes focused straight ahead. I was in a dead run as soon as I turned the corner. I made it to the bedroom and slammed the door, engaging the flimsy lock that would only buy me a minute or two while I stared at my shaking hands. Before I could will my claws to come back out, I felt the brunt of something hard come down on top of me, making the room go dark.

I didn't actually lose consciousness, but I did see a lot of stars as I was lifted off the ground and tossed over someone's shoulder like a sack of potatoes. I kept hearing an annoying sound as he carried me across the room.

He was humming. No, he was purring.

With a violent thrust, I flew backward and landed on the bed. The mattress sagged as he climbed on top of it and straddled me.

"Wake up, princess," he said, patting my cheek roughly. "I remember you being tougher than this."

Kaleb.

The fog in my head started to clear as the pain subsided. I could hear the dragon moving down that long tunnel, coming closer as I tried to open my eyes.

Suddenly Kaleb moved back onto the mattress, kicking my legs apart with his knees and yanking me down the bed toward him.

My eyes flew open as the dragon lunged from the dark tunnel into the light. I gasped and filled my lungs with air, trying to scurry out of Kaleb's grip. He just held on tighter.

"Yeah," he hissed, his voice husky. "I figured that would do it."

He took his time climbing off me, running his hand down the length of my torso before resting it between my legs. "We'll get to that a little later."

He turned and walked across the room, giving me a view of

that tattoo on the back of his head. He was almost as tall as Jackson, but not as lean. More muscular. A steroid junkie, I would have thought if I didn't know what he was. He sat on top of the dresser and pulled a cigarette from his jacket.

"Just tell me what you want," I said, hoping to buy some time while the dragon made up its damn mind about what it wanted to do as it vibrated just beneath the surface of my skin.

"You don't mind if I smoke, do you?" he asked, lighting up before I could answer. He took a long drag and scratched the edge of his chin, studying me. "What are you?"

I opened my mouth to feed him some bullshit.

"No, no, no," he said, tightening his brow. "That wasn't an actual question. I know what you are." His voice dropped about two octaves. "But I sure as fuck don't see it." His demeanor changed significantly as he hopped off the dresser and extinguished the barely smoked cigarette on my hardwood floor. Then he started to walk back toward the bed, his eyes growing dark as he got closer. I noticed the tips of his fangs protruding from his upper lip as his mouth opened slightly and his tongue worked the corner. "Come out, little dragon," he taunted with a lilt in his voice.

Climbing to my knees, I moved farther back on the bed until I hit the headboard. There was only one way out, and it was through the bedroom door to my right.

"I know you think you've found Mr. Right," he continued. "But you see, Jackson already has a family. In other words, you're a problem that needs to be solved." His dark eyes flashed and shifted from nearly black to glimmering amber. "Kara wanted to take care of that little problem herself, but I convinced her to let me pay you a visit. You see, I have plans for you, Katie. Don't make this difficult."

My heart was pounding so fast I thought I was going to pass out on the bed and make it real easy for him. But then he reached for the zipper of his pants and my eyes began to burn. The room went up in a blaze of emerald, and I felt that old familiar sensation of my claws trying to punch through my fingers.

When I felt the light blasting from my eyes and my senses turn razor sharp, I glanced at my ordinary hands that hadn't quite caught up yet. Kaleb stopped when I shifted my gaze to him, targeting him with a beam of emerald. He leered at me from the foot of the bed, and I could sense his excitement.

"There she is," he sneered, rubbing the bulge beneath his half-lowered zipper. A wicked grin flashed across his face as he lunged toward me.

I bolted off the bed and ran through the bedroom door, down the hallway as the sound of Kaleb's laughter shifted into a deep, guttural growl. I reached the patio door and yanked, the floor vibrating under my feet as his heavy paws paced down the hallway after me. It wouldn't open.

The metal rod.

The taste of adrenaline flooded my mouth as I sank to the floor and closed my eyes, waiting for the strike. He was on top of me in an instant, digging his massive claws into my back and tearing at my tattoo. The pain faded as my mind slipped into some safe place inside that dark tunnel.

And then I saw it.

Moving silently through the black corridor, the dragon flew out of the darkness, smashing into me like a freight train. The impact jarred me, rendering me unconscious. When I came to and opened my eyes, I was on top of something, slashing at the animal beneath me. I kept digging my talons into its sleek black fur, tearing at its flesh with a violent ripping motion until there was more red than black.

The muffled sounds in the room suddenly rose into a crescendo of screams. My screams. I let out a piercing screech as the cat's teeth punctured my neck, sending a spray of blood across the room. I went still. A second later I teetered sideways, and the room disappeared.

———————

"BABY, YOU GOT TO WAKE UP!"

I heard Sugar's voice, but the only thing I could see was a hazy film covering my eyes. I willed my fingers to move, and then I lifted my arm to signal for her to come closer. Her blurry frame came into view, but when I tried to speak, my voice was barely a whisper.

"Sweet baby Jesus!" she sang out. "Thank you!"

I tried to sit up but quickly fell back to the floor when my head started to feel like the inside of a washing machine on the spin cycle. It was like someone had spun me around before kicking me off a cliff.

"Where the hell am I?" I eventually muttered.

"Baby, you lying on the floor in a puddle of blood. But I don't see no cuts or bullet holes anywhere, so I don't know whose blood this is."

Against her protests, I shoved myself up on one arm and waited for the excruciating pounding to subside. "I'm gonna throw up," I announced, using her body to pull myself off the floor. I stumbled to the kitchen and emptied the bile from my stomach into the sink.

"I don't know what the hell's going on around here, but you're scaring me. Where's Jackson?"

"Jackson?" I repeated. *Jackson!* "What time is it, Sugar?"

She looked at the clock on the stove. "Almost ten thirty. I stopped by the shop and Mouse said you hadn't shown up yet. Said you stood up a client, and girl, I ain't never seen you stand up a client."

"Damn it!" I dropped my forehead against the edge of the sink when my brain started to spin again.

A few seconds later, I heard the door open. Jackson walked inside and dropped a duffel bag on the floor. He looked at the damage in the room and spotted the blood. When his bewildered eyes circled back to mine, all I could do was look down at that bag.

"Is that the money?"

14

Jackson was scary quiet, standing in the entryway with a neutral look on his face. He waited for me to explain why the place was a wreck and there was a significant amount of blood on the walls and floor. I suspected the only reason he was so calm was because I appeared to be intact.

"Kaleb stopped by last night," I said matter-of-factly, turning my head sideways to discreetly spit some blood into the sink. "I made him leave when he lost his manners."

"You made him leave?" Jackson said, clearly not buying my casual act.

"That's what I said." I tried my damnedest to look normal as I walked over to the bag he'd deposited on my floor, then bent down to lift it. "So this is what two million dollars feels like," I practically coughed out.

He gave me a stern look. "Don't change the subject. What happened?"

"Can we just do something with this bag before we get into all that?" I said. "I really don't feel comfortable with this much money just lying on my floor."

I thought Sugar's eyes were going to fall out of her head the way they popped when Jackson lifted the duffel bag on top of the kitchen island and opened it.

"You okay, Sugar?" I asked.

She stared at the money neatly secured in half-inch bundles like the ones you see on TV when a bank is being robbed.

"I'm fine," she said, still gazing at it. "I just ain't never seen that much money up close." She glanced at Jackson as her fingers twiddled over the pile of cash. "Mind if I touch it?"

Jackson shrugged. "Climb in the bag and roll around in it if you want."

She reached inside and pulled out one of the stacks, bouncing it in her hand as if trying to guess the weight. Then she noticed the paper band wrapped around it identifying the amount. "That's all ten thousand dollars feels like? Damn! A few of these is a shiny new car."

While Sugar fondled the cash, Jackson walked over to the patio door and bent down to dip his finger into one of the pools of blood that was beginning to thicken and dry. He smelled it and looked back at me. "This isn't Kaleb's blood."

I gave him a puzzled look. "I find it very disturbing that you just said that. How exactly do you know what Kaleb's blood smells like?"

"I don't, but I know what yours smells like."

The fact that he knew what *my* blood smelled like was just as disturbing. "Got a little vampire thing going on that you haven't told me about?" A bonus that came with his Superman powers, his hearing was superior to most people's. I guess it shouldn't have been a surprise that his sense of smell was superior too. Right up there with a black bear's. He'd just never mentioned it before.

Ignoring my remark, he walked back over and started manhandling me. When he couldn't find any wounds on my arms and legs, he took a step back and reached for my hair. He lifted it off my shoulders to expose a faded pink mark on the back of my neck where Kaleb had bitten me. I'd healed almost immediately, as soon as my claws disappeared and the dragon retreated back to that dark cavern in my head.

"He marked you," he hissed under his breath like he was making a note to himself.

Sugar dropped the stack of bills back into the duffel bag and got a good look at my neck. "Is that where all that blood came from? I'm surprised you ain't dead."

Jackson and I locked eyes, tuning Sugar's voice out as she rattled on. I wasn't sure what he meant by "marked," but I had a good idea and didn't like it.

"You mean like... he's got dibs on me?" I joked, shrugging. I didn't feel any different, and I sure as hell wasn't planning to dump Jackson for a shifter who turned into a black panther when he got a little horny or had a taste for tourist meat. "Don't worry. I'm pretty sure I'm immune to that kind of thing." I snorted. "You know, with the dragon and all."

"Well, I don't know about that," Sugar muttered. "That dragon ain't been too impressive lately."

We both shot her a wicked glare, compelling her to shut up.

"It's foreplay," he said. "It means he's got designs on you."

"Designs?" I repeated, snickering. "Good luck with that." The grave look on Jackson's face put a halt to the jokes. "Come on, Jackson. Don't tell me you're worried about my getting all dreamy-eyed for Kaleb. If it makes you feel any better, he repulses me." That wasn't completely true. As much as I wanted to be repulsed by a killer shifter who had no regard for anyone, especially women, there was something about him that was alluring. Kind of like a train wreck you couldn't stop looking at.

"It's not you I'm worried about. I know him, Katie. When he sets his sights on something—or someone—he doesn't stop until he gets it."

I looked back and forth between the two sets of eyes that were gawking at me. "Okay, you two need to chill. I don't give a shit what Kaleb thinks this little bite means," I said, running my hand over the spot on the back of my neck where the mark was healed but still raised above my skin. I was getting a little annoyed at their lack of faith in my ability to defend myself. The last time a guy tried to take something from me without asking, I killed him.

"Fuck the dragon," I hissed under my breath, suddenly furious.

Jackson looked at me oddly and grabbed my wrist. I flinched and pulled away, catching a glimpse of my right hand. The morning sun reflected off the sharp talons protruding from my fingers. My eyes were on fire. I inhaled sharply and let out a steady hiss from somewhere deep in the back of my throat.

"What's happening, Katie?" I heard Jackson say somewhere in the distance.

The pounding in my head had returned, but it was different. I felt weak. Sick. Defensive. The dragon rumbled through the tunnel, shaking the cavern as it stalked closer. The glow that surrounded me suddenly faded, and I was left in complete darkness, the sounds of the beast and the heat from its skin circling me. It was angry. Frustrated.

Without warning, the dragon swung its tail, sending me flying against the wall in the black tunnel. I jumped to my feet and swung my claws, blind in the darkness as I felt its hot breath graze my skin.

"Katie!" Jackson growled, knocking me out of the way with his powerful forearm. I flew backward, landing near the patio door. When my eyes cleared, Jackson was hunched on the ground a few yards away next to Sugar. She wheezed and coughed violently, her wig slipping from her head as she rolled to her side and exposed a gash on the back of her skull.

I gasped, revealing the blood running down my palm as I opened my hand. "Sugar, I—"

Jackson stood up and stalked toward me. For a second I

thought he was about to hit me, but he extended his hand instead. I took it and let him pull me to me feet.

"I don't know what the hell's going on with you," he said, staring at me with a deeply disappointed look in his eyes. "If you're lucky, she won't be afraid of you for the rest of her life."

I glanced past Jackson to where Sugar was sitting on the floor, stunned and bleeding from the wound. When she saw me walking toward her, she backpedaled across the floor and then started to crawl toward the front door.

"I don't know what happened," I said, shaking my head in disbelief, reaching for her.

Jackson grabbed me by the wrist. "Don't."

I yanked my arm out of his grip and looked at Sugar, pleading with my eyes for her to let me explain. She stopped crawling toward the door and reached for my hand to pull herself up. Then she stood tall and straightened her shirt, wincing as she touched the open wound on the back of her head.

"You out of your ever-lovin' mind!" she spat out, taking a few steps back. Then a flood of rare tears burst from her eyes.

I'd only seen her cry once before, which made me want to cry too. Sugar avoided sappy sentiment like the plague, making it difficult to decide how to mend the fence I'd just plowed through. I gambled and took a step toward her with my arms wide.

"Don't you touch me!" She held her hand up to stop me from coming any closer.

"I was lashing out at the dragon, Sugar. You've got to believe me." I glanced at Jackson and then back at her, whispering discreetly under my breath, "It just happened again. You know, what happened yesterday."

She must have pieced it together, because her wounded look got real curious. "You mean at your aunt's house?" she said with about as much discretion as an elephant in the kitchen.

"Somebody better start talking," Jackson said.

I let out a dramatic sigh and groaned. "We went to see my aunt yesterday," I said without turning around.

"And?"

I finally turned to face him. "The dragon is getting stronger. The problem is we don't know how to sustain it. We don't know how to feed it."

Understandably, he looked confused. "I'm not going to like this, am I?"

"Well, that depends on how much you like having the dragon around," I said. "Have you noticed we haven't gone to the beach lately? To let it loose?" We used to go to the beach at night so I could fly over the ocean. We hadn't done that since the ritual. I was surprised he hadn't questioned it but figured it was due to how chaotic our lives had been since the Sapanths hit town.

He thought about it for a few seconds before answering. "Are you telling me it's dying?"

I shook my head. "The only thing I know for sure is that it's weak. It can't come all the way out. You saw what just happened. It gets right up to the edge of me, but then it hits a wall and eventually collapses."

He glanced at Sugar and back at me. "I still don't understand why it attacked Sugar just now."

"It didn't. It attacked me."

Sugar's eyes flew wide. "What the—"

"I think it's angry. I don't think it was trying to actually hurt me, but it was damn sure trying to get my attention." I smiled feebly at Sugar. "You were in the way when I defended myself."

"How long have you known?" he asked.

I'm sure he was thinking about my trip to Mojo's on Saturday night. Before I could explain that my suspicion started the night we were at Forsyth Park, Sugar hit the wall hard.

"Whoa!" She moaned, with her hand cradling the back of her head. "I think I need to sit down."

Jackson seemed as concerned about Sugar as I was. We helped

her to the couch where he examined the gaping wound on her head.

"Looks pretty deep," he said. "We need to get you to a doctor to stitch it up."

Didn't that make me feel like a piece of shit. I'd nearly given her a concussion at Mojo's Saturday night, and now I'd just mauled her like a wild animal.

"Mama's the only doctor I need." She started to get up but fell back down on the couch. "Just give me a minute here, then I'll drive myself out there."

"You're not driving anywhere," Jackson informed her. "Katie's gonna call May and let her know we're coming. We'll drop you off on our way to Cairo's place."

I'D CALLED Abel to let him know I had a little emergency and wouldn't be in. With Sea Bass still out, it wasn't the optimal time to take a day off, but under the circumstances I didn't have any other options. Jackson needed to stash his money at Cairo's place, and we needed to discuss our next move. Besides, Jackson wanted Cairo to confirm that Kaleb had actually marked me and not just given me a nasty nip in the middle of our fight. Being a shifter himself, Cairo would be able to distinguish a mark from your run-of-the-mill bite.

Jackson followed us on his bike while I drove Sugar to May's house in the Eldorado. May was waiting on the front porch when we pulled up. She took one look at her child and shook her head, leading Sugar into the house.

As I headed back down the porch steps, she stuck her head back out the door. "Watch out for them cats."

"Thanks, May. I'll keep that in mind."

I climbed on the back of the bike. We drove toward Cairo's place with me wedged between Jackson's back and the duffel bag strapped to the rack behind me. I had visions of taking a sharp turn and sending two million dollars flying onto the highway. A breath of relief shuddered out of me when we finally turned down the long dirt road that doubled as Cairo's driveway.

Cairo met us out front when we pulled up to the house. Easter, Jackson's former dog, was at his side. Angela and Cairo had agreed to dogsit for a while when Jackson first moved down to Savannah but since then had decided to keep her.

Jackson dropped to one knee and welcomed the large mutt as she greeted him enthusiastically, wiggling like a squirrel in his arms.

"Don't get too attached," Angela said, leaning against the doorway. "You're never getting her back." She looked over at me and grinned. "Come on, Katie. Let's have some frozen margaritas out on the dock while the boys decide where to hide the treasure chest." She glanced at the duffel bag strapped to Jackson's bike and then glanced around her large property, complete with a barn and a herd of alpacas. "I like what it bought us, but that money is nothing but trouble. Either bury it deep enough so Kaleb won't find it, or get it off my property, Jackson."

I started to follow her inside the house, but as soon as I got within a few feet of her, she stopped in her tracks and turned around. A strange sound slipped from her mouth as she glanced at Cairo, who was glaring at me the way a dog trains his eyes on an unwelcome intruder.

"I was about to mention that," Jackson said. "It's one of the reasons I brought Katie out here."

"What the hell's going on?" Angela demanded. Her eyes turned hard, like two stones.

Cairo stepped closer and gave me a good whiff. Then he looked at Jackson and snorted. "You got something you want to tell me, bro?"

I reluctantly lifted the hair off my neck, revealing the pink mark that would probably fade completely by evening. "Kaleb paid me a visit last night."

"He marked you," Angela hissed through clenched teeth.

Being female, she took appropriate offense to a male of any species helping himself to a woman's neck without an invitation. As beautiful as she was, I imagined she knew personally what it was like to have someone try. I sure as hell wouldn't want to be the guy on the receiving end of her wrath.

"He tried to do a lot more than that," I muttered.

Jackson was trying to maintain his composure, knowing how I hated a Neanderthal reaction out of him. But I understood exactly how it made him feel. Hell, I'd had a similar reaction to seeing Kara in his apartment the day I paid him an unannounced visit. But she didn't try to hump him in the middle of his apartment. At least not to my knowledge.

"Well, fuck me," Cairo said, nodding his head. "He's got some real balls, man. And for that, the motherfucker shall *die*." He looked at me sympathetically and lost his cocky smile. "I give you my word, Katie. He'll pay for putting his fangs on you."

Jackson sneered. "Yeah, he's definitely gonna die. In fact, that's one of the reasons we're here. You been watching the news?"

Cairo drew a deep breath. "Not if we can help it."

"A couple of tourists were found down by the river Sunday morning, gutted and half eaten. Cops are spinning it as an animal attack."

"The Sapanths," Angela chimed in. "I bet they were good and hungry after making that mess in Forsyth Park. It probably killed them to leave those reporters floating in that fountain. Whet their appetites."

Jackson nodded his head. "And you know what they need after a good night of killing."

Cairo grinned widely. "A good catnap."

"That's right," Jackson replied. "We need to find that lair. And then we're gonna kill them all."

"Come on, Katie," Angela said. "Let's give these boys some privacy while they make that money disappear. Trust me, it's best that we don't know where it is, just in case someone tries to torture it out of us."

I chuckled nervously and followed her inside to make those margaritas she'd offered. On the way to the kitchen, I made a detour to the bathroom. Once I was inside, I grabbed the bar of soap from the edge of the sink and scrubbed the pink spot on my neck until it was nearly raw.

15

I was almost afraid to open the door and walk inside. My business was beginning to suffer from all the drama keeping me from doing my job, and with the added bonus of Sea Bass losing his mind, I needed to be here more than ever instead of drinking margaritas while Jackson played bury the bone with two million dollars. It was almost ten a.m., so not only had I skipped work the day before, I was coming in late too. The thought of walking in there to face my employees' admonishing glances was just icing on the cake of shame I was about to eat.

"Boss," Abel said as I walked past him and headed for the computer.

No time like the present to see how much damage had actually been done. I pulled up the schedule and cringed from all the blank appointment slots on the calendar. Mouse's schedule was full, but Abel could only work on clients under my supervision until I was satisfied that he'd earned his wings. That could take months.

"I canceled your clients," he said as he walked up behind me. "Wasn't sure if that emergency of yours would take another day."

I shrugged off the sick feeling in my gut. It didn't help my dilemma and only made me feel worse. "I need to find that Help Wanted sign. I think I shoved it in the desk in the back."

Abel looked surprised. "You shittin' me, boss?"

"Bills need to be paid, Abel. If I don't have employees, I don't have customers." I closed the schedule and glanced at Mouse, who was working on a client. "We could use another set of hands around here anyway, even if Sea Bass comes back."

Abel seemed a little uncomfortable, and I realized what must have been going through his mind.

"Don't worry, Abel, you're still working on clients. And you'll have seniority over anyone new I bring in here."

He nodded, clearly relieved he wasn't being relegated back to full-time apprentice.

Mouse glanced up from her client to look at me. She had that usual neutral stare on her face, but there was a hint of judgment in her eyes. She'd been taking the brunt of the work since Sea Bass had his meltdown, and now I was slacking off too. I made a mental note to have a talk with her after we closed that night, to let her know I appreciated the extra help.

I was heading for the coffee machine when Mouse finished her client's tattoo. She wiped the excess ink from the woman's skin and told her she could stand up and take a look in the mirror. She'd been lying facedown while Mouse worked on her.

Climbing off the table, she shook her hair and sent a wave of strawberry blond cascading down her perfectly toned back. "How does it look, Katie?" she asked, pulling all that gorgeous hair aside. Kara turned around to look at me before walking over to the full-length mirror to see for herself.

Mouse glanced to me, her mouth hanging open the way it always did when something had her undivided attention. Her eyes panned back and forth across the room between me and her client.

Kara moaned her approval, preening in front of the mirror a little longer than necessary to admire the electric-blue scorpion on her right side. That's when I noticed the mark between her shoulder blades. It was hard to make out from across the room, but the pronounced lines telegraphing through her skin were unmistakable. Jackson had told me about the mark the night he showed up on my patio for the first time, insisting on seeing for himself if I had that same mark on my own back. It was the mark of a Sapanth. We'd just met, and he wanted to make damn sure I wasn't one of Kaleb's pack sent down from Atlanta to find him.

Through the reflection in the mirror, her eyes flicked from her new tattoo up to me. "You haven't answered my question. Do you like it?"

Who the hell cares. Eat shit.

"Do *you* like it?" I asked her in return. *You're the client, bitch.*

Refocusing her eyes on her perfect skin with her perfect hair falling gracefully over her perfect shoulders, she practically purred. "I love it."

"Then you can pay for it and get the hell out of my shop."

Mouse's jaw slackened even more, and Abel muttered something under his breath as he anticipated the impending storm.

A growl snaked through the room as Kara's golden eyes went a couple of shades darker. I'd hit a nerve. She strolled over to where I was standing and came within a few inches of my face, allowing me to feel the full impact of the threat in her eyes.

"I think I'll hang around for a few minutes." She looked at the chair next to the side table with the stack of outdated magazines. "To see if Jackson shows up," she added, glancing at the clock on the wall before smiling at me with about as much warmth as an ice cube. "He should be stopping by pretty soon. Right?"

Well, what do you know? Kara seemed to know a lot about Jackson's habits. Knew his timing too. An uneasy feeling came over me as it dawned on me that she'd probably been watching us. I don't know why that surprised me, but it definitely pissed me off. She'd crossed a line.

The tips of my fingers itched as my eyes began to burn, sending a threat right back at her. But there was no need to start a fight in the middle of the shop just because she was trying to get a rise out of me. Unfortunately, it was working. I tensed up, staving off the erratic beast and that growl that was crawling up the back of my own throat.

She cocked her head like a dog when she heard it. "Daddy told me you were a wild one. He likes his women rough in the sack even more than Jackson does." Her eyes flashed in mock surprise. "Said you were a real handful the other night."

I tried to hide the rush she'd just sent careening through my veins, but animals can smell adrenaline, and mine was threatening to come pouring out of my mouth if she didn't back off.

Still locked eye to eye, I managed to break the visual hold she had on me to glance over her shoulder at the back door. Sea Bass came waltzing in, carrying a bag from the deli down the street, smiling sheepishly at me before heading over to the counter at the back of the room. He grabbed a small carton of chocolate milk from the mini-fridge and smelled it, deciding it was past its prime before tossing it in the trash.

"What?" he said, looking up at all the faces staring at him. "I brought donuts." He held up the bag and jiggled it, shrugging when no one seemed interested.

"I'll take one," Mouse said, getting up and heading for the kitchenette.

I interpreted the look she gave me as she passed by as asking *should I call Jackson?* I wasn't proud of it, but I was feeling a little territorial and didn't want Jackson anywhere near the psycho bitch, so I was hoping she got my visual reply to leave it alone. She apparently got the message and made a beeline for the bag to grab a jelly donut. Then she leaned against the counter to watch the show.

By the time I turned back to Kara, she'd decided to back off and give me some room. In fact, she was practically out the front door. The look on her face was downright feral. Her eyes were back to their bright golden color, and the elongated slits that suddenly ran the length of her irises pulsed wildly. Something had spooked her.

I looked over my shoulder to see what had gotten her attention. Sea Bass and Mouse were in her direct line of sight. Mouse furrowed her brow and stared back at her client, but it was Sea Bass she was looking at.

"That tattoo is on the house," I said, dragging my eyes away from Sea Bass to look back at her. "Get out."

She backed up to the door and grabbed the handle to leave, but not before delivering a final threat. "You think you're winning, don't you?" she said with a condescending smile that sent a shiver down my back. "But I have a surprise for you, Katie Bishop." She flashed her cat eyes one more time and then shot out the door so fast I thought the glass would shatter.

"What the hell was that all about?" Abel asked.

Without answering his question, I turned around to look at Sea Bass. "What the hell's going on with you?"

He stood there like a deer in headlights with half a donut stuffed in his mouth, chewing it for a few more seconds before swallowing. "Was that who I think it was?" he asked, drawing questioning looks from Mouse and Abel.

"Yes, it was."

He looked a little too pleasantly surprised. "Damn, Katie. That was one good-looking woman."

"Thanks, Sea Bass." I shot him an eat-shit grin.

Staring at me for answers, Abel and Mouse were still trying to figure out what was going on. "That," I blurted out to satisfy their curiosity, "was a shifter." Sea Bass had told them about the Sapanths the day Mira, Kara's spy, walked into the shop. "A Sapanth to be specific."

Mouse looked unimpressed. "I knew there was something

funky about her." She snorted. "Her skin was too tight, and she had these random little hairs on her back."

That made me feel better. *Hairy bitch.*

Sea Bass was staring at the wall when I looked back over at him, but it was like he was looking right through it. His temporary recovery seemed to have vanished.

"All right." I waved my hands dismissively. "Let's break it up and get back to work." Abel and Mouse glanced around the empty room, passing each other snide looks. "We'll have a walk-in coming through that door any minute now," I added for emphasis. What I really wanted was some privacy to talk to Sea Bass, to find out why he'd come strolling back into the shop like nothing had happened. When Davina picked him up on Sunday morning, he was half out of it and had no idea where he'd been for two days.

Like clockwork, the front door opened and one of Mouse's regulars walked in. Now I just needed a diversion for Abel.

"Do me a favor, Abel." I walked over to the register and pulled out a twenty. "Mind going over to the deli to get some donuts?"

He looked at the bag Sea Bass had deposited on the counter. "Sure," he replied sarcastically, getting the message and grumbling on his way out of the shop.

Not wanting to lose my window of opportunity to have that little chat, I grabbed Sea Bass by his wrist and led him to the back of the shop. "I'd take you out back, but I don't feel like running into Kara again if she's still sniffing around."

I sat in the chair next to him and watched him look everywhere but at me. "What are you hiding, Sea Bass? You know my deepest secret and you're one of my best friends, and yet you won't talk to me."

His face flushed with a little shame.

Good, I thought. *You should be ashamed.*

"Grams says I'm just following in my mom's footsteps," he

began. "She's an alcoholic. A dangerous one. Grams said that's why they sent her back to the mountain. To keep her sober."

Sea Bass had told me about losing his mother at a young age. Not literally, but to the distance between them. She'd moved back to the mountain. The Ozarks. He talked to her occasionally on the phone, but he hadn't seen her in over ten years. Davina had raised him ever since, and now I knew why.

"She said Mom got plowed one night and nearly killed me. Took me out to the woods and just left me there in a clearing. If they hadn't found her passed out behind Gram's house, they wouldn't have even known I was missing. Jesus, Katie. I'd probably be dead if they hadn't sent out a search party to find me." He dropped his face in his hands and ran his fingers over the top of his head before looking back up. "I guess I should be thankful that I don't remember any of it. Grams said I was just a toddler when it happened."

I wrapped my arm around his shoulders and pulled him against me. "I'm sorry," I whispered. "I had no idea."

"Looks like I inherited her alcoholism gene. Shit, Katie! How the hell am I supposed to give up drinking? I love drinking!"

"The same way I gave up cigarettes," I replied.

He pulled away and gave me a puzzled look. "I ain't never seen you smoke a cigarette."

"There you go," I said. "Nicotine is a hell of a lot more addictive than alcohol, so if I could quit smoking, you can quit drinking." I left out the fact that I was sixteen when I started, and I was only a closet smoker for one summer.

"I'm real sorry about all this, Katie. And don't think I'm not grateful for you letting me keep my job."

I snorted a laugh. "You didn't think I'd actually fire you, did you? Just don't disappear like that again."

"I wasn't lying when I told you I didn't remember where I was for those two days. I'm just glad I didn't hurt anyone. Well, except for Maggie. I put her through the wringer. Thank God she didn't leave me." He stood up and let out a long, therapeutic breath. "I need another one of them donuts."

About that time, Abel came back into the shop with a bag in his hand. He walked over and handed me my change. Then he shoved the bag into Sea Bass's chest. "Here. Have another donut."

I THOUGHT the day would never end. With my appointments canceled thanks to Abel, and Sea Bass not having any to start with since he wasn't expected back for a while, we spent most of the day cleaning. The floor was so spotless I could have performed surgery on it. The second half of the day was spent calling customers to let them know the shop was fully staffed again—a desperate measure if I wanted to pay my bills at the end of the month. That two million that Jackson had buried thirty minutes south of the city was starting to look good.

Since we had a strict rule about no more than two lunch dates per week, Jackson was coming over around ten for a very late dinner. It was a space thing, me needing some boundaries so I didn't lose my identity to our relationship. I'd done that before, and I'd vowed to never let it happen again.

I fed Jet and unpacked the ground beef and buns I'd picked up on the way home. It was burger night. Jackson was going to need something substantial after a day of trying to hunt down the Sapanths' hidden lair. All I wanted to do was have a good meal and then curl up next to him for the night, making me wish he would hurry up. I was kind of surprised he hadn't called already to let me know he was on his way. But then there was the part I wasn't looking forward to. Our pleasant evening would probably end as soon as I told him about Kara showing up at the shop. I considered not telling him at all but figured lying by omission was a bad idea. We couldn't afford to have any more secrets between us.

I grabbed the remote to turn on the news while I prepped for dinner. As I sliced a tomato, a reporter was going on about a body found in a cemetery. Nothing unusual about a body in a cemetery unless it's not one of the deceased that belongs there. Something about an unsolved case. In the midst of all the background noise coming from the TV, I heard a name I thought I'd never hear again. I sliced the ripe fruit as the name came out of the reporter's mouth a second time and sawed straight through the soft tip of my index finger. I dropped the knife and looked down at the red cutting board, unable to distinguish the juice of the tomato from my own blood.

A few seconds later my phone rang. I looked at Fin's name on the screen, and I knew why he was calling. As I reached for it with my uninjured hand, the doorbell rang. Jackson would have used his key.

"Fin," I said into the phone as I headed for the door. The headlights from the patrol car blinded me when I opened it.

"Katie Bishop?" one of the officers asked.

"Yes, that's me," I said, knowing my time was up and feeling oddly relieved that it was finally over. I set the phone on the table next to the door, oblivious to Fin on the other end. Then I held my hands out so the officer could cuff me.

"You're under arrest for the murder of Christopher Sullivan."

16

Christopher's face stuck in my mind like a brand, his shocked expression as he went lifeless in front of my eyes. His last word had been my name as he stared at me in disbelief, trying to understand what he'd done to make me leave him dying on the floor at my feet. What he didn't remember was the demon that had taken up residence in his body. In that brief moment before his death, he had no memory of trying to possess and suck the life out of me.

I'd killed Christopher Sullivan earlier that summer in self-defense. The dragon had.

I was taken to the same interrogation room as the one they'd put me in the first time they brought me in for questioning. Empty walls, a stark table with a few folding chairs, and a large window that I was pretty sure obscured faces watching me from the other side.

The door opened, and in walked Detective Frank Ryan, the same detective who'd made it very clear to me that he thought I was a murderer—which I was. He took a dramatic breath, which I was sure was meant to set an intimidating mood for our impending interview.

It didn't work. I'd been through this before.

"Katie Bishop," he said, grinning smugly. "Now why am I not surprised to see you again?"

The last time the detective and I met was at a funeral. Chase Stone, one of Fin Cooper's business partners, had been murdered. Detective Ryan was there to see if he could get any leads on the killer. Why did murderers tend to show up at their victim's funeral? Fin said it was an ego thing. Killers liked to get a front-row seat to view their handiwork—and to prove how clever they were at outsmarting the police. Little did the detective know, the killer was sitting right next to him that day—the grieving widow.

Detective Ryan pulled out one of the rickety chairs and slid it over to mine. I turned away from him as he sat down next to me and leaned his elbows on his knees. "You must be tired, Miss Bishop. We can end all this very quickly if you just tell me what happened between you and Christopher Sullivan. I'm sure you had a good reason for killing him."

I'd been watching the news just before the police knocked on my door. If my memory was correct—although I was a little foggy at the time from the shock of hearing Christopher's name —the reporter had said the body was found buried in someone else's grave. Apparently something had dug up what was left of him, and some poor visitor to the cemetery had made the discovery.

"Maybe we should start with his arms, Miss Bishop. The body didn't have any."

I whipped my head around to look at him, suddenly horrified by the memory of ripping those arms off Christopher's body. In my defense, he was using them to try to rape me before ultimately killing me.

Ryan smirked, pleased by my reaction to the gruesome remark. "How did you remove them?" he asked. "Did you dismember him before or after you killed him?" The detective's face had gone from curious to disgusted by the end of the question. "We can stay here as long as it takes, Katie."

It's Miss Bishop, asshole!

"How about that phone call," I said, looking him square in the eye. "I don't think I want to talk to you anymore, Detective."

Ryan sat up in his chair and shot me a cocky grin. "I don't suppose you'd be willing to give us a DNA sample, would you? We could clear this all up right now."

I took the bait. "Why?"

He seemed to be waiting for that question and gladly answered. "Because of that pretty little scarf we found wrapped around the victim's neck. Soaked in blood," he added, leaning back in his flimsy chair, drawing out the moment as long as possible. I think he expected me to break from that revelation. When I didn't, he continued. "Something tells me we're going to find your blood on that scarf, Katie."

My mind started to race. I didn't own a scarf, and only a masochist would wear one in the middle of a Savannah summer, which was when Christopher died and Fin got rid of the body.

"If that's all you have, I'd suggest you let me go before my lawyer gets here." I didn't have a lawyer, but Fin had been on the other end of the phone when the lovely officers arrested me, so I expected council to come walking through that door at any second. "I'm not saying another word until I have my lawyer present."

Detective Ryan smirked and stood up to walk over to the two-way glass, but it was only to stretch his legs and have some kind of visual conversation with whoever was on the other side. He cocked his head to the right, cracking his vertebra as he stretched his ear toward his shoulder. Then he did the same on the other side.

All limbered up, he turned back around and popped a piece of gum into his mouth. "Want one?" he asked, holding the pack out to me.

I ignored his outstretched hand and defiantly smirked back, refusing to say another word. He shoved the pack of gum back into his pocket and milked the silence in the ice-cold room a little bit longer. The last time I'd sat in the room, it was sweltering, but tonight I found myself wishing I had on a sweater instead of a thin tank top.

He reached for the back of his chair and dragged it around to the other side of the table before taking a seat again. As he sat down and leaned back, I felt a rush of dread scurry up my spine. I knew something was about to come out of his mouth that would change the course of our little chat. I could see in his smug eyes that he hadn't dropped the real bomb yet.

"I guess you're wondering what grounds we had to cuff you and haul you in here tonight," he said, taunting me.

Without consciously doing it, I rubbed my wrists. The officer had removed the handcuffs when he put me in the room, so I suspected the dramatic arrest was more to intimidate me than to protect the fine officers from harm. If they'd known what I was, they would have left them on.

"Yeah, I was kind of wondering, Detective," I said, trying to sound aloof. "No telling whose blood is on that scarf." It wasn't mine, so what grounds did he have?

He glanced at that window again and smiled at the interlopers on the other side. Whatever he was about to tell me had fortified his confidence. "Where were you the night Christopher Sullivan disappeared?"

My mind began to race again and my heart rate escalated. Did he ask me that the first time I was brought in? More importantly, did I give him an answer? There's an old adage that if you tell the truth, you don't have to have a good memory. Unfortunately, the truth could put me on death row.

Seeing that I was clamming up and guessing that I was probably going to invoke my rights again, he finally got down to playing hardball. "We have his cell phone."

I tried to steady the tremor that was starting to travel up my legs, because my foot was about to nervously start tapping against the floor.

"We were a little surprised that it was still working after sitting in his pocket under all that dirt for months. A little more rain over the summer could have rusted it right out." The smug look on his face gave away the fact that I was screwed. Like half the population, Christopher was a phone junkie. We'd had a date at MacPherson's Pub the night he disappeared, and I knew that date was on his phone calendar with my name right next to it. "That phone just needed a little juice. Started right up."

The door to the interrogation room opened, and in walked a woman I'd met once before. It was Valerie Stephenson, one of Fin's pricey attorneys he had on retainer. He'd arranged for me to consult with her the first time they brought me in for questioning. That was the first and last time we met, because there was no evidence to tie me to the disappearance. I'd been cleared.

But now they had their evidence. At least enough to add me back to the prime suspect list.

"Miss Bishop," she said, walking past me and dropping her briefcase loudly on the table. She was an imposing figure, tall and sharply dressed, with an aggressive presence that hit you like a backhand when she targeted you with her gaze. "Has this detective been questioning you without council present?" Her eyes trained on Ryan as she asked the question, and I caught the contempt on his face. He probably considered lawyers nothing but bottom-feeders. Accomplices to their clients' crimes.

"I was just about to ask for my lawyer," I replied. "Again."

She cocked her head at Frank Ryan. "You should know better than that, Detective."

Picking her briefcase back up, she turned to me. "Let's go, Miss Bishop."

Ryan's head shot to the other detective standing just outside the open door. The look on his face said *not so fast*, but the other detective shook his head and stood aside for us to pass. Someone had pulled some pretty thick strings to get me out. Probably Fin. He practically owned Savannah, and there was no one you wanted on your side more than Fin Cooper if you were in a jam.

We left the police station and headed for her black Mercedes. As we walked toward the car, I expected an officer to come running out after us to handcuff me again, saying they'd made a mistake and had enough to hold me. But that never happened.

"Where are we going?" I asked.

She started the car and headed out of the precinct parking lot. "To the society."

FIN WAS WAITING in the living room when we walked inside. I don't know what got into me, but by the way I stalked up to him, you would have thought I was getting ready to clock him. Believe me, I wanted to.

"What the fuck, Fin!" I backed off when he met my growl with a warning look. We were tight, but not that tight.

He headed for the bar and poured some fancy scotch into a glass. "What are you drinking, Val?"

She dismissed the offer with a wave of her hand and dropped down into one of the wing chairs. "I have to be in court early in the morning, so let's just get down to business."

"Where's your sidekick?" I asked, referring to Lillian.

"Hosting some pretentious fund-raiser for dolphins or sea turtles," he replied. "It's for the best. No need to drag the whole damn coven into this mess."

I gave him a dangerous look when he walked over and handed me the glass, but I took it anyway. "What the hell did you do with that body, Fin?" I asked, quickly realizing I had no idea how much Valerie Stephenson actually knew about Fin's involvement in my felony.

Before Fin could implicate himself in the crime, Valerie stood up and headed for the door. "I'd advise you to wait until I'm out of earshot before continuing," she said. "Call me tomorrow afternoon, Fin, so we can figure out how to salvage this clusterfuck and save Miss Bishop's ass."

The second she was out the door, I turned back to Fin. "You buried Christopher's body in someone else's grave? And you left his cell phone in his pocket for the cops to find?"

He poured himself a glass of bourbon and took his time before answering the question. Fin didn't respond well to demands, considering he was usually the one in charge. "If you want to hide a body, Miss Bishop, you want to put it in a place where no one will be digging it up in the future. Conveniently, someone else's final resting place usually falls well within the no-dig zone." He took a sip of his drink, not hiding his annoyance well. "Although that cell phone was a little sloppy." Fin Cooper didn't like loose ends, and someone or something had just unraveled the whole ball of yarn. "The question you should be asking, Miss Bishop, is who did that digging?"

"They said there was a bloody scarf wrapped around the body's neck. I don't suppose you put it there?" I laughed mirthlessly, trying to hide my nerves.

"Wasn't me," he answered. "Lose any blood lately?"

I glanced at the bandage wrapped around my finger. "I did slice my fingertip just before the cops knocked on my door. I was bleeding like a stuck pig, but they were decent enough to give me a Band-Aid before I bled all over the back seat of the patrol car." A conspiracy theory suddenly entered my mind. "You don't think they would—"

"Frame you by scraping the back seat of that patrol car?" Fin finished. "I don't think the Chatham County PD is smart enough to pull that off. They have enough trouble solving murder cases with legitimate evidence."

It took me about two more seconds to remember the pool of

blood resulting from that bite Kaleb had given me. "You son of a bitch," I muttered.

Fin raised his brow. "I've been called worse."

"Not you." I was about to rehash the whole story when the doorbell rang.

"That would be Jackson. I told him to meet us here."

I would have called him myself, but my phone was on the table next to my front door. It was either that or the police would have confiscated it the minute I stepped outside. I'm sure Jackson had been frantic when he came over and found a pound of ground beef on the counter and a half-sliced tomato with traces of blood on the cutting board. Finding my car parked outside with me nowhere in sight probably had him thinking Kaleb had come back to finish what he started a couple of nights earlier.

Jackson walked into the room, escorted by the housekeeper. She didn't look very happy about entertaining us, especially when her boss wasn't even home.

"You can retire now, Vivian," Fin said. "I'll lock up on my way out."

She glanced at me briefly, then nodded to Fin before leaving the room.

"That woman hates me," I said.

"Are you all right?" Jackson asked.

I shrugged. "Nothing this can't fix." I shook my glass and turned it up to drain the last drop of expensive scotch. "Mind if I help myself to another?" I asked Fin.

He swept the glass out of my hand and headed for the bar. "What are you drinking, Jackson?"

Jackson shook his head. "I'm good."

Fin refilled my drink and delivered it to me before walking over to the window to stare out. "We were just talking about the suspicious evidence found on Christopher Sullivan's body. I'm afraid someone is gunning for Miss Bishop's ass."

"They found a bloody scarf wrapped around his neck. We

didn't put it there," I added, glancing at Fin. A thought suddenly occurred to me. "Who were those men with you the night you showed up to take care of Christopher's body?"

He sipped his bourbon and took his time responding to my accusation. "You're barking up the wrong tree."

Jackson's eyes were fixed on me when I looked back at him. I knew what he was thinking. Kaleb had bitten me and left blood all over my house. It would have been so easy to take a scarf and rub it in my blood while I was out cold.

"How would Kaleb even know about Christopher?" I asked.

That got Fin's attention. "One of you two want to let me in on your theory?"

Without taking my eyes off Jackson, I explained. "Jackson thinks Kaleb did this. That *is* what you're thinking, isn't it?" He didn't need to answer the question. It was written all over his face. "You see, Kaleb paid me a visit the other night. He attacked me and bit my neck." I laughed nervously. "You should have seen all the blood."

"This isn't a joke," Jackson said with a grave face.

My expression sobered. "No, it isn't. But right now I feel like the subject of a Salvador Dalí painting. I've just been framed for murder." Realizing the irony of what I'd just said, I laughed even harder.

Fin chimed in. "Before we tumble too deeply down this rabbit hole, let's consider the fact that we don't even know whose blood is actually on that scarf. Neither do the police." He shot me a glance as if something unpleasant had suddenly occurred to him. "You didn't by any chance give them a DNA sample while you were in custody?"

I shook my head, relieved that the interrogation hadn't escalated to that point. "Detective Ryan brought it up, but Valerie showed up before he could try to pressure me into giving them one."

"I'm gonna have to cut this short," Jackson said, standing up. "We need to go. Cairo's meeting me in an hour."

Fin's brow arched. "You boys doing a little hunting tonight?"

"We need to find the Sapanths before they start killing again. Right about now they're probably starting to get a little hungry, and something tells me it won't be cattle dropping like flies when that happens."

I finished my drink and followed Jackson out the door. On the ride back to my house, I couldn't shake the uncomfortable feeling that those cops could show up at my front door at any moment with irrefutable evidence that I'd killed Christopher Sullivan. I wanted to murder Kaleb with my own two hands for what he'd done to both of us.

"Will you be back tonight?" I asked Jackson as I climbed off the back of his bike.

"Depends on what we find." He looked a little uncomfortable before letting me in on the next bit of news. "I've got someone watching the house. Just until we find them," he added as I predictably opened my mouth to argue with him about it.

I glanced around the dark street. "Who is it?" I decided to tolerate it for the time being for the sake of Jackson's sanity.

"One of Cairo's clan."

I kissed him and gave him a long look. "Just bring your ass home in one piece. Can you promise me that?"

"I'll be fine," he said. "We're just scouting tonight. We'll save the actual hunting for later."

As I walked to the front door and turned back to watch him pull out of the driveway, I got the strangest feeling I was being watched—by an animal.

1 7

The last thing I needed was more alcohol and a bad night's sleep, but I was about as tired as an insomniac injected with espresso. Not to mention the fact that I was worried sick about Jackson.

My phone was on the table where I'd left it before being escorted down to the precinct. The message light was blinking. I was pretty sure it was Sugar, but I didn't dare call her back this late.

I fed Jet and grabbed the bottle of scotch from the cabinet. It would probably taste like rotgut after drinking Lillian's high-end alcohol, but I figured after a drink or two I wouldn't notice anymore.

I was turning into a real alcoholic.

"Come on, Jet." I opened the sliding glass door and sat down in one of the chairs, still feeling a little uneasy about the darkness with all those bushes. Jet was always a good barometer of danger, and as long as he was content, so was I. And then there was Cairo's guy out there, probably parked down the street with his eyes trained on my front door.

Jet lay on the patio next to my feet. I looked down when I

noticed his tail twitch back and forth a couple of times. "What's the matter, Jet? Too hot?" The air was finally starting to cool down a little. But cooling down in Savannah at the tail end of summer was still pretty miserable, and I imagined wearing a fur coat twenty-four seven was no picnic.

The first sign that something wasn't right was when Jet's tail went from intermittent swishing back and forth to full-throttle windshield-wiper mode. A low growl snaked out of his mouth, followed by a loud hiss as he bolted back inside through the cracked door.

A jolt of adrenaline suddenly hit me, and a chill shot through me. Something was out there, and it had managed to get past my babysitter. My eyes were beginning to burn like they always did when the dragon smelled a threat, but I saw and heard nothing.

"Time to go back inside," I muttered to myself, wondering if I was just being paranoid. But my cat sure as hell wasn't paranoid.

I stood up abruptly and darted for the sliding glass door. That useless door that wouldn't stop an amateur thief was about to be the only thing between me and whatever was coming out of that row of bushes bordering the patio.

Something reached over my shoulder before I made it inside, pulling me away from the door. The smell of musk and dirt hit my nose as hot breath rolled across my face. I managed to pull myself out of its grip and stagger back to my feet, catching its reflection in the glass. I gasped at the sight of the creature standing behind me on its hind legs, coal black with a set of golden eyes. The smell of it made my stomach lurch. A raccoon or a possum, but it looked more like a bear.

Jet darted back outside but let out an ungodly screech when he saw the creature. He retreated back into the house a second later.

The thing snorted wildly and came at me again, pawing at me aggressively with its powerful claws.

I whipped around just as my talons sprang from my fingers.

With a powerful thrash, I sliced through the creature's thick fur, ripping all the way through to its flesh. It let out a strangled howl and stumbled back against the table before regaining its legs and coming at me again. I lashed out a second time. It just stumbled backward again, this time falling to the ground. The creature rolled sideways and went still, moaning with an eerie cadence that sounded like nothing I'd ever heard before.

"Where the hell are you?" I hissed, referring to Cairo's guard who was either sleeping behind the wheel or worse.

The creature stirred. I took a cautious step toward it, careful to stay out of striking range. I jerked back when it righted itself and crawled toward the edge of the patio, cowering and clutching its wounded arm. I needed to strike while it was down, before it regained its strength and came at me again.

With a growl, I leaped toward it with both hands fanned wide to extend my long talons into slicing machines. But before I delivered the deadly blow, the creature opened its mouth and blurted a strangled string of words. I thought my mind was playing tricks on me.

"Kay-*tee*," it called out, emphasizing the second syllable of my name with difficulty. "S-see."

I stopped and gazed at the strange creature huddled on the ground "What did you say?" My breath hitched when I looked into its eyes. The golden color had faded and turned a shade of light blue, and the black fur covering its face had started to recede back into its skin. "Sea Bass?" By the time I reached him, he was half man and half beast, curled up on the ground like a frightened animal.

"Katie," he managed to get out of his mouth. "It's me. Sea Bass."

"I know, I know," I kept repeating, suddenly realizing he was the victim. I kept shaking my head, stunned at what I was looking at and wondering if it was real.

A minute later, he was huddled up, cold and completely

naked on my patio. I ran inside and grabbed a blanket to wrap around his shivering body. Then I helped him up and into the house. I led him to the couch and ordered him to lie down.

"Call Grams, Katie." A few seconds later he was sound asleep, exhausted from whatever had just happened to him.

Davina McCabe was the one person we both agreed needed to be summoned. She'd lied to me, and I wondered if Sea Bass had a clue about what had just happened to him.

Someone knocked on my front door. I hesitated to answer it, but then I remembered about Cairo's clansman. When I opened it, I was surprised to see a woman.

"Are you Katie?" she asked.

"That would be me," I replied without inviting her in. "Are you my babysitter?"

"Yep." Her cocky smile faded as her nostrils went up, sniffing the air like a hound. "Can I come in for a minute?"

I had a feeling she was prepared to alert the National Guard if I refused, so I let the door swing open and took a step aside. "Why not."

"I'm Elizabeth," she said, walking past me and making a beeline straight for the smell, which was no longer detectable to my nose now that the creature had disappeared. "You can call me Liz." She walked over to the couch and peered down at Sea Bass. "Heard some strange noises coming from the house. You sure you're okay?" She went to jab his arm with her index finger, to rouse him I assumed.

"Don't touch him," I warned. "He's sick."

"Yeah, no shit." She snorted. "What's wrong with him?"

Her presence was starting to annoy me, and I needed to call Davina. "Look, I'm not trying to be rude, but you need to leave. As in go home. I'm fine. Jackson's just a little overprotective."

She gave me a smug look. "Suit yourself. Jackson isn't going like it though."

"Jackson's my boyfriend, not my keeper."

She followed me to the door, glancing back at the couch before turning her eyes back to mine. I think she was trying to read between the lines to see if I was in any way under duress, like any good bodyguard would do under the circumstances.

"Nice to meet you, Katie," she said as she headed down the sidewalk toward an empty street. Her car must have been parked a few houses down.

"Hey, Liz." I waited for her to turn around and look back at me. "Thanks."

Davina knocked on my door twenty minutes after I called her. I'd offered to drive Sea Bass over to her place, but she instructed me to leave him on the couch so he could sleep it off.

"Sebastian," she called out, taking a seat on the edge of the couch while nudging him. "Time to wake up, sleepyhead."

I'd expected a different reaction to her finding out her grandson had turned into a smelly beast on my back patio, but her reaction to my description over the phone had been on the quiet side. She knew exactly what had happened to Sea Bass, and it was time for her to let me in on his little secret.

"Cut it out, Maggie!" He opened his eyes and realized he wasn't at home and that the finger prodding him wasn't his girl-friend trying to wake him up for work. "Grams?"

"That's right, boy. In the flesh." She reached into her purse and pulled out a small paper bag containing some dried herbs. "Here," she said, shaking a small pile of it into his palm. "Chew on it."

"You want me to chew on some dried-up leaves? What is it?"

"Exactly what you need right now."

Not one to argue with the woman who raised him, he popped the leaves into his mouth and began to chew as instructed. "Tastes bitter."

The blanket fell away from his shoulders and revealed the nasty gashes I'd inflicted before I realized it was him. Even I was a little shocked at how deep they went. I wasn't too happy about the crime scene all over my couch either. I'd probably have to buy a new one.

"What the hell happened?" she asked, glaring at me.

"Don't go all Cujo on me, Davina," I shot back at her. "Your grandson here came up behind me on my patio and attacked me first."

Sea Bass looked horrified. "I did not! Shit, Katie, I was just trying to get your attention. I was coming out of Mojo's when it happened. One minute I was walking home, and the next I was down on all fours."

My house was somewhere between Mojo's and Sea Bass's apartment. It wasn't the first time he'd shown up on my patio on his way home from that hellhole.

"Are those his clothes?" I asked, nodding to the tote she'd set on the floor. I'd warned her that he was naked and asked her to bring some clothes from his old bedroom at her house.

Davina reached for the bag and handed it to Sea Bass, who by now was starting to gag. "All right. Spit it out." She held out her hand, and he took her up on the offer, spitting out the chewed herbs that apparently had turned intolerable in his mouth.

"God in heaven, Grams! What did you put in my mouth?"

"Just a little monkshood."

I glared at her in disbelief. "Monkshood is poisonous, Davina!"

"Not to a howler, it ain't," she replied, nodding her head once. "Monkshood will help get it under control."

"A what?" Sea Bass and I both said in unison.

She sighed dramatically and slapped her hands on her thighs. Then she got up and walked toward the kitchen. "You got any booze in this place?"

I glanced at the broken bottle of scotch next to the patio

table. "There's some red wine on the counter and a fresh bottle of tequila in the cabinet over the microwave. I think there's some beer in the fridge too."

She retrieved the tequila and a bottle of beer. "Go change into them clothes, boy. We'll meet you on the patio."

By the time Sea Bass came outside, dressed in a pair of shorts and a T-shirt from his younger days, Davina and I had righted the overturned table and cleaned up the broken scotch bottle on the ground. He sheepishly sat down.

Davina handed him a bottle of beer and a shot of tequila. "Drink up, boy. You'll be needing it."

She sat down in the other chair while I stood. I was too wired to sit.

"Let's see," she began. "How am I going to put this?" After a minute of contemplation, she got straight to the point like she always did. "Sebastian, honey, you're a howler. A mountain howler, which is a hell of a lot better than a river howler."

He stared at her blankly, like her words hadn't caught up to his brain yet. "Okay," he eventually said, nodding his head with a confused look on his face.

"Are you hearing me, boy?" She leaned across the table to give him a pointed look. "You turn into a big hairy beast that looks like a cross between a werewolf and a black bear. We all do. You're just a late bloomer. Most of us turn on the first full moon after our eighteenth birthday. But you were always difficult," she added with a nervous grin.

Sea Bass and I both looked up at the bright moon over our heads. It was indeed full. I could see that it was finally sinking in for him. Being a beast myself, I knew all too well what it felt like to find out your life had been one big secret.

"Those squirrels that used to sit around the dining room table when I was a kid," he began to ask her, thinking back to the memory of seeing strangers sitting at the table one minute, then seeing a bunch of squirrels in those same chairs upon a second look. "Were they—"

Davina nodded, sighing. "Yes, they were."

He'd told me that story the day he introduced me to his grandmother, but I just assumed he was a kid with an active imagination.

"You said we all do. Does that mean you're a howler too, Grams?"

She nodded her head. "But I've been in complete control of mine for over fifty years. It only comes out when I let it. I'm getting too damn old for all that carousing, so that ain't very often." She looked up at the full moon and grinned. "See?"

His eyes went soft, and I could almost read his thoughts. As much as he tried to hide it, I knew how devastating it must have been to lose his mother to the mountains of the Ozarks when he was so young. I could see it in his eyes every time he mentioned her. Davina had fed him that bullshit story about his mother's alcoholism, but I guess it was a little more complicated than that.

"Was it all a lie?" he asked. "You plan on telling me the real reason my mother went back to the mountain?"

For the first time since I'd met Davina, she seemed a little fragile. It was unsettling to witness such a private moment between them.

"Your mama never did learn how to control it," she began. "It was like a dark cloud was always over her head." She poured herself a tall shot of tequila and drank it before continuing. "You'd snuck out in the middle of the night like you always did. Thirteen going on thirty is what you thought you were." She laughed quietly at the memory of her delinquent grandson. "It was a full moon. You went out into the woods that night looking for your friends, but they never showed up. Something else did though." She drank her second shot and looked him in the eye. "Your mama almost killed you. If I hadn't gone looking for you that night, she probably would have succeeded."

Sea Bass looked like he's just been kicked in the gut. "That was my mother?" he said, remembering the encounter. "That thing in the woods was Mama?"

She reached over and patted the back of his hand and gave it a good squeeze. "She didn't know, honey. Your mama was out of her mind that night. That beast inside her is about as powerful as any to ever come off that mountain. That's why she left. She was getting more unpredictable by the day and couldn't bear the thought of hurting you." She grinned at him and gave his hand a final squeeze before letting go. "Your mother is a living legend on that mountain."

He took a shuddering breath and then let it out along with all the pent-up emotions waiting to burst out of him. "So all that stuff you told me about trying to keep her sober was a lie?"

"What did you expect me to say, boy? That your mother was a wild animal and we were all just waiting for you to turn too?"

He looked at her incredulously. "Well, yeah. You could have at least warned me. Hell, I could have killed Katie tonight."

I snorted a sarcastic laugh but decided to keep my mouth shut.

Sea Bass scratched his head and cringed. "Shit! What am I supposed to tell Maggie? That her boyfriend is a werewolf?"

Davina smacked her hand down on the table, making both of us jump. "If that girl loves you as much as she says she does, she'll turn lemons into lemonade. Won't be the first time an outsider got inducted into the McCabe clan."

He seemed to have a little faith in that statement and nodded his head. "I guess you're right, Grams." Sea Bass was easy like that, laid-back and nonconfrontational. Then he let his shoulders sag as he sank back into the chair, looking at the empty shot glass next to him on the table. "Does this mean I'm not an alcoholic?"

18

I had the worst headache when I walked into the shop the next morning. It was hard to say whether it was from all the alcohol I drank the night before, lack of sleep, or if the arrest and subsequent revelations were the cause of all the pounding going on inside my head. It was almost morning before Jackson got in, after another unsuccessful scouting mission for the Sapanths' lair. By the time I finished telling him about Sea Bass's family secret, it was time to get up and go to work.

The morning glare coming through the window assaulted my eyes the instant I took my sunglasses off, forcing me to snap them shut for a second. When I reopened them, I noticed Sea Bass hunched over a drawing at the desk in the back.

"Morning, boss," Abel said as I walked past him and headed over to talk to the boy wonder, who a few hours earlier had been covered in shaggy fur and smelled like a possum.

I walked up behind him and examined his bare arms where I'd done some pretty significant damage the night before. Davina had told me the wounds would heal quickly. She wasn't kidding. There were a couple of faint pink lines where my claws had opened his skin, but other than that he looked perfectly fine.

"Hey, Katie," he said when he noticed me standing behind him. He turned back around and continued drawing on the paper. They were those same red circles he'd been obsessively drawing the morning he showed up after his two-day disappearing act.

"What are you doing here?" I asked.

The faint smile on his face suddenly vanished, replaced by a look of fear. "Well, you told me I still had a job." Then he glanced around at the others and lowered his voice to a whisper. "Am I fired?"

"Hell no, you're not fired." It irritated me that he thought I could be so petty and fire one of my best friends because of a little medical emergency—and that's exactly what it was. Then I grinned and tried to lighten up all the gloom and doom glowing around him like a bad aura. "Are you kidding me? Feels good not to be the only freak in the room."

He exhaled the breath he was holding. "Thank God. I was getting ready to head over to Tattoo Haven to see if they were hiring."

"You'd last about an hour in that overpriced boutique," I said. "I just figured you might need a day to rest after what happened last night."

"What happened last night?" Abel asked, hearing our conversation as he swept the floor within earshot.

"Nothing!" Sea Bass snapped. "This is a private conversation between Katie and me, so go clean the toilet or something."

Abel didn't take offense. Men could tell each other to go fuck themselves and then five minutes later act like nothing happened.

I glanced at the desk where his hand was still gripping the red pen. "Why do you keep drawing those?"

His palm spread over the piece of paper and then crumpled it into a ball. "Doesn't mean anything," he said, looking embarrassed, almost self-conscious, about doing it. "I'm just doodling."

Doodles were usually a random distraction, but he was as

focused as a laser beam every time I caught him drawing those circles.

Sugar came flouncing into the shop like a hurricane before I could interrogate him further about the mysterious circles. She spotted us in the back and made a beeline across the room.

"Great," I muttered. "Here we go."

She was in a sixties mood today, wearing a black-and-white-checkered sheath dress with matching white heels that clacked across the floor as she walked. She exhaled dramatically as she approached us, her pale pink fingernails coming to rest on her hips.

"Since you standing here looking all alive and well, I guess I can rule out finding you dead on your living room floor." It wasn't a question, but it definitely required an answer. Her brow went up when I didn't immediately respond.

"Good morning to you too," I replied. "I was just about to call you." It was a little white lie. She'd been blowing up my phone since around ten the night before, but since I was busy being arrested and interrogated by Detective Frank Ryan and then had to deal with Sea Bass when I finally got home, returning her calls was way down on my list of priorities.

"I know you ain't ignoring me, girl."

"Could I ever ignore you, Sugar?" I walked over to the front desk to check the schedule. "I've got a client in thirty minutes. That gives us about fifteen to go out back for a chat." Sugar followed me toward the back door without opening her mouth, which was difficult for her. Before walking out the door, I looked over at Sea Bass. "You want to tell her, or should I?"

He grumbled something under his breath and scratched his forehead. "Might as well. She's gonna find out anyway with all them big mouths over at the society. Hell, she probably already knows."

His comment suddenly made me wonder if Fin and Lillian had known all along what he was—or was about to become.

Maybe the whole coven knew. I turned around and glared at Sugar. If they all knew that Sea Bass was a walking time bomb ready to explode into a beast at any moment, maybe she was the one who had some explaining to do.

"Why the hell you looking at me like that?" she asked.

I grabbed her arm and practically dragged her outside. The second the door shut, I started the inquisition. "Did you know all along about Sea Bass's little family secret?"

She looked genuinely startled by the way I was manhandling her, quickly yanking her arm out of my grip and taking a step back. She slung her purse over her shoulder and smoothed her disheveled black wig. "What in Hades is wrong with you?" she asked, her bewildered eyes turning angry. "You better have a good reason for going all caveman on me. I love you, girl, but I'm about to whip yo' ass if you do it again."

I backed off and gave her some space. "Sorry, Sugar, but I'm just a little bit on edge this morning. I spent the first half of the night in an interrogation room down at the police station. Then I came home and found Sea Bass in my backyard, smelling and looking like something out of *Underworld* or *The Howling*."

Based on her confused expression, I could see that she was having trouble keeping up. I wasn't sure which part had her more dumbfounded, so I decided to back up and tell her about my arrest first. "They arrested me for Christopher Sullivan's murder last night. Well, they tried. Fin sent one of his fancy lawyers down to remind them that they didn't actually have enough to detain me."

She shook her head and twisted her brow. "Baby, did you say *Underworld*?"

"Yeah, never mind about my arrest." I snorted.

"I just don't know if I can handle all this without a strong cup of coffee in my hand. I ain't even had breakfast yet."

I groaned and shut my eyes.

She relented and confessed. "I know about his crazy mama.

Hell, half the town knows about that loon. They just don't know why she's crazy."

"And you do?"

She hemmed and hawed for a moment before coming clean. "Whole damn society knows about Sarah McCabe. That woman is a card-carrying member of the Sasquatch club."

"Well, apparently Sea Bass is a Sasquatch too," I whispered, not knowing why since we were the only two out here.

Her eyes went wide. "No shit! Sea Bass too? My boy?"

"I wish I was kidding. He showed up on my patio last night in full howler mode. The poor guy didn't even know what he was. I had to call Davina."

"I just can't believe it," she whispered back. "I'm gonna give Mama a piece of my mind if I find out she knew."

I flattened my back against the building and stared off into space. The fatigue was starting to get to me, and it wasn't even noon. "They found his cell phone."

She leaned against the wall next to me. "Sea Bass's phone?"

"Christopher's," I said with a halfhearted laugh. "They found his body in some graveyard outside town, where Fin buried it Mafia style. Someone dug it up. His cell phone was in his pocket. It just needed a little charge, and there was our date on his calendar the night he disappeared."

"That don't mean you killed him," she said. "Well, you did, but it was self-defense, and they don't have any hard evidence to prove it."

I rolled my head to the side to look at her. "They also found a bloody scarf wrapped around his neck. I didn't put it there, but I have a bad feeling that blood is going to match mine. I am so screwed, Sugar."

"Well, how the hell did your blood get on a scarf around his neck?" She thought about it for a second and seemed to have the same epiphany I'd had when Detective Ryan had told me about the evidence. "You don't think it was one of them shifters?"

My house had looked like a crime scene the morning after Kaleb attacked me and bit my neck. I was out cold for hours, and God knows what had happened between the time I passed out and the time Sugar came banging on my door the next morning. He could have done all kinds of things to me that I preferred not to think about.

I stared at the parking lot and nodded my head.

"That son of a bitch!" she hissed.

We stood against the wall in silence and let it all sink in. Hearing Sugar verbalize exactly what I was thinking only cemented my theory. Kaleb had soaked a scarf in my blood and then dug up Christopher Sullivan's body so he could frame me. The only reason for doing that was to hurt Jackson. Revenge for walking away from the Sapanths. Maybe he thought losing me to a life sentence in prison would weaken Jackson enough to bring him back to the club.

He didn't know Jackson as well as he thought he did.

"Katie," Sugar said, cocking her head, "how do you think them shifters knew about Christopher Sullivan? That man disappeared months ago, and them assholes just rode into town last week. And how the hell did they know where Fin buried the body?"

"That's a real good question. I haven't figured that out yet."

The back door opened, and Sea Bass stuck his head out. "Your client just walked in, Katie."

We went back inside, and Sugar put her arm around Sea Bass's shoulders. "Why don't you let Sugar buy you a cup of coffee over at Lou's? You can tell me all about it."

JET DIDN'T GREET me when I walked inside the house. I tossed my mail on the table next to the door and went straight to the kitchen to feed him. Even if he wasn't interested in seeing me, he was always interested in a bowl of food.

"Jet," I called.

The hair on the back of my neck stood up as I heard his faint chatter coming from the living room. It was an odd staccato sound that came out of his mouth when he watched birds or squirrels through the patio door.

I set the unopened can of cat food on the counter and reached for the glass on the towel next to the sink, my heart racing as I filled it with water to quench my dry mouth.

"Come on, Jet," I called again, staring at the tile backsplash behind the faucet, hoping he'd come bouncing into the kitchen but somehow knowing he was preoccupied.

His chattering trailed off into a low growl that climaxed into a hiss, and I turned around to survey the dark living room where I could barely see his tail swishing back and forth in the sliver of moonlight shining through the glass door.

This scenario was getting old.

"I don't think that cat likes me." Kara stepped out of the darkness and into the dusky space between the living room and the dimly lit kitchen. "Strange, since we're so much alike."

"I guess he doesn't like alley cats."

She ignored the insult and walked toward the kitchen. Her long hair swept across the granite surface in a wave of amber and gold as she bent down to rest her elbows on the kitchen island separating us. "No Jackson tonight?" she asked, flicking her caramel eyes up to mine.

"What do you want, Kara?"

"No, no, no," she said, shaking her head slowly as she lifted off the edge of the island. "That is such a cliché question. Especially when you already know the answer."

The only thing I knew for sure was that she wanted Jackson. But since he wasn't here, I was more concerned with her immediate motives for breaking into my house. Her daddy had been a handful, which meant she'd probably be just as difficult to remove from my kitchen if it came down to it.

She walked over to the patio door and gazed out into the backyard. "You should get this door fixed."

"For Christ's sake," I said, squeezing my tingling left hand into a tight fist, the other gripping the glass so hard I expected it to break. "Let's just get this over with so I can send you on your way and eat my dinner in peace."

She glanced down at the floor. "I didn't think all that blood would clean up so easily. It must have taken some real elbow grease to get it out of the wood grain." By the time she looked back at me, her irises had stretched to the outer edges of her eyes, and her pupils had elongated into thin slits. "My father spared me the hassle of biting you myself. To get that blood," she added with a menacing grin.

Jet darted into the bedroom when I dropped the glass on the floor. It shattered, sending water and shards in every direction. The sound of her voice dimmed as the rush of my blood filled my ears. My eyes burned, and the familiar sensation of my talons trying to force their way out through the tips of my fingers jolted me.

Kara's eyes flashed when she realized what was happening to me. "Too bad that dragon of yours is such a pussy these days. Not at all like the beast I remember seeing before you cut off its balls." She took a deep breath and turned around to face me. "But," she continued with mock caution, "those claws of yours can still do some damage. My father can attest to that."

"I guess it was you that planted that scarf." I ran my eyes along her lean and toned body, noticing her perfectly painted black fingernails. "I bet there's still dirt under those nails from all that digging. The stench of death is all over you," I added just to piss her off.

Her cocky grin flattened for a second but reappeared quickly as she tried to hide the reaction I'd gotten out of her. But not before I got a satisfying glimpse of it.

"I'm curious," I said. "How did you know about Christopher?"

She seemed surprised by the question. Like I'd asked something so obvious that it didn't warrant an answer. "You didn't really think I'd let Jackson just walk away and start a new life?" Her brow twisted as she obliged me with the details. "I know everything about you. I know what you are, who you work with, where you had lunch on the first Tuesday of last month." Her face went cold as her voice deepened into a guttural growl. "Jackson shouldn't have taken you to the beach. The sea shifters were ours!"

On our first date, Jackson had taken me to Tybee Island to see what I thought were loggerhead hatchlings, flapping under the moonlight as they raced toward the water's edge. What I hadn't expected to see were those tiny hatchlings shifting into birds to make it out to the ocean, to the safety of deep water, where they'd shift back into turtles. Jackson called them sea shifters. He'd also said he used to bring Kara there when they were still together.

"That was the first night you fucked him," she continued matter-of-factly. "I wanted to kill you that night, but that would have been too easy. I had a better plan that would make you suffer."

"You're mighty confident." I knew damn well I could have beaten her at the time, before my dragon started going through its little crisis. Maybe she knew it too. But now it was a different ball game. Her daddy was one thing, but the jealous rage of a scorned woman was another, especially when that woman had her own set of sharp claws.

"Capable is more like it," she replied with a roll of her eyes.

I'd never seen a cat roll its eyes before. It was kind of creepy.

"So you're a Peeping Tom too? Been stalking us all summer?"

I thought she was about to lose her cocky composure when I likened her to a common pervert, but a humorless laugh burst from her mouth instead.

"I even know when you pee," she sneered.

"Obsess much?" I blew her off.

She snarled, and for a brief second her leopard spots flashed vividly on her arms and face. I thought she was about to shift, but then I heard the key jiggle the front door.

I turned around as it opened, and Jackson walked inside. When he didn't seem surprised, I whipped back toward Kara. The patio door was open, and she was gone.

"Did you see—" I stopped when I noticed the grave look on his face. He shoved the key back in his pocket and gazed at me. "What's wrong, Jackson?"

He glanced at the cell phone in his other hand. "I just got a call from Cairo. Angela's gone."

19

Jackson had thrown some clean clothes into a bag the night before, trying to convince me to go with him to Cairo's place. Under the circumstances, I'd decided not to mention Kara's visit. He would have insisted on taking me with him, and I would have argued the fact that I had a business to run the next day. That would have only conflicted him and forced him to choose between me and his best friend, who clearly needed him more than I did at the moment. Besides, Kara wasn't coming back. At least not right away. I had no doubt about that.

Sea Bass eyed me with concern when I dragged myself through the back door. He headed straight for the coffee machine and poured a cup. "I'd run over to that fancy shop down the street for some of that espresso if I thought you could hold out that long," he said, handing it to me. It was cheap but got the job done. "Damn, Katie, what did you do last night?"

"Nothing," I said, not wanting to bring up my visit from Kara. "I haven't been sleeping much lately. It's just catching up to me, that's all."

"No shit," he said. "Don't take this the wrong way, but you look like hell."

"And that's exactly how I feel." I flashed him a wide grin and took a deep swallow of the mediocre coffee, feeling the high-octane caffeine kick in almost immediately.

My nine o'clock client walked in and nodded to me. Being a few minutes early, he took a seat and grabbed one of the magazines from the table.

"You can go over," I said to him, motioning toward my station. I finished the coffee and shook my head back and forth to shake off the haze that had clouded me since I woke up from my two hours of sleep. Did I really want to work on a client feeling like this?

"How do I look, Sea Bass?"

"Like a zombie who shouldn't be putting permanent ink on someone's skin right now."

"That bad?" I cringed at the thought of how I must have looked. "I actually feel a lot better than I did ten minutes ago."

He didn't look convinced. "You sure you don't want me to do that tattoo, Katie? I don't have any clients till this afternoon."

"No," I said, pondering the offer. "I think work is exactly what I need this morning."

I collected some supplies and walked over to my station. I'd started the tattoo on his pectoral muscle a couple of weeks earlier, so all I was doing this morning was filling in a few spots. Piece of cake.

"You doing okay, Katie?" he asked as I sat down and pulled on a pair of gloves.

"Okay is a relative term. But for the purposes of finishing that eagle flying across your chest, I'll be just fine."

He eased back in the chair, and I hit the power switch to start filling in the last section of the bird's wing. As I came within a half inch of his skin, I lingered and stared at the humming gun while a mild tremor made its way up my hand and into my arm.

It was a tattoo artist's—or a surgeon's or bomb specialist's—worst nightmare.

"Everything all right?" he asked, looking a little concerned by my hesitation. Then his eyes followed mine.

"I'm fine. Just give me a minute."

He swallowed hard, and I could see the discomfort growing on his face.

A hand covered mine, and I looked up as Sea Bass gently took the tattoo gun out of my hand and turned it off. "I told you to rest a little more before coming back to work, boss. That stomach virus is doing a real number on folks all over town."

Keith looked relieved. "It's okay. I can come back in a few days when you're feeling better."

"I can finish it up for you, if you want," Sea Bass offered, glancing at me for approval.

I was already heading toward the back of the room, trying to escape everyone's eyes before I broke down in tears. "Sure. Go ahead," I managed to get out before ducking into the bathroom. Once I was inside, I locked the door and gripped the edge of the sink, staring at my reflection in the mirror while I came to terms with what had just happened. I was losing it.

"You all right in there, boss?" Mouse asked through the door. "Keith rescheduled. He's gone, so you can come out now if you want."

The last thing I wanted to do was walk out there and face my employees.

"I'll be out in a minute."

I sat on the toilet with my forehead pressed into my palms, wondering what the hell had just happened to me. Sea Bass had covered for me nicely, but maybe he was right. Maybe I needed to spend a few days in bed. But I'd been out of the shop more in the past few weeks than I had since we opened the doors for business. At this rate, I'd be closing those doors by year end.

Another knock came. This time it was Jackson. "Open the door, Katie."

I reached over and unlocked it. "It's open."

He swung the door open and leaned against the frame, waiting for me to either come out or invite him in. When I did neither, he took the liberty and came inside and shut the door behind him, which was a feat considering his size in the small space. Kind of like trying to maneuver your suitcase inside an airport stall.

"Any word on Angela?" I asked as he leaned back against the edge of the flimsy sink.

Without answering, he reached over and lifted my chin to raise my eyes up to his. "What's this all about?" He glanced around the tiny bathroom and brought his eyes back to mine.

"I just had a little problem with my hands shaking, that's all." The thought of the damage I could have done to a client's skin made me feel like a bag of shit. "Jesus," I muttered quietly, remembering the oath I made to myself that when the day came that I couldn't do exceptional work, I'd give it up. I'd expected that day to come in thirty or forty years though.

He stared at me without saying a word, reading between the lines like a seasoned bullshit detector.

No time like the present, I figured. "Kara showed up at my house last night."

He straightened up so fast I thought the sink was going to dislodge from the wall and crash to the floor. "After I left?"

"Just before you showed up actually. She was standing in the living room when you stuck your key in the door, but she slipped out through the patio before you walked inside."

He opened the door, grabbing my wrist on his way out. "Come on." On the way to the entrance of the shop, he glanced at Mouse, who was working on a client. "She'll be back in a little while."

We went across the street to Lou's. Jackson ordered coffee at the counter while I grabbed a booth. By the time he slid into the seat across from me, I was starting to feel a little more composed and capable of carrying on a rational conversation.

"You never answered my question," I said. "What's going on with Angela?"

"We'll get to that, but you need to tell me what happened with Kara first."

I took a sip of coffee and eased back into the seat. "Kaleb didn't wrap that bloody scarf around Christopher's neck. It was Kara."

"She told you that?"

"She didn't come right out with it, but she made it pretty clear. She also made it clear that she's been stalking us since you showed up in Savannah. That's how she knew about Christopher."

His jaw tightened, and I thought he was about to crush the paper coffee cup in his hand. "I'm sorry I dragged you into this mess, Katie, but I'll make it right. By the time I'm through with Kara, she'll wish she had never heard your name."

"Angela?" I asked for the third time.

"She was gone when Cairo got home last night. Her car was parked outside, and her purse and wallet were still on the living room table. No one's seen her since Cairo drove into town to meet me."

From what Jackson had told me, Cairo and Angela were inseparable. A mated pair is how he'd described them. Apparently Dimensional shifters bonded for life, death being the only thing that could break that bond once they were married.

"Jesus, Jackson. You don't think Kaleb had something to do with her disappearance?"

His eyes went cold as the name triggered him. "He called Cairo from Angela's phone this morning. He wants the money."

"What money? I thought you said Cairo spent most of his on that big spread of property he owns."

When he hesitated, I knew I wasn't going to like what he was about to say. "He has some of it left. Said he can call in a few debts and scrape together about a million, but Kaleb wants the whole two million."

"Or?"

"Or he'll kill her." He turned to look me straight in the eye. "They'll play with her for a few days. Make her wish she was dead. I won't go into detail about what a pack of shifters can do to a woman."

I'd seen Cairo and his clan pull off some pretty amazing tricks with their ability to shift into objects. Seemed reasonable to think that Angela could just throw herself up as a brick wall or something else the Sapanths couldn't penetrate.

"Can't she just—"

"No," he said, knowing where I was going with the question. "They work as a team. One of them starts to build, and the other one serves as an anchor at the other end. It's like energy being thrown into the universe. It always lands somewhere, in some other form, unless it's harnessed. He read the confusion on my face and simplified it. "Imagine Angela throwing herself over a river, like a bridge. Cairo would have to be on the other end to hold down and harness her energy until she reached the other side."

"What would happen if he wasn't on the other side?" I asked with strange curiosity.

His grave look hinted at the answer. "It's a dangerous gift to throw around without a little forethought. One poorly calculated move and you could find yourself drifting through space, landing in ten different places in ten different forms."

"Jeez," I muttered. "I think I'd try to give that little gift back."

"You mean like your dragon?"

"It's not like I have a choice about that." As soon as the words left my mouth, I realized the point he was making. None of us had a choice about our gifts. I couldn't hand over the dragon any more than Jackson could relinquish his strength or Cairo and his clan could ignore their abilities. "Point taken."

"I'd give Cairo my money, but Kaleb wants mine too. Four million in exchange for Angela's life."

"So what now?"

"We give them the money," he said, taking a sip of his coffee. "I'll get the extra million. From my father," he added a second later. "The son of a bitch owes me."

I shut my eyes for a second and considered my words carefully, trying not to sound like a selfish bitch. The money was irrelevant, but my concern for Jackson wasn't. "I hate to even ask, but why are you doing this? I know they're your friends, but can't Cairo call in a few favors?"

"Because I owe them. They took me in when I was on the run. Shit, Katie, they took my dog in."

He made me laugh, which was exactly what I needed. "You're right. I shouldn't have even questioned it. I guess I'm just a little worried about you driving all the way to New Orleans to grovel to your asshole father. Is there a plan B if he says no?"

"If he doesn't give it to me"—he shrugged—"I know where he stashes the washed money."

"Oooh, not a good idea, Jackson. The part about stealing the dirty money, I mean. Last thing we need is the mob rolling into town."

"It's not me they'll be coming after." He grinned slyly, but it wasn't funny. Seeing the concern on my face, he tried to put me at ease. "Don't worry about it. The bastard will give me the money—charge me interest too. Randall Hunter never passed up an opportunity to make a profit in his life."

"When are you leaving?" I asked, suddenly feeling a little vulnerable about having him so far away when things were getting so hot around town.

"Right after I walk you back to the shop. I'll reach New Orleans by tonight. I'll get a few hours of sleep after meeting with my father, then I'll hit the road and be back here by tomorrow night."

He made no attempt to talk me into going with him. He must have thought I was safer here, with a pack of killer shifters stalking me, than in the presence of his own father. That realization only escalated my fears.

We finished our coffee and Jackson walked me back across the street. I hadn't been back for more than ten minutes when Detective Ryan walked through the door.

Being an ex-cop, Abel could smell one from a mile away. That ability wasn't necessary today though.

"Officer Ferguson," Ryan said, cocking his head at Abel like he couldn't quite put two and two together. I'm sure the bald head with all those tattoos was a bit confusing to the detective, seeing how Abel had covered them up with a headful of hair until the day he quit the force.

Abel nodded to him. "It's just Ferguson now."

Detective Ryan looked amused. "I heard something about your leaving the force." It must have suddenly dawned on him that Abel worked for me, because he squinted his eyes and nodded, doing his best to rein in his grin. The shop broom that perpetually lived in Abel's hand must have confirmed it.

"Can I help you with something, Detective?" I asked.

He pulled his eyes away from Abel and looked at me. "You certainly can, Miss Bishop." He snapped his fingers at his partner before opening his hand. The other detective produced a folded piece of paper and slapped it in Ryan's outstretch palm. "I'm here to collect a DNA sample from you."

My heart instantly began to race. While I was being questioned the other night, he'd suggested that I might want to offer one. Lucky for me, Valerie Stephenson showed up before the conversation escalated, and I walked out of the precinct without giving them my DNA.

"Got a warrant?" Abel asked, glancing at the piece of paper in Ryan's hand.

"I sure do," he replied with a smug grin, extending the document to me. "If you'd prefer a little discretion, we can take this out back."

What a nice guy, trying to spare me the embarrassment. "That's not necessary, Detective."

Abel snatched the warrant out of his hand before I could. He read it twice before folding the paper back up and handing it to me. "It's legit."

My mouth froze up when I tried to speak, but Abel was ready with a suggestion. "You got a lawyer, boss?"

I nodded. "Sure do."

"Then you need to make a call before you do anything," he advised me, giving the detective his own smug grin.

I regained my senses and took his suggestion. "Be right back, Detective." I held up my index finger.

Ryan was on my heels as I headed for my cell phone at the front desk.

"What's the matter? Afraid I might flee?" I said without looking back at him. Thankfully I had Valerie's number stored in my phone.

After reading her some pertinent information off the warrant, I hung up the phone and walked back to the two detectives and Abel. "My lawyer told me to comply with the warrant but nothing more. So don't think this is your opportunity to interrogate me again."

What Valerie Stephenson actually said was a little more colorful than that. Something about scumbags and bloodsuckers.

Ryan did that rude finger-snapping thing again, and the other detective pulled out a plastic bag with DNA written in bold blue letters across the front. Ryan pulled on a pair of silicone gloves and peeled back a wrapper containing something that looked like a giant Q-tip.

"What are you planning to do with that?" I asked.

"Open your mouth, Miss Bishop."

I glanced at Abel, who nodded for me to do it.

Opening my mouth wide, I grimaced as Ryan inserted the long swab past my lips and rubbed it around the inside of my cheek, a little rougher than necessary if you asked me. When he was finished, he placed the sample in the plastic bag that already had my name written on it.

Confident bastard.

"Are we done?" I asked, running my tongue along the area he'd just poked, waiting for him and his partner to finish up so they would get the hell out of my shop before a client walked in.

He handed the sample to his lackey and then leaned in a little too close for my comfort to deliver a departing message. "I bet you thought you got away with it," he sneered. "But I've got you now, Katie."

It's Miss Bishop, asshole!

2 0

By the time we closed the shop, Jackson had called to let me know he'd reached New Orleans. The games were about to begin as he prepared to see his father for the first time in years. I just hoped his father was a reasonable man so Jackson wouldn't have to resort to stealing mob money.

My cell phone rang while Sea Bass and I were heading out to the parking lot after locking up. It was Fiona MacPherson. Before answering the call, I motioned for him to take off as he waited for me to get in my car.

"Hey, Fiona," I said, anticipating bad news. Fiona would be at the pub on a Friday night, so she was either calling to invite me for a drink—which was unlikely—or something had happened to Lillian or Fin and she was in charge of the phone tree to notify the society members.

"I think some of Jackson's shifter friends just walked into the bar," she said.

I slowed down and tried to reconcile what I'd just heard. "Right now? In MacPherson's?"

"Yes, ma'am. Three of them, and they look like trouble."

Maybe they were just part of some biker club passing through. "How do you know they're Sapanths?"

"Because one of them has a tattoo on his forearm that says SAPANTHS in big black letters." She snorted into the phone. "Mind telling Jackson to get them out of my bar? I don't think they'll leave quietly if I ask, and Johnnie will just get his ass kicked if he tries to go up against the three of them. They look kinda mean."

With his imposing size and Irish fighter blood, Johnnie—MacPherson's cook and occasional bouncer—could be pretty ferocious when he needed to be. Especially when a nasty drunk got out of hand in the pub. But even a formidable guy like him was no match for a pack of shifters.

"Jackson's in New Orleans right now."

"New Orleans? What's he doing there?"

"Long story," I replied, sliding into my car. Their visit to MacPherson's could actually be an opportunity as long as Kaleb wasn't with them. I doubted I'd be able to recognize the ones I'd seen at Forsyth Park since it had been night and I'd stayed in the shadows. I was banking on them not being able to recognize me either. And if they got drunk enough, they might lead me straight back to where they were hiding out without even knowing they were being followed. "Does one of them have a shaved head with a tattoo on it?" I asked.

"No. These guys have plenty of hair," she said. "I asked them if they were new in town and one of them said they got here two days ago."

That cleared up any question about whether they'd recognize me. The bikers at the pub had to be the late arrivals Jackson had talked about, which solidified my plan.

"Keep feeding them drinks and don't let them leave. I'll be there in ten minutes."

She barked out a laugh. "Right. I'll barricade the door."

A few minutes later, I pulled into the parking lot behind

MacPherson's. Based on the number of cars out back, the place looked crowded, as usual for a Friday night, which could pose a problem if I was recognized and things got ugly in there. I'd seen four bikes parked outside when I drove past the front of the pub. The extra bike could have belonged to a regular who happened to ride a motorcycle, but it could also mean another Sapanth had shown up in the ten minutes it took me to get here. I prayed it wasn't Kaleb's bike.

I pushed open the green door with the word BEWARE written on the front. As soon as I walked inside, I was hit with a cloud of smoke filling the air. I suppressed a cough and glanced over at the bar where Fiona was pouring a drink. She pointed to the stool she'd been saving for me.

"Christ, Fiona," I said when I made my way over. "You'd think there was a fire in here. I'll have to wash my clothes when I get home."

MacPherson's was a classic Irish pub in a town built off the backs of slaves and Irish immigrants. You got all kinds in a place like this, including the occasional tourist or student, but it was a working-class bar with a regular clientele that fit right in with the charming dive interior.

"Yeah, no shit," she said, sliding a glass of scotch in front of me before glancing at the alcove on the right side of the room. "Your buddies over there are chain-smokers."

There were four guys walking around the pool table, each looking exactly like you'd expect a dangerous biker to look. They were all wearing faded jeans and T-shirts, and three of the four had on combat shit-kickers that looked like they could bust a liver with a swift blow. The fourth guy was wearing metal-tipped cowboy boots. But the real telltale sign that you were looking at a bunch of outlaw bikers was the leather vests they were wearing. The word SAPANTHS wasn't plastered in bold letters, but the demonic panther skull that took up a good portion of the backside made it clear that these guys weren't your garden-variety bike enthusiasts slumming it in the neighborhood dive.

I discreetly glanced over to get a good look at each one, but none of them looked familiar. One of them stretched his arm along a pool cue as he bent down to take a shot at the eight ball. His eyes lifted up over the table and landed directly on me.

"Are you kidding me," I said under my breath. My plan was to stay under the radar, but the look on his face was classic male horniness. "Is he coming over here?"

Fiona glanced over my shoulder and grinned. "Yep. Want me to run a little interference?"

"Bless you."

Fiona MacPherson was a walking conversation piece, beautiful but a bit intimidating until you got to talking to her. Her grandfather on her father's side owned the place, and if there was any doubt about whether she could hold her own in a pub like this, all you had to do was test her one time to get your answer.

She leaned on the bar, her breasts telegraphing through the fabric of her scant tank top, giving everyone a good look at the tattoo on the top of her shaved head. That alone was enough to make any guy think twice about playing her for an easy lay.

The biker stepped up to the bar and squeezed between me and the guy sitting to my left. The leather from his vest squeaked and released a familiar smell that reminded me of Jackson. But that's where the familiarity ended.

"Can I get you something, honey?" Fiona purred, leaning in a little closer to accentuate her cleavage. "Maybe a drink?"

Good one, Fiona.

His eyes trailed down to the deep groove between her girls, and then he glanced back up at the horned god inked on top of her head. "Yeah, give me a Jack Daniel's," he ordered, suddenly losing interest.

He turned sideways in my direction and leaned his arm on

the bar. "You looking at me, baby?" he asked, flicking his head toward the pool table where he'd caught my eye.

I shrugged. "I was looking at the pool table. You just happened to be in my line of sight."

"Oh yeah? You play?" he asked, all polite and friendly like he didn't want to bend me over the table and do me.

Fiona set his drink in front of him and gave me a wink. I hoped that meant she'd added a little something extra to it, like a spell or some of that Irish moonshine she kept behind the bar.

I'd plastered a bogus smile across my face and turned to continue with the fake banter when a hurricane of hair and boobs brushed up against me on my other side. Carmen Santos, Blackthorn Grove's resident seductress, shimmied up to the bar and drummed her hands on its surface.

"Give me a drink, baby," she said before leaning over it to plant a kiss on Fiona's mouth. She was your typical man-eater who had no problem snuggling up to other women's boyfriends, Jackson being one of her recent targets. In his defense, he'd been under the influence of some sneaky magic at the time and had no control over his indiscretions.

"What's going on, Katie?" she asked, glancing at the biker as she turned around and leaned against the edge of the bar on her elbows. Her grin suggested a mischievous mood.

"Carmen," I said, sipping my drink. "What kind of devious business have you been up to tonight?"

She looked like she'd just swallowed the canary. "Who? Me?" she said, feigning innocence. Then she let out a laugh. "I just took one for the team, Katie."

Before I had a chance to delve deeper into what she meant by that, Mr. Biker lost interest in me and walked around to my other side, squeezing into the space between me and Carmen with his back to my face. I couldn't hear what he was saying, but whatever it was didn't appeal to her.

"Yeah, you wish," she huffed, pushing off the bar and walking around to the other side where Fiona was serving drinks. She ran her hand over Fiona's perfect ass, letting the guy know she was of a different persuasion for the evening.

Did I mention that she was a woman-eater too?

Rejected by the Latin bombshell, he turned back to me and continued as if nothing happened. "You want to play a little pool?"

Are you kidding me?

I swallowed my pride for the sake of the mission, which was quickly turning into something a little more dangerous than I'd originally planned. "Why not?" I shrugged.

Fiona gave me a cautionary look, but I ignored it and headed over to the alcove with my new friend. He shoved his buddy away from the table and grabbed the pool cue from his hand. Then he racked the balls into a tight triangle and chalked the end of a second cue before handing it to me.

"Why don't you break," I suggested. "I might not be able to hit those balls hard enough."

He grinned and leaned into the table to aim his cue at the white ball, unsteady from the booze and whatever else Fiona had given him. Then he slammed it into the triangle and sent the other balls ricocheting across the green felt. He landed a few shots in the pockets and then walked over to me.

"Your turn," he said, slipping behind me as I leaned over the table. He bent down over me and put his hand on mine to guide my cue while his other hand snaked around my waist. I could smell the Jack Daniel's creeping over my shoulder and feel his crotch press against my ass like a dog mounting a bitch.

I wanted to hike that pool cue backward right into his junk.

We finished in record time, with him running the table to win the game. "Let's get out of here," he said as soon as he sank the eight ball.

The voice of reason inside my head was screaming at me to decline his charming offer, but my dragon side was telling me not to waste the opportunity to find out where they were hiding. Sober, I doubted he'd be stupid enough to take me back to his lair, but he was pretty sloshed. I hadn't suffered through all that groping just to go home empty-handed, and I had no intention of going inside if he was inebriated enough to take me there. I just needed him to show me where it was, and then I'd knock him out and take off while he slept it off.

"Give me a second to say good night to my friends." I walked back over to the bar and finished off the drink I'd left sitting there.

Fiona gave me a questioning look. "I hope you're not planning to leave with that piece of shit."

I nodded once. "We need to find out which rock they're hiding under. And that asshole seems just drunk enough to show me. What did you put in his drink, anyway?"

She smirked. "Something that'll put you in the designated driver seat tonight." She leaned back against the wall behind the bar and folded her arms. "Don't be a hero tonight. You're messing with something dangerous."

"Yeah? Well, so is he." Even half comatose, my dragon could still take that drunk bastard waiting for me over by the pool table. "Don't worry. I'm not planning to do anything stupid. I'm just going to see where he takes me, and then I'm dumping him. He'll be so hungover tomorrow morning he probably won't even remember what I look like." I could tell she wasn't on board with my decision to play detective, but that wasn't my problem.

When I turned around, he was waiting for me by the entrance. A fluttering of nerves suddenly threatened to make me throw up that drink, but I pushed through it and gave him an insipid smile as he held the door open for me.

He headed for his bike as soon as we were outside.

"I should probably drive," I said, knowing how difficult it was to separate a hardcore biker from his Harley, let alone convince him to leave it in a public place on a strange street. "This probably won't take too long," I said with a suggestive grin. "And your friends are still inside."

He'd won the lottery, a woman who wanted to get down to business and have him back in time to catch his buddies on their way out.

Without giving him a chance to argue, I turned the corner and headed for the back lot. I was relieved when I heard him walking behind me.

We climbed inside my Honda and I started up the engine. "Where to?"

"Your place," he said. It wasn't a question.

"That's going to be a problem," I said. "My boyfriend is home."

His grin widened. Not only did he think he was getting laid, he thought he was getting a slut as a bonus.

"Just drive," he said. "I'll tell you where to turn."

I followed his directions out of the parking lot and onto the main road. As we drove in the opposite direction of town, the hair on my neck began to stand on end. Other than an occasional instruction to turn, not a word transpired between us for a good fifteen minutes until he eventually told me to stop in the middle of the deserted road we were on.

"What are we doing here?" I asked, searching the surrounding area for signs of anything other than the eerie trees lining the empty road. His gaze was hard and lucid when I looked at him. Gone was that hazy expression in his eyes, and his pupils were elongated.

I suspected he was about to shift.

Without warning, he clocked my right cheek, smashing my head into the side window, sending an explosion of pain through my head as my eyes slammed shut. The next thing I knew, he was dragging me out of the car by my shirt.

"What—" I tried to speak, but I couldn't get past the first word.

"You thought you could get me drunk and fuck with me!" He gave a barking laugh. Then he lifted me to my feet and yanked my head back by my hair, painfully twisting it until I thought my scalp was going to rip away from my skull. "I know who the fuck you are. You're Jackson's little whore!" He dropped me back down on the ground and stepped back to unzip his jeans. "But I'm still gonna get what I came here for."

A memory suddenly flashed through my mind. It was my twenty-first birthday, and I was lying on my back in an alley behind a club on the Lower East Side of Manhattan. Some guy was standing over me with a knife in his hand and his pants down around his knees. He'd drugged me back at the bar. A second later I was on top of him, gripping his neck as blood sprayed all over my face. My talons had punctured his flesh.

I tried to shake the memory. When I opened my eyes, the biker who hadn't even told me his name was gasping for breath beneath me. His skin had sprouted fur on parts of his body, and his eyes had completely shifted along with his teeth.

With the swift movement of a leopard, he managed to slash the skin of my torso with his massive claws. I rolled sideways in pain, which was all the time he needed to turn the tables and meet me head-on in the glare of the car's headlights. Then he shifted completely into an enormous cat and lunged. I fell back against the ground and felt his hot breath hit me in the face as he roared and came within an inch of my neck, lashing at it with his sharp fangs. The light was starting to dim, but it was me losing consciousness from his claws restricting my neck. I nearly passed out, and my eyes began to close for what I thought would be the last time.

From the corner of my eye, something caught my attention. Down near my right thigh, a glimmer of metal protruded out of the dirt. A rusted license plate. With all my strength, I gripped it between my talons and yanked it out of the ground, driving it into his back between his shoulder blades. He reared up and screamed, giving me the precious few seconds I needed to roll over on top of him.

"You're gonna die now," I gritted out between my clenched teeth, plunging the tips of my talons into his heart like skewers. It took about thirty seconds for him to stop convulsing underneath me, his fur and fangs receding as the life left his eyes. I wasn't sure if it was the license plate or the talons that killed him. I didn't care.

I sat back on his motionless legs, trying to slow my breath before I had a heart attack. Something smashed into the back of my head a few seconds later, knocking me out cold.

2 1

In the distance I could hear a commotion. The sound of things colliding. Ungodly sounds that made my skin crawl. I could hear it clearly, but my eyes wouldn't open. Sleep paralysis, I thought. Then I remembered where I was and why.

Lying halfway in the road with the lights from the car beaming in my face, I rolled sideways and finally managed to open my eyes, coming face-to-face with a dead man whose cloudy, lifeless stare was fixed in a look of surprise.

I gasped and pushed myself away from the corpse, spotting the blood covering my arms and torso. The license plate protruding from his back lessened my fear when I realized the blood was his.

I shoved myself off the ground and tried to get my bearings. I turned toward the scene illuminated by the headlights and tried to see through the hazy film covering my eyes. The pain radiating through my head made it difficult to focus. About a dozen yards in the distance, where the snarls had culminated into a single high-pitched scream, I saw what I thought was a mountain lion on its back. On top of it was something much larger, caging it against the ground and ripping at its throat with its massive claws. A black beast.

Too weak to climb to my feet and run, I let my head fall back down to the ground. A moment later my eyes shut and the sickening sounds faded away.

I THOUGHT I was dreaming when I heard a familiar voice call my name, but then someone ran a damp cloth over my face and snapped me back to life.

Emmaline was sitting on the edge of the bed when I opened my eyes. "Welcome back," she said, looking down at me with her ghostly gaze. "We were starting to worry about you."

I rustled under the sheets, pushing myself up on my elbows. Bad idea. I fell back down on the mattress, my eyes wandering around the palatial room. "Where are we?" I asked, but I had a pretty good idea whose bed I was lying in.

"We're at Lillian's house."

My gaze continued to travel around the room and spotted an audience looking back at me. Fin was sitting in a chair in the corner, and Davina was walking through the door with a tray in her hands. At the foot of the bed stood Sea Bass.

"It was you," I said.

He gave me a modest grin and flushed a little before averting his eyes.

"Don't be so damn shy about it, boy," Davina said, setting the tray on the table next to the bed. "If it wasn't for my grandson, God knows what would have happened to you."

The memories of the previous night—I hoped it was the previous night—were beginning to flood my head. On my second try, I managed to sit up and lean back on the mountain of pillows stacked behind me. The scent of lavender hit my nose as I sank into them. A second later I bolted straight up. "Jet."

"Don't worry about Jet," Sea Bass said. "I stopped by this morning to feed him. He's doing just fine."

"Please tell me I haven't been here for days." I groaned. Then I realized Jackson wasn't in the room. He probably hadn't made it back yet, so it had to be early Saturday. Either that or he was gunning for Kaleb like a crazy man in retaliation for his men nearly killing me.

Emmaline verified the timeline. "Sea Bass found you last night."

I glanced at him, recalling the creature I'd seen just before the lights went out in my head for the second time. "How did you know where I was?" Before he could answer, I furrowed my aching brow and tried to reconcile the fragments of what I could remember. "What the hell happened to me last night?"

"You nearly got yourself killed," Fin said from across the room. "If Sea Bass hadn't followed you, there's no telling what those shifters would have done to you."

"You were following me last night?" I glared at Sea Bass as he swallowed hard and looked like a puppy who'd piddled on the floor. "Don't get me wrong, I'm thankful you did, but you were *following* me? Please tell me you haven't done that before."

"God no!" he snapped, looking horrified. "I swear. It's just that I could sense something wasn't right." When I kept staring at him, he explained. "When you got that call from Fiona last night, it was like an alarm went off in my head. I've been having these weird extra senses ever since… you know."

I snorted. "Next time just say something."

"Yeah right." He snorted back. "Like you would have listened."

"Would you two stop going at it like an old married couple," Davina spat out. "You should be grateful, Katie. You might have taken out that first shifter you left MacPherson's with, but one of his buddies showed up and didn't appreciate finding his packmate dead. He smashed you in the head with his pistol. Sea Bass took care of him before he could finish you off."

I felt the back of my skull and cringed from the pain of barely touching it. "I guess that's why I feel like I've been run over." Then I looked at Sea Bass again. "I thought you could only shift during the full moon?"

Davina answered for him since I assumed he was still in the amateur stages of his education. "Shifting usually lingers for a couple of days after a full moon. Lucky for you." She handed me one of the cups from the tray she'd brought in. "Drink this. It'll help with the pain."

"What is it?"

She dismissed my question with a wave of her hand. "It's not going to kill you. Just drink it."

I complied, sipping the hot liquid as the ounce of strength I'd managed to muster started to evaporate. Flipping my right leg over the side of the bed, I set the cup down and tried to get up. I had to go to the bathroom. That's about as far as I got though. The room started to spin, and I fell back down against the mattress, a wave of nausea threatening to bring the liquid back up.

"I don't think you should try to get up yet," Sea Bass warned. "That shifter poured something down your throat after he knocked you out. By the time I got to you, he'd already emptied that vial into your mouth."

My tongue automatically swept around the inside of my cheeks. Maybe it wasn't just the knot on the back of my head making me feel like I'd been run over.

"It was poison," Emmaline informed me in her demure voice. "Not like rat poison or strychnine though. Mandrake. A pretty powerful dose mixed with something else I haven't been able to identify."

"Enough mandrake will kill an ox," Davina said.

My heart rate picked up as my imagination started to run wild. Had they been preparing me to die? Feeding me a tonic to ease the pain of death? My mouth went dry, and I looked Emmaline in the eye. "Are you telling me I'm dying?"

She gazed at me for a moment with a blank stare. Then her eyes grew wide as a small gasp left her lips. "No!" she blurted. "I don't think he was trying to kill you. I think he was just trying to knock you out and keep you that way for a while. It's not easy to sedate a dragon."

"Then deliver you to Kaleb," Fin added.

"Don't worry," Emmaline continued. "I already gave you something to flush most of it out of your system. I guess I should have mentioned that before I scared the bejesus out of you."

Sea Bass let out a nervous laugh and muttered something under his breath.

"What's so funny?" I asked.

He sobered up quickly. "Nothing. Ain't nothing funny about any of this." Then he looked at Emmaline and sighed. "I guess you better go ahead and tell her. You got to do it again, right?"

The room went quiet. Even Davina was momentarily at a loss for words.

"You're all starting to make me real nervous," I said, glancing around the room at the faces staring back at me. "And right now my head feels like it wants to explode, and I'm about to pee all over myself."

Gaining her cantankerous voice back, Davina chimed in. "Well then, Emmaline is about to fix you right up."

Emmaline's pale skin took on a rare flush of pink when I turned back to look at her. She pulled at the edges of her long sleeves, inching them farther down until her hands were practically hidden by the black fabric. It was a nervous habit I'd seen her display on several occasions.

She glanced at Fin. He nodded to her and she averted her

eyes to her hands, which were now resting in her lap. A moment later, she reached for her right forearm and began to push her sleeve back, raising her arm up to her slightly parted lips. I watched in horror as a set of fangs descended from behind her upper lip and she bit into her wrist.

"Don't be frightened, Katie," Lillian said, walking into the bedroom with Esrial following behind her. "Emmaline is keeping you alive."

Esrial was a priestess with Blackthorn Grove. While Lillian had provided a home for Emmaline after her parents died, it was Esrial who'd raised her to be the witch she was today. Her parents had tried to murder her when she was a child, because of her powers. Some backwoods preacher had brainwashed the former witches into thinking their own daughter was the devil. But Emmaline had unleashed her telekinetic powers and turned the tables on them when they tried to plunge a knife into her belly. She was nine years old. The grove knew how special she was. Based on what I was seeing with my own two eyes, I had a feeling I was about to find out just how special.

She pulled her wrist away from her mouth, revealing a set of small holes that oozed with her thick crimson blood. "You have to drink it," she said, moving her arm toward me. "It's the only thing that will get rid of the rest of the poison. I couldn't give it to you all at once last night. It would have been too much."

I instinctively shrank deeper into the pillows behind me. Then a memory flashed through my mind of Pearl May Mobley feeding Sugar a jar of vampire blood when she was nearly blinded a few weeks back. It restored her sight in a matter of minutes.

"You need to drink it," Sea Bass said firmly. "I think this is why I've been drawing them red circles. They're premonitions about the blood. Besides, you already had one dose right after I brought you here last night and it didn't kill you."

"You're a—" I began to ask, suddenly realizing the possible ramifications of what Sea Bass had just said. "Dear Lord," I prayed, shutting my eyes. "Please don't tell me I'm about to turn into a vampire."

"Well, that's just silly," he scoffed. "It doesn't work like that."

"I'm a half-breed like you, Katie," Emmaline said with a weak smile, looking a little embarrassed by it all. As extraordinary as she was, she was the most modest human being I'd ever met. If there was an ounce of evil bloodsucker inside her, it was wasted on a woman who didn't have a malicious bone in her body.

"I don't understand," I said, shaking my throbbing head. "I thought your parents were—"

"Crazy lunatics?" Esrial interjected, sparing me the awkwardness of coming up with a suitable label for the people who'd tried to murder their own child. "Emmaline was adopted. The Gilberts were respected members of the coven at the time, and her birth mother was one of us. My sister. She died the moment Emmaline was born." That explained her deep connection to Emmaline. "You're wondering why I didn't adopt her myself," she said, pulling the thought right out of my head. "At the time, I wasn't in a position to legally adopt a child. Marlene and Jimmy were the perfect nuclear family. None of us could have predicted what would happen when they left the coven to follow that heathen who called himself a man of God."

"The first eight years of my life were wonderful," Emmaline said, glancing at Esrial. "I had everything. Parents who loved me, Aunt Esrial, the grove." She lost her faint smile as the memories of that dark time must have resurfaced in her mind. "They were victims too."

"Emmaline's father was something very different," Esrial continued. "Dark. A vampire with a taste for witches. A half-breed birth is extremely rare and dangerous. It wasn't easy keeping him away after my sister died, but we convinced him it was in his best interest to forget he had a daughter."

"Now that everyone's skeletons have been dug out of the closet," Lillian interjected, hijacking the conversation, "I'd suggest we get back to business before Miss Bishop's condition takes a turn for the worse."

Esrial shot her an aggrieved look. Lillian had been the one to offer Emmaline all the tangible comforts money could buy, but Esrial was the one who taught her how to use her gifts, how to truly fly. The tension between the two women was palpable.

I decided to defuse the conversation. "How much do I have to drink until the poison is out of me?" I asked, feeling a little sick again.

The disgusted look on my face must have made Emmaline feel like some kind of freak. The shame clouding her eyes confirmed that I was being a real asshole. She was the last person I wanted to offend, and she was offering me her rare gifts when she could have just let me die. I just wished it didn't involve drinking blood, something I wasn't even sure I could do consciously without gagging.

"Just a little bit more should do the trick," she said.

Fin, who had been quiet for the most part, got up and walked over to the window. "Drink the blood, Miss Bishop, before Emmaline bleeds all over the bed. We need you alive."

I inhaled sharply to fortify myself before nodding my head at Emmaline. Awkward was the best way to describe it when I tentatively reached for her arm. "How do we do this?" I'd never sipped anyone's blood before, so the proper etiquette escaped me. "Do I hold your wrist?"

"If you'd like," she said, holding her arm out to me.

Hesitantly, I took her wrist and raised it to my mouth, running the tip of my tongue over the small pool of blood collecting on the surface of her skin instead of just diving in. I expected it to taste like iron. Copper pennies. Imagine my surprise when the flavor bloomed in my mouth like a fine red wine. My eyes shut as my lips wrapped around her tiny wrist and I began to suck the wound. As the thick liquid slid down my throat, the room disappeared. All I could hear was the blood coursing through Emmaline's veins, continuing into mine where it evoked every sense in my body.

A light inside my head flickered and then exploded into of sea of fire, creating the strangest sensation of being at the center of the flames. I turned to see where they were coming from and saw my dragon in the distance, its emerald green eyes glowing back at me as it lifted into the sky. My dragon was very much alive.

I fell back against the bed and let the blood race through me while patterns of the most vivid colors filled my mind like a kaleidoscope, the sound of my beating heart a soundtrack to the fantastic fireworks going off inside me. Every nerve ending vibrated with pleasure, and I couldn't wipe the smile off my face.

"Hold her down!" I heard someone say.

My peace faded quickly when I felt my arms being restrained. My eyes flew open as Fin wrestled my left arm in a death grip and Sea Bass shoved his knee into my chest as leverage to get control of my other one.

"Get her out of here!" Fin yelled.

Emmaline's wrist started to pull away from my mouth, her skin tearing as my teeth dug deeper into her flesh. She glanced back at me while Esrial ushered her quickly toward the bedroom door. Her pale face had turned an icy blue, and her hazel eyes had dulled to gray.

"Let go of me!" I screamed, flying off the bed toward the door. A familiar pressure was building inside me, and my eyes were on fire. This time it wasn't my talons fighting to come out— it was the dragon. I had to get out.

In all the time I'd spent in Lillian's house, I'd never been past the first floor. I glanced up and down the hall, spotting a set of finials that marked the top of the stairs. As I ran down the winding staircase, my fingers began to split. "Not again," I whispered, vividly remembering the last time I shifted into the dragon while inside this house. The damaged wall in the ballroom was still under renovation.

Without a second to spare, I ran out the front door. My foot stepped over the edge of the landing at the top of the stairs as my wings expanded and lifted me into the sky.

Emmaline's blood had set my dragon free.

22

What good was it to have my clothes shift right along with me if everything in my pockets was left behind? Either my cell phone was somewhere in that bedroom, or it was lying on the concrete of the landing where I'd taken off.

Being reunited with my wings after a dry spell felt amazing. I spent the afternoon flying over my favorite spot—the Atlantic Ocean. Jackson used to bring me out here late at night to let the dragon loose. If I flew far enough out, I could blend in with the sea birds to anyone spotting me from land.

I touched down on a remote section of the beach along Tybee Island, figuring it was the safest place to land without an audience. The spot was familiar, since I'd landed there numerous times over the summer.

"Damn it!" I hissed, realizing I was barefoot. Of course I didn't have shoes on when they put me in that bed. I was just thankful I wasn't in my underwear.

I headed for the pavilion about a quarter of a mile north to beg someone to let me use their phone. Jackson wasn't due back until evening, so I decided to call Sugar. She'd picked me up the last time I flew the coop and landed on Tybee Island.

The walk up the beach was cathartic, giving me time to reconcile everything that had happened over the past twenty-four hours, including my killing one of Kaleb's men and drinking Emmaline's blood to stay alive. I wondered how long the power of that blood would last and if the dragon would need more to thrive. Right now I could feel it under my skin, restless and very much alive.

By the time I reached the pavilion, I was starving. Not counting Emmaline's blood, I hadn't eaten in almost a day. I was thankful that the first person I asked let me borrow her phone to call Sugar, although I wasn't too thrilled with the way she stared at me the whole time, like she was afraid I might take off with it. I guess I looked a little rough. She probably thought I was homeless and took pity on me.

After Sugar agreed to come get me, I asked her to pick up some fast-food burgers on the way, Emmaline's blood stirring my carnivorous cravings.

Never having gotten the opportunity to relieve myself back at Lillian's house, I headed for the pavilion restrooms. I glanced in the mirror on my way to the stall and spotted my glowing green eyes in the reflection. They hadn't shifted back yet.

"No wonder," I muttered, recalling the woman's expression. She was probably too scared to say no when I asked to use her phone.

I averted my eyes to the deck on my way back out of the pavilion. They stood out like beacons, and being a Saturday afternoon, the pavilion was packed.

Sugar showed up about thirty minutes later, meeting me at the parking lot by the edge of the beach. She was a speed demon and probably would have made it in twenty if I hadn't asked her to stop for food.

Her eyes went wide when I climbed into the Eldorado. "Well,

I guess the dragon is feeling a whole lot better," she said as I flashed her with green.

I hadn't given her the details over the phone, especially not the part about the vampire blood. "Yep. The dragon is definitely back," I said matter-of-factly, reaching for the bag of food on the seat. "Did you get any ketchup?"

"I'll give you some ketchup right up your ass if you don't start talking," she said, shifting the car into park.

All I could think about was shoving those french fries in my mouth between bites of hamburger. "Tell you what," I said around a mouthful of food. "Get me home and I'll tell you everything over dinner. My treat."

"Dinner?" She glanced at the bag in my lap, the one that still had a second burger inside. "Girl, don't tell me you're pregnant."

"Yeah right." I snorted. "Just get me home, Sugar."

We drove the twenty miles back to my house in silence. I was too busy savoring my food as I stared out the window. I still couldn't believe that I'd consumed vampire blood and my dragon seemed to thrive on it. More important, did I need more?

"You better start talking the second we walk inside that front door," Sugar said as we climbed out of the car. "You know I ain't got no patience."

It was a little past seven p.m. when we walked inside. I dumped some food into Jet's bowl and then dropped down on the couch.

"Were you ever going to tell me about Emmaline?" I asked.

"What about her?" she replied evasively, sitting down next to me.

"About her parents," I said. "Her real ones. About her being half vampire."

Sugar had told me about Marlene and Jimmy Gilbert, the psychos who'd tried to kill their young daughter because she was different. But she'd never mentioned the part about Emmaline being Esrial's niece and her interesting paternal bloodline.

"You know about all that?"

I smirked. "How do you think I got my dragon back?"

Her expression went from cagey to shocked as she started to put the pieces together. "I know you ain't about to tell me what I think you is."

Leaning sideways to look her in the eye, I told her point-blank what had happened. "I drank her blood. Twice." I thought her eyes were going to pop out of her head.

"Well, why'd you do that?"

"I was attacked last night by a shifter. One of Kaleb's. I woke up at Lillian's house this morning, and Emmaline fed me her blood to stop the poison."

"Poison?"

"It's a long story, Sugar," I said, hoping to avoid a complete retelling of the details. "The Sapanths kidnapped Cairo's wife, Angela. They want four million dollars, or they'll kill her."

"Four million?" she said. "Lord Jesus! Who the hell's got that much money lying around?"

"Fiona called me last night and said some of Kaleb's shifters showed up at MacPherson's. I got some stupid idea about following them back to where they were holding her."

She cocked her head at me. "And Jackson didn't have a problem with that?"

"Jackson's in New Orleans getting the rest of the money."

Before I could continue, I heard the key in the front door. Jackson walked inside and dropped his duffel bag on the floor. It was the same one he'd used to transport his money from Atlanta a week earlier.

I got up and met him halfway. He took my face in his hands and examined my glowing green eyes. "Fin called me before I got on the road this morning. Said a shifter attacked you." He looked back and forth at my pupils. "What the hell did they use on you?"

"Emmaline said it was mandrake."

He kept staring at my eyes, eventually asking about the bright glow. "The dragon?"

I nodded. "You're probably going to freak out about what I'm going to tell you, but don't. Everything's okay. Better than okay, actually." I thought about the best way to tell him I'd consumed vampire blood without him thinking his girlfriend was about to start sleeping during the day and snuggling up a little too close to his carotid artery at night. There was no easy way to say it. "I'm alive because Emmaline fed me her blood."

He looked at me blankly. "You want to tell me why?"

"Because she's a half-breed. Her father is a vampire. Her blood saved me. I'd be dead right now if she hadn't given it to me."

It took a moment for it to sink in, but eventually he nodded his head and dropped his hand away from my face. "Okay. Does this mean you…"

"That was my first question too," I said. "But I've been assured that I won't be turning into a vampire."

He tried to hide the look of relief on his face, but it was obvious.

"Baby, I would've been a bloodsucker a long time ago if that's how it worked," Sugar said. "Mama gave me my first dose of that medicine when I was just a kid."

Medicine. So that's what May had been talking about.

"I guess your mama was right, Sugar. The medicine was on its way."

A light bulb seemed to go off in her head. "Mama's always right."

"Fin said it was one of the Sapanths," Jackson said, bringing the conversation back to the attack.

"It was one of the late arrivals," I said. "But I got him before he got me. Unfortunately, one of his buddies showed up a little later to get in on the fun. He knocked me out and forced that mandrake down my throat. Thank God Sea Bass showed up and took him out."

He looked confused, which was completely understandable. "What do you mean, Sea Bass took him out?"

"You missed a lot while you were gone. And yes, Sea Bass came to my rescue. I'll tell you all about it later."

"You did something real stupid, didn't you?"

"Sure did," I replied with a satisfied smirk on my face. "But there are two less predators on the street, and I've got my dragon back."

"You sure about that?" I could see the doubt in his eyes, questioning the reliability of my secret weapon. "Maybe it's temporary. I should take you to the beach tonight to find out for sure."

"I just came from the beach. The dragon came out as soon as I drank Emmaline's blood. The secret sauce," I joked. "Wings and all. I headed straight for the ocean."

"Yeah, that vamp blood is some powerful shit," Sugar said, still staring at the bag on the floor. "Don't tell me you've been driving around all week with all that money on the back of your bike. Baby, you got to be out of your mind."

I glanced at the bag and wondered if we now needed to keep both eyes open while we slept—one for the Sapanths and one for the unsavory owners of that money.

"Did your father give you the loan?"

"Yeah, wants interest too."

Sugar looked confused. "That ain't the same bag of money you walked in here with a few days ago?"

I walked over to the bag and unzipped it. "That's another million. Jackson just took a ride to New Orleans to borrow it from his father."

"Well, what the hell for?"

"To get Angela back. Jackson now has three, and Cairo is coming up with the rest of the four million."

"Well, ain't that nice of you, Jackson," she said.

"Give me your phone," I said to Jackson. "I lost mine."

I needed to confirm if the dragon was cured of its fatigue or if we'd be needing more of that blood.

AUNT MARIANNA KNOCKED on my door an hour later. She took one look at my eyes and shot me a wicked grin. "Somebody's feeling frisky."

"I don't know if I'd call it frisky. I do feel energized though."

"So, what's this all about?"

I'd called and asked her to stop by because I had something important to talk to her about, deliberately leaving out the part about the vampire blood. That was a detail I preferred to discuss face-to-face.

Jackson and Sugar were at the kitchen island eating pizza.

"You hungry?" I asked.

"I just ate. But thank you."

We joined them in the kitchen and I got straight to the point. "See this?" I pointed to my eyes, which seemed to be growing more vivid by the hour. "I think I found the solution to the dragon's lethargy. In fact, I'm a little tired right now from flying all morning."

"Mm-hmm." Sugar muttered, "More like hungover from all that vamp—"

I shot her a look warning her to keep quiet.

My aunt glanced at me curiously. "Something you'd like to tell me, dear?"

"It's complicated," I said. "In a nutshell, I was given a dose of vampire blood last night. I drank some more this morning. The dragon came out after the second dose."

Her expression went unchanged for a minute. Then she cocked her head and asked, "Where on earth did you get your hands on vampire blood?" She glanced at Jackson and Sugar and then back at me. "Should I be concerned about you? I understand it's quite addictive."

I realized what she was thinking. "No, no," I said, vigorously shaking my head. "I'm not *using* vampire blood." I'd heard of people ingesting it as a drug. And based on how euphoric it had made me feel, I understood why. "I got attacked last night by a couple of shifters. One of them poisoned me with mandrake, so I was given the blood to counteract it." I huffed a laugh. "Damn if it didn't feel good though."

"Who gave it to you?"

"A witch with Blackthorn Grove. I found out this morning that she's also half vampire. It was her blood I drank."

"I see," she said, nodding her head thoughtfully. "Then the blood came from a safe source. No back-alley vampire strapped for cash."

I'd never thought of that.

"It's common knowledge that vampire blood is a powerful restorative," she continued. "It can cure disease. I've even heard of it used in necromancy rituals to raise the dead."

"What about the dragon?" Jackson asked. "Do you think the blood has restored its strength permanently, or is it as unpredictable as ever?"

"Unfortunately, I don't know." Her brow furrowed deeply as something seemed to distract her. "But I recall a case in Austria several decades back. The woman was like us," she said, looking at me. "She was killed, but a few weeks later her dragon was spotted flying over the mountains. I remember the rumors about a dragon who answered to a cult of vampires. The rumors implied that it was the blood of those vampires that kept it alive."

"So you're saying I might need to feed it vampire blood on a regular basis?" I prayed she'd laugh and tell me I was being silly.

Shrugging, she gave me a sympathetic look. "I wish I could answer that. But at least for now you know what it needs."

"I guess I need to have a talk with Emmaline. Maybe she

won't mind serving as my emergency blood bank," I said, laughing humorlessly.

Emmaline was about as selfish as Mother Teresa. I knew she'd roll up her sleeve anytime I needed blood for my dragon, but at what cost to her? It never dawned on me until that moment that the donation might be taxing on her physically or mentally. I definitely needed to have a talk with her about the possibility of needing more in the future.

"I bet Emmaline would give you a whole bag of it to keep in your freezer if you asked her," Sugar said. "Mama probably still has a little bit tucked away too."

"I'll keep that in mind."

She glanced at me and pursed her lips. "What you really need right now is a good pair of shades. Gonna scare the hell out of people if you walk into the shop looking like that." She got up and walked over to her purse on the hall table. Reaching inside, she pulled out her coveted Versace sunglasses, the tortoiseshell pair with the gold trim. "Now, I don't think I need to tell you what'll happen if you lose these."

23

Jackson hung up his phone and shoved it back in his pocket. "Cairo's on his way. They want us to bring the money tonight."

"Where?" I asked.

"He'll fill me in when he gets here."

"So much for bed." After Sugar and my aunt left, all I wanted to do was get a little sleep. But with Angela's life on the line, I doubted there'd be much rest for any of us.

Jackson grabbed the bottle of tequila from the cabinet and set it on the counter.

"Think that's wise?" I said. Getting buzzed on tequila just before delivering four million dollars to a bunch of murderous shifters seemed like a bad idea. Especially when your girlfriend was responsible for the death of two of their packmates.

"It's not for me."

"Okay. Maybe Cairo shouldn't be getting drunk before walking into the lion's den. For all you know, Kaleb could be planning to take the money after he kills both of you."

He grabbed a shot glass and set it next to the bottle. "His wife's life is on the line. Let the man have a drink."

I shrugged it off. "Just trying to be the voice of reason here, but I'm not his mother. He can drink the whole damn bottle if he wants to." A second later, I whipped around and pointed my finger at him. "But you better come home to me in one piece. You got that?" If Cairo was ready to walk in there with guns blazing, I hoped he had the decency to spare his best friend from getting caught in the cross fire. Of course, Jackson would gladly volunteer to storm the place right next to Cairo.

How do you save a man from himself?

Cairo made it to my house in record time, knocking on my door twenty minutes after hanging up the phone with Jackson. He must have been doing double the speed limit. A recipe for death.

"Jesus, Cairo," I said when Jackson motioned him in. "Ever hear the expression arrive alive?" I looked behind him, expecting to see a small army of Dimensionals walk through the door behind him, but it was just Cairo. "You didn't bring your clan?"

He gave me a halfhearted smile and dropped a duffel bag on top of the counter. It was the original two million dollars that Jackson had hidden on his property, plus the extra million Cairo was able to liquidate. "Kaleb's instructions were pretty damn clear. No clan."

Suddenly he was staring at me like he'd just noticed that my eyes were the color of glowing emeralds.

"It's the dragon," I said, brushing it off as something insignificant compared to the pressing matter of Angela's ransom exchange. When he couldn't pull his eyes away from mine, I reached for the sunglasses and put them on. "Is this better?"

He nodded absently from the distraction of my unworldly eyes. Then he turned and looked at Jackson for a minute before reaching over to give him a man hug. "I owe you, brother. I know it wasn't easy for you to ask your old man for that money."

"You don't owe me shit," Jackson replied. "This doesn't begin to cover my debt to you and Angela."

I felt like an interloper watching them solidify their loyalty to each other, and it was clear there was more to that loyalty than Cairo just giving Jackson a place to hide out when he first ran from the Sapanths. I decided in that moment to never ask. If Jackson ever did talk to me about the real glue that bonded them, I'd take that as a sign that we were soul mates. Right now simple love was enough.

Cairo glanced sideways, catching the bottle in his periphery. "Is that for me?"

I grabbed two more shot glasses and smirked at Jackson. "The hell with it. Let's all have a shot." I set the glasses down on the counter and looked at the bowl containing a single apple and a black-speckled banana. "I don't have any limes, but I do have salt."

"Salt and lime is for pussies," Cairo said, quickly apologizing. "Sorry, Katie. My potty mouth just doesn't know when to shut up."

"Said the sailor to the sailor," I replied.

Jackson poured a shot and handed it to Cairo. "You get a pass on being an asshole for a while."

Cairo wasted no time downing the tequila and holding out his glass for another. Jackson obliged and then poured two more, handing one to me.

"Where do they want us to deliver the money?" I asked.

Jackson shot me a questioning look. "What do you mean *us*?"

I swallowed the shot and ran my tongue along the edge of my lip to catch a stray drop. "I'm going." It wasn't a request.

Jackson laughed incredulously, kind of pissing me off. "No, you're not."

I took a step back and put my hand on my hip. "Why not?"

He let out an exasperated sigh, getting ready for the argument. "Because the last thing I need while I'm trying to help Cairo save his woman is to worry about mine. You haven't seen Kaleb when he turns his mean side loose."

With dramatic flair, I whipped my sunglasses off and glared at him. "And he hasn't seen me when my dragon is completely turned loose. In fact, I have the advantage. He has no idea, Jackson."

Apparently Kara had seen the dragon in its full glory since she'd been stalking us all summer, but to my knowledge Kaleb was still a virgin to the true beast.

Cairo cleared his throat. "You need to let her come, Jackson."

Let me?

The look on Jackson's face made me wonder if I was about to come between friends.

"One of Kaleb's instructions was to bring her along. I don't know why, and I don't like it. To be honest, I wasn't gonna comply with that, even if it meant—" He choked a little on the thought of what Kaleb might do if he didn't follow the instructions to the T.

"What the hell are you telling me, Cairo?"

"Kaleb wants Katie at the exchange. I don't know what he's up to, and I wasn't planning to find out. But Jesus, look at her. She's scaring the shit out of me right now with those eyes. She could probably take every one of us out."

Before Jackson could respond, I made the decision for him. "I'm coming with you. End of discussion."

"Katie—"

"I'm coming, Jackson!" I barked. "There's nothing he can do to me."

That statement wasn't completely true. While the beast was formidable and capable of reducing the Sapanths to a pile of ash, it did have its weaknesses. I'd learned that from a couple of dead witches who'd rendered my dragon helpless not too long ago through the use of some pretty powerful bone magic. I doubted that Kaleb and his pack of shifters were skilled in that kind of warfare though. So if it came down to a good old-fashioned fight, they'd lose.

Jackson backed off and bowed his head, a wordless truce from a wise man.

"The oil terminals at the river," Cairo said. "We need to leave now."

Jackson's jacket swung open as he bent down to pick up the duffel bag with the million he'd brought back from New Orleans. Protruding from his side pocket was a pretty big gun. I knew he had one, but this was the first time I'd actually seen it.

He followed my eyes and stood back up, glancing at the .45 tucked in his inside pocket. "You know how to use one?"

I looked at the gun again and then gazed at him for a moment with my dragon eyes. "I've never needed one."

"I guess not," he replied with a grin edging up one side of his face.

"Jackson can pick off a grasshopper from a hundred yards," Cairo said with a straight face, hefting the bigger bag off the counter as he flashed the weapon concealed under his own jacket. "You should see what I have in my boot. Now let's roll. I got a wife to get back." His expression turned deadly as a side of him I'd never seen before made an appearance. Something told me that Cairo could be your best ally or your worst enemy, depending on which side of his fence you were on. I was glad to be on the right side.

I grabbed my sunglasses off the counter as we headed for the door. No need to give Kaleb a warning until we needed some leverage.

———

THE OIL TERMINALS were located northwest of the Talmadge Bridge on the Savannah River. The area was largely industrial, which meant that for the most part we'd be isolated. Kaleb's instructions were to meet in the center of four specific oil tanks where we'd hand over the money and they'd hand over Angela.

The lights stringing up and down the river and the ones illuminating the bridge created a deceptively benign backdrop for what was about to happen.

"Kaleb!" Cairo yelled as we stood in the center of the giant tanks like sitting ducks. "Where the hell are you?"

I heard something move. When I looked at Jackson, whose hearing was superior to mine, he was staring up at the top of the tanks. On the catwalk between the two tallest ones stood Kaleb. Four large cats perched on the tops of the tanks, looking down at us like sentinels guarding a castle.

We were surrounded.

"What kind of game are you playing, Kaleb?" Cairo said, his lilting voice laced with aggression. It was the same deceptive calm you'd expect from a tame tiger just before it dug its teeth into you.

Kaleb laughed wildly and clapped his hands, seeming to recognize exactly what his former comrade wanted to do to him. "Cairo, you burly fuck!" he shot back, losing his jovial smile. "You look like shit. I don't know what she sees in you. A woman like Angela deserves, well… a man like me."

Her name coming out of his mouth nearly destroyed the mission. Fortunately, Cairo had the good sense to reel in his fury. Clearly his love for Angela was stronger than his need to rip the beating heart from Kaleb's chest, something he'd probably save for another day.

"Drop the bags," Kaleb ordered, noticing one in each of their hands. "Then you can have Superman over there slide them about forty feet in my direction."

"Tell you what," Cairo said. "Why don't you come down here and get them? Bring my wife while you're at it."

Kaleb did exactly as Cairo asked. He climbed over the railing of the catwalk and jumped, shifting before landing on all fours as he dropped a good thirty feet to the ground. A few seconds later, his black fur vanished. He stood up and dusted the dirt off his hands before looking up and turning his attention to me.

With a cock of his head, he studied the sunglasses I was wearing. "Vampire?"

I figured it was meant to be a bad joke. If he only knew what kind of blood was coursing through my veins...

Cairo took a step toward him. "Where's my wife?" he hissed, losing patience.

One of the cats on top of the tank nearest to us positioned itself to jump. Kaleb's hand went up to stop him. "No," he said with a smug smile. "Cairo knows he'll never see his wife again if he does anything stupid. Isn't that right, Cairo?"

Cairo stepped back like an obedient dog. It was obviously killing him, but he didn't dare speak the words that were on his tongue. I wondered how Kaleb would escape when this was all over, because I believed with every ounce of my being that Cairo would eventually make him pay for the mere inconvenience he'd caused to Angela. God help him if one hair on her head was missing.

"Why am I here?" I asked, wondering why my presence was part of the instructions.

He smirked and then took a deep breath. "I wanted to see the woman who killed my brother."

Brother? Jackson never mentioned anything about Kaleb having a brother. I wanted to say something along the lines of *I guess the apple doesn't fall too far from the tree*, or *the scumbag deserved what he got*, but under the present circumstances, that would have been stupid and detrimental to saving Angela.

"Self-defense," was all I said. "He tried to rape me. Can't blame a girl for defending herself."

Out of the corner of my eye, I saw Jackson visibly flinch. I hadn't told him about that part.

"Well," Kaleb continued. "Can't blame a guy for wanting an eye for an eye. You do realize I can't let that go unpunished? I haven't determined yet what the proper restitution should be, but I'll think of something. You know, cats are solitary creatures. The whole pack thing comes from our human genes. But we do like to share. Isn't that right, Jackson?" he said without taking his eyes off mine.

There was that damn reference to sharing again.

After a long, lecherous gaze, he turned to look at Jackson. "When I take you back to Atlanta and marry you off to Kara, I'll find a nice place for Katie."

I heard a female laugh come from somewhere above us. Kara was standing on the catwalk, her arms leaning against the rail. "Sorry to disappoint you, Daddy. I think Katie is going to be busy for the next fifty or sixty years."

Kaleb stiffened, and I wondered if Kara's attempt to have me thrown in prison for murder was something she'd done without consulting dear old dad. Looks like he'd had other plans for me.

I pulled the sunglasses off to give Kaleb a good look at what he was up against. He'd seen the dragon's eyes before, but not like this. God help me, I wanted to unleash the beast on him right then and there, but the terrified look on Cairo's face made me back down. The last thing I wanted to do was jump the gun and get Angela killed.

Relieved that I wasn't about to sprout my wings, Cairo stepped up to Kaleb. "I'm gonna ask you one more time. Where's my wife?"

"What are you going to do?" Kaleb shot back with a smug glare. He leaned closer, whispering in a cold taunting voice, "You were always impatient, Cairo. But you'll just have to wait until I count my money."

"That wasn't the deal," Cairo gritted out, forced to hold back his rage for the sake of Angela.

"What's the matter, Kaleb?" Jackson said. "Don't trust us?"

Kaleb snorted. "I don't trust my own mother."

He snapped his fingers and two of the cats descended from

the top of one of the tanks. They shifted back to human form before picking up the bags and disappearing through the narrow space leading to the river. Kara jumped from the catwalk next. I thought she was about to break her neck, but the drama queen shifted into a leopard seconds before hitting the ground. She followed the others, growling viciously as she looked back at me.

With a cocky smile, Kaleb gave his last instruction. "You'll hear from me by morning if the money is all there. A dollar short and I'll have to make adjustments to our deal." Then he turned his eyes on Cairo. "Don't worry, old friend. Tomorrow she'll be all yours."

24

I offered to put Cairo up on the couch when we got back to
my house because he refused to leave the city until we got
the call from Kaleb with instructions on where to find
Angela. It was either that or a bench in one of the town squares.

"Anyone hungry?" I asked.

Jackson's phone rang before either of them could take me up
on the offer.

"That was Fin," he said, ending the call. "Said he thinks he
knows where they're hiding."

Cairo's face lit up like a flare. Not only did it mean we might
not have to wait for that call to get Angela back, it also meant
we'd been handed our opportunity to kill the sleeping cats. It was
the only way to stop Kaleb from a lifetime of extortion. He had
no intention of leaving Savannah without Jackson, and Jackson
wasn't going anywhere. The war would never end as long as Kaleb
was alive.

"Fin's meeting us at Lillian's house in twenty minutes. Said he
has a map to show us."

"A map?" I said, suddenly feeling uneasy. "I don't like the
sound of that."

Jackson nodded. "That's what he said."

I expected him to argue with me as I followed him out the door. Instead, he handed me a helmet.

"Aren't you going to give me the whole spiel about why I shouldn't come?"

"Spiel?" he said, cocking his brow. "Would it work?"

I put the helmet on and climbed on the bike. "Just drive."

We drove off and headed for Lillian's place. I kept my eye on Cairo's bike the whole way, trying to fathom what it must have been like for him, not knowing what they were doing to his wife. He was funny and gracious, a man who knew how to throw a party and enjoy life. But I had a feeling I'd see the vicious side of Cairo tonight. The side you didn't want to meet.

Fin was smoking a cigar at the top of the steps when we pulled up to the house. "Miss Bishop, Jackson," he said, looking curiously at my sunglasses. He glanced at Cairo as he climbed off his bike. "Just the three of you?"

"That depends," Cairo replied. "Let's see what you got."

He extinguished his cigar in the planter next to the stairs. "Don't tell Lillian I did that." Then he reached for something in the dirt that caught his eye.

"That's my phone," I said, grabbing it from his hand. The dirt had cushioned its fall, sparing me the cost of fixing a cracked screen. "Huh. I lost it when I ran out of here this morning."

"Lucky you," he said.

I dusted the dirt from the screen and followed him inside.

Lillian was waiting in the library. "You're looking a hell of a lot better than you did this morning," she said to me on her way over to the bar to pour us some drinks. It was an automatic reflex when guests entered her house. Southern hospitality. "But I guess you're still not completely back to your old self, judging by those sunglasses you're wearing."

I flashed her a smile. "The dragon is still feeling a little frisky.

Then I lifted the glasses above my eyebrows to give her a peek. "Feels good though."

"I guess so," she replied. "I'll be sure to thank Emmaline for you, yes?"

"Of course. I'd thank her myself, but I'm sure you'll be seeing her first." Although I'd be talking to her sooner rather than later to discuss a little arrangement for the dragon.

"What's everybody drinking?" she asked, pouring me a glass of scotch automatically.

Jackson waved her off, but Cairo took full advantage of the stocked bar. "Bourbon, if you have any."

A brief grin crossed her face as she poured him a glass. "Asking a Savannah hostess if she has any bourbon is about the same as asking a car if it has gasoline."

Cairo took the glass from her hand. His initial reaction to the taste reminded me of my own reaction the first time I was treated to the exorbitantly priced liquor in that bar.

The clock was ticking, so Jackson got down to business before the opportunity slipped away. "The map?"

"Yes," Fin said, getting up to retrieve a piece of paper from the desk on the other side of the room. When he returned, he slid it across the table to Jackson. "Savannah has a series of tunnels underneath her streets. Some folks refer to them as the catacombs, but the only dead things down there are the rats."

I'd heard the rumors about tunnels running under the city, but like so much of Savannah's infrastructure, the actual history behind them was a mystery.

"Are you talking about the tunnels where the old hospital used to be?" I asked. "On Drayton Street?"

He nodded toward the map. "The tunnels I'm talking about are a little farther north. There's an entrance at the south end of the cemetery. You'd walk right past it unless you knew what you were looking for." He leaned back in his chair to put his feet up on the table, but Lillian gave him a warning look in anticipation of his predictable bad habit. "You won't find these tunnels on any tour guide's itinerary."

Jackson and Cairo studied the map.

"What makes you think the Sapanths are in there?" Jackson asked.

"There's a police station over on Habersham Street, on the east side of the cemetery. One of my contacts over there said they had an interesting report the other night from a homeless woman. She kept saying the city was being invaded by cats."

"And?" I said when he left it at that and decided to light up another cigar.

"Mountain lions and leopards, Miss Bishop. The woman insisted that she'd seen several of them ducking behind one of the tombs. When she decided to investigate—fully inebriated of course—she saw the top of the tomb lifted off the base."

"And they believed her?"

"Well, this particular citizen does have a history of reporting all kinds of interesting activity in the cemetery at night. I believe it was a pirate walking along the path the last time she made a report. But since it was right outside their back door—and out of curiosity —a couple of officers decided to take a walk and see what had gotten her all riled up. As expected, the top of that tomb was right where it belonged. Some of those stones can weigh a quarter ton.

"And you call that a lead?" Jackson said, looking irritated for being called out to Lillian's house for nothing. "You're wasting our time."

Fin took a draw of his cigar and blew the smoke back out before responding. "Normally I would agree with you. But under the circumstances, I don't think we can afford to disregard the ramblings of this particular delusional woman."

"Why's that?" Cairo asked.

Fin smirked. "Because she also said one of them was wearing a leather vest and was walking on its hind legs. A black panther, to be specific. And by the way, I've confirmed that there is a tunnel structure under the cemetery."

That sealed it for me. I leaned over Jackson's shoulder and looked at the map of Colonial Park Cemetery, the same cemetery where we'd discovered the portal to the crossroads a few weeks earlier. All kinds of supernatural things were drawn to that place, so it was serendipitous for Kaleb and his crew to discover a nice little hiding place within its gates.

"This may be a naïve question, Mr. Hunter," Lillian said as she listened to the conversation. "Is it even possible for them to lift that massive slab of stone so easily to get in and out of that tunnel?"

"Shifters? Are you kidding me?"

Cairo stood up and finished his bourbon. "Well? Let's do this," he said, heading for the library door.

Jackson got up to follow him.

"Now hold on," Fin said. "Don't you think it would be wise to come up with a plan instead of going all commando into that tunnel?"

Cairo pulled out his phone and dialed. "We got them," he said to someone on the other end. "Meet me at Lafayette Square." He hung up and shoved the phone back in his pocket. "How's that for a plan?"

Jackson turned to Fin. "Clan's on the way."

"You call that a plan?"

CAIRO'S MEN were already there when we got to Lafayette Square. Six men and two women, one being my babysitter from the other night.

"Good to see you again, Liz," I said.

She saluted and grinned up one side of her face. "Should be a fun night." She started to walk toward Cairo but turned around. "Hey, how's your friend doing?"

"Much better," I said.

He's a mountain howler.

Better to leave that part out for now. We had enough on our hands tonight.

Cairo did the talking, instructing his team to stay above-ground at different checkpoints around the cemetery. There was no way to know if the Sapanths were actually down there or if they were still out feeding. Jackson had mentioned before that they liked to snooze as a group, leaving a single sentinel to stand watch while the others slept. He'd also said they needed to sleep after a night of shifting. I'd say our rendezvous at the oil termi-nals qualified as a night of shifting. Besides, Kaleb had a lot of money to count, which was probably the perfect nightcap before he slept it off.

While Cairo briefed the clan, Jackson pulled me aside. "You don't have to go down there. You're just as useful up here keeping watch."

"Bullshit. I'm going down there with you. They can't touch me now. Not like this." I tapped my glasses to remind him that the dragon was back and stronger than ever. Granted, letting the dragon loose down in that tight tunnel was probably a bad idea, but I still had its strength, and Jackson and Cairo were gonna need me if they got ambushed.

"I can't stop you, can I?"

"Nope, but I'll lag behind. That way you two will get it first," I said, snickering. I sobered up and took his face in my hands. "If I lost you tonight, I'd never forgive myself for not being down there with you."

He nodded once. Then he reached inside his boot and pulled out a dagger. "You think you can use this if you have to?"

I took it from his hand tentatively. "What about you?" Then I remembered that .45 in his inside pocket. "Oh yeah. I forgot about the gun."

"The gun will stun a Sapanth, but it won't kill one." He glanced at the knife in my hand and chills shot through me. There were two ways I never wanted to die: by drowning or by the blade of a knife. The thought of a dagger plunging into my organs was terrifying. Funny coming from a dragon with razor-sharp talons.

"You remember the mark I told you about?" he asked.

"The one between their shoulder blades?"

The first time he showed up on my patio months ago, after our rocky introduction at the shop, he'd asked me to lift my shirt to prove I wasn't one of Kaleb's women sent down from Atlanta to track him. Sapanths bore a mark between their shoulder blades. I'd compromised that night and let him look down the back of my shirt to prove that I wasn't one of them.

"The tip of the blade has to pierce straight through the center of that mark. Before they shift completely," he added. "The mark will disappear once they've shifted. Then it's too late. Once you get the blade into the flesh, you need to keep pushing it deeper until it reaches the heart. That's the only way to kill a Sapanth. Your fire won't even kill them. It'll stop them in their tracks for a few minutes, but the knife is the nail in the coffin. Kind of like a vampire getting staked."

"Then that gun of yours is useless," I said, handing the knife back.

He lifted the bottom of his jeans on his other leg, revealing a second knife in his left boot. "Don't worry about me." Running his thumb over my lower lip, he gauged the hesitation on my face. "Can you do this?"

I shrugged. "Wouldn't be the first time I skewered someone."

"Okay. Time to hunt."

The plan was for Cairo, Jackson, and me to go down into the tunnel. Since space would be at a premium down there and an army of Cairo's people would spoil the surprise, the others would remain aboveground until they got the signal to attack. Angela's safety took priority over the need to kill Kaleb.

With Cairo's people in place, the three of us headed for the tomb Fin had marked on the map.

Cairo watched as Jackson wrapped his hands around the edges of the stone top. "Need any help with that, man?"

Jackson scoffed. "Fuck no."

With his supernatural strength, he lifted the top a few inches off the base and tilted it on its side against the tomb, exposing a deep hole and a set of concrete stairs that descended into the darkness below.

Still pumped with Emmaline's blood, I pulled my glasses off. I grabbed Jackson's arm as he moved toward the steps, shaking my head and pointing to my eyes, which had dulled slightly but still gave off enough of a glow to lead the way without announcing us. "I can see. Let me go first." We couldn't afford the risk of using a glaring flashlight that would beam through the dark tunnel like a beacon, and one of the benefits of being a dragon was my night vision. So much for lagging behind.

He hesitated but relented when he couldn't argue with the logic. "You signal if you see so much as a rat down there."

I nodded and headed down the steps. At the bottom, the tunnel terminated into the darkness about twenty feet ahead. The walls were straight and squared off, probably built before the cemetery was seeded with its first graves over two hundred years earlier. God knows what the tunnel was originally used for.

After Cairo and Jackson made it down the steps, I started to move forward. Poor Jackson. He was so tall that his head scraped the ceiling where it dipped every few yards.

We'd made it about a hundred feet into the tunnel when Jackson grabbed my arm to stop me, cocking his head.

"Do you hear something?" I whispered.

He put his finger to his lips to quiet me and then continued to listen. Then he turned to Cairo and held up two fingers, letting him know there were two Sapanths up ahead.

We rounded a corner and a flare of light flashed from the far end of the tunnel. I reached for the dagger I'd stuffed in my boot when I noticed Jackson pull his out. Cairo was wielding a gun in one hand and his dagger in the other. As we closed in on the light, my heart began to race at a dangerous speed. Not from fear but from some predatory instinct that must have been a combination of the dragon's bravado and Emmaline's blood.

I saw the back of a man's head as we crept closer, shielded by the glare of the light that was working to our advantage. Before I could think straight, Cairo was on top of him, wrestling the shifter's own knife from his hand. The other one let out a yell as Jackson grabbed him, struggling to slam him face-first into the wall.

The damage was done, and the howl of a giant cat reverberated through the tunnel, bouncing off the walls as it traveled through the long corridor and filled the space around us. I could hear the pounding of paws as the accumulation of growls and hisses grew louder.

"They're coming!" I said.

It seemed like only a second passed before I felt something graze the back of my skull. My attacker grabbed me from behind before I could react. He grasped my chin while his other hand gripped the side of my head. A gasp slipped from my throat.

With my head locked in a death grip, I caught Jackson from the corner of my eye, still struggling with his own shifter. He flipped the guy against the wall and tore his shirt to expose the mark on his back. Then he plunged the dagger between the shifter's shoulder blades, driving it deep. After he delivered the fatal push, the shifter slid to the ground and went still.

Suddenly my eyes lit up like flares, filling the room with a blinding light that sent my attacker stumbling backward. While he struggled to regain his footing, I turned and punted the tip of my boot between his legs.

"Mother *f...uck*!" he roared, hitting the edge of the wall. A second later he was on top of me, sneering with a twisted grin that told me I was going to regret doing that. "I'm gonna fuck you up, bitch!" His face began to morph as colored spots flashed over his skin. He was starting to shift.

"Hell no," I squeaked out as his grip tightened around my throat. He was doing his damnedest to strangle me before his fingers turned into paws. The urge to release the dragon was almost unstoppable, but people would die. Jackson and I could survive the implosion it would cause when I crashed through the stone walls, but Angela and Cairo would be crushed.

With my dragon's strength—and that vampire rocket fuel running through my veins—I sent the heel of my palm into his throat, crushing his windpipe and sending him slamming against the wall. It cracked under the impact and sent him to his knees. I scrambled to my feet and reached for the knife in my boot, holding it high above my head as I squeezed the handle tight and ripped the shirt off his back. The blade cut through his skin like butter but stopped when it hit bone. He let out a horrific sound and reared back. If I didn't finish this now, he'd kill me. With my full weight, I drove the blade past the bone until the hilt was flush with his back. He slumped to the ground and his spots began to recede. He looked pretty dead to me.

I stood up and whipped around. Jackson was plunging his dagger into his second victim, and Cairo was against the wall, about to take a knife to his gut from a massive shifter suspending him two feet off the ground. Yanking my dagger from the dead shifter's back, I charged the one attacking Cairo. I blindly drove the blade into his leather vest, praying I'd hit the spot. He dropped Cairo to the ground, but the damage was done.

"That fucking hurt!" he spat out, reaching over his shoulder to yank my one and only knife from his back. "Good thing you brought me a spare," he snickered, glancing at his weapon buried in Cairo's stomach. As big as Jackson, he stalked toward me with a sadistic grin. "I'm gonna fillet you now."

I didn't consider myself a religious person, but that didn't stop me from saying a silent prayer.

Backpedaling, I tripped over my victim's body and landed on my ass. The Sapanth straddled me with his boots on either side of my hips and bent down on one knee, copping a feel between my legs as he leered at me and lifted the dagger into the air. The blade came down hard and dropped to the floor next to my head. A sharp pain hit me in the chest as he fell on top of me and then rolled off to the side. He lay faceup, the tip of a knife protruding from his chest.

Jackson extended his hand and pulled me to my feet. He kicked the guy hard to turn him over. The hilt of his dagger was buried a good six inches inside the shifter's back, guaranteeing a direct hit to the heart either from the blade or his bare fist.

"Sorry about that," he said, noticing the tear in my shirt and the trace of blood where the tip of the blade had pricked my skin.

I stood there staring at him in disbelief, a pathetic laugh bursting from my mouth. Then I remembered the knife in Cairo's stomach.

"Cairo!" I rushed over to him as he was pulling it out. "How deep is it?"

He shrugged. "Meh. Just a scratch." He opened his shirt and revealed the oversized belt buckle with HARLEY embossed on the front. The tip had hit the metal and slipped into his leather belt, barely protruding through to his abdomen. "I have a feeling that would have ended differently if you hadn't jumped the son of a bitch like a pit bull. I owe you."

"My pleasure."

Jackson helped him up and we cautiously rounded the corner to see what was coming for us next. The light coming from the room at the end of the tunnel had gone out. We crept down the corridor without making a sound. To the right was a large room. Jackson pulled out a pocket flashlight and switched it on.

"Don't!" I hissed.

"They're gone, Katie." He surveyed the spot where the Sapanths had been making camp. "There's another exit point over there." He motioned to a second tunnel on the other side of the room.

I looked at Cairo, who was on his knees next to one of the makeshift beds on the floor. In his hand was a clump of long black hair. It looked like someone had cut it off just above the turquoise-studded barrette that held it together. It was a beautiful barrette that I'd seen before—on Angela.

25

We tried to entice Cairo to come back to my place for the night, but he declined the offer. Still gripping the clump of black hair, he climbed on his bike and started the engine.

"You gonna be all right?" Jackson asked. It wasn't really a question. We both knew Cairo wouldn't be all right until Angela was safe at home and Kaleb was lifeless at the end of a knife.

Cairo slowly lifted his eyes up to Jackson's. "I'm fine, man." His stare was cold. He revved the engine of his bike and kicked the stand back. "I'm gonna get my wife back. Then I'm gonna kill them all."

"If I know Kaleb, we'll be hearing from him by morning," Jackson said. "He knows what will happen if he doesn't hold up his part of the deal. The last thing he wants is to end up on your shit list."

A twisted grin formed on Cairo's face, but his expression went blank a second later as he carefully folded and tucked Angela's severed hair into his front pocket. I could visibly see the effects of the adrenaline rushing through his veins, the tremor in his hands as he gripped the handles of his bike, the tensing of his jaw. I could smell it.

"Be careful, Cairo," I said.

He studied me for a moment and nodded once. Then he drove off, the sound of his bike fading as he floored it and disappeared into the night.

"Should we be worried about him doing something stupid?" I asked.

Jackson thought about it for a second and then released his pent-up breath. "He'll swallow his pride and wait like a good boy because he knows how Kaleb plays the game. Angela is all that matters right now. After we find her, Kaleb won't be able to run fast enough."

I WOKE to the sound of Jackson's phone ringing. He fumbled for it on the nightstand.

"Yeah?" he said, sitting up to answer it. The call lasted less than a minute, with Jackson staying perfectly quiet until he hung up.

"Who was that?" For someone to call him at five thirty in the morning, it had to be pretty important. By the look on his face, I figured it was either Cairo calling with bad news or Kaleb with instructions.

"Kaleb." He stood up and headed for his jeans, which were tossed over the arm of the chair. "He told me where to find Angela."

I climbed out of bed and headed for the dresser to grab some clothes, catching my reflection in the mirror. My eyes were back to normal, thank God. "Why did he call you instead of Cairo?"

"Because I'm the one he's playing this game with. Cairo's just a pawn."

"Well, he can't be too insignificant to them if they kidnapped his wife." The look on his face was starting to make me feel uncomfortable. "Why are you staring at me like that?" I asked, pulling a shirt over my head.

"It could have been you, Katie. If it weren't for the dragon, Kaleb would have taken you. But you made it a little too difficult, so he took the next sure thing that he knew would get him that money."

The night he broke into my house and attacked me, he made a comment. *I have plans for you, Katie. Don't make this difficult.* I guess his plan wasn't as easy as he'd anticipated. Separated from her shifter husband, Angela was a much easier mark.

Wait until he met the real dragon.

"Let's go," I said, putting the rest of my clothes on and heading for the door.

No argument from Jackson this morning. I think he was finally convinced that I was his equal in every way. That primal need to protect me was overshadowed by the knowledge that I could probably kick his ass in hand-to-hand combat. He was Superman, but the dragon was back and drinking rocket fuel now.

Jackson had called Cairo on our way out of the house to let him know the Sapanths had dropped Angela off in the middle of Bonaventure Cemetery, a few miles outside town. He said it was typical Kaleb style to leave her in a place that also held a message —you're a dead man if you don't cooperate.

I automatically headed for his bike, but he stopped me and motioned to my car. "We don't know what condition she's in. If I know Cairo, he was on his bike before he hung up the phone, and she might not be able to ride."

We drove as fast as we could without getting pulled over, hoping to beat Cairo to the cemetery. There was no telling what they'd done to her, and getting there first would give us a chance to buffer the reunion. A man might be the last thing she needed to see right now, even if it was Cairo.

It was still dark when we pulled up to the entrance around six a.m. The cemetery didn't open for another two hours, so we had to scale the brick wall to get around the closed gate. Jackson laced his hands together and offered to boost me up, unintentionally catapulting me over the top.

"Jesus!" I squealed, my fall barely cushioned by a long hedge growing along the other side.

He climbed over the wall like Spider-Man and helped untangle me from the sharp branches of the boxwood. "You okay?" he asked, lifting me effortlessly and lowering me to the ground.

"Yeah, if you like sharp twigs up your ass."

He grinned and brushed some green stuff from my hair. "Sorry."

"Which way?" I asked, glancing at the sea of graves.

"That's a good question."

With over a hundred and fifty acres, Bonaventure was huge. It wasn't like we could just survey as far as the eye could see and spot a woman waiting patiently for her ride. Angela could have been cowering behind any one of the thousands of headstones and tombs. Fortunately, the sun was getting ready to rise, which would make it easier to find her.

"Maybe we should wait for Cairo," I suggested.

Jackson gave me a look that for some reason made me uncomfortable. He slowly scanned the cemetery before bringing his eyes back around to mine. "He'll see the car and come looking for us."

We headed down the main drive, the gravel road crunching under our feet and the majestic live oaks lining the path on both sides. It was a spectacular sight with the sun just beginning to peek over the horizon.

"Angela!" Jackson called out in his deep baritone voice. There would be no mistaking it if she heard him, but the mind can play funny tricks on you when you've been terrorized by a pack of bloodthirsty animals.

There was no answer.

We headed toward the center of the cemetery. My guess was that Kaleb wanted us to find her quickly, to see his handiwork as payback for the night before. I pictured her with that beautiful hair chopped off. Goddamn animals.

I heard a motorcycle in the distance. Cairo had arrived.

Jackson stopped walking and glanced to his left. Something caught his eye, and he turned down one of the side roads lined with large Victorian tombs. The graves along the road were like tiny yards with even tinier gardens and benches. Some of them housed entire families, with miniature fences or stone walls bordering the neighboring plots.

They didn't bury people like that anymore.

"Where are you going?" I yelled as he wandered off.

He ignored me and kept heading toward whatever had caught his eye. I started to follow him, but he raised his hand to stop me. A hollow feeling filled my gut when he turned into one of the plots about halfway down the road. One with an aboveground casket-like tomb protected by a three-foot-tall iron fence.

"You're scaring me, Jackson. What is it?"

"Katie," Cairo said as he approached me from behind.

I turned to look at him, glancing back at Jackson and feeling an overwhelming sense of dread. I wanted to shield Cairo from something. Turn him around and walk him back toward the front gates.

"Katie?" he said again, furrowing his brow and glancing at Jackson in the distance.

Before I could do anything to stop him, he headed down the road. "Where is she, Jackson?" he asked, the timbre in his voice growing shaky.

Jackson turned to see Cairo heading straight for him. He

walked away from the tomb and pressed his hands against Cairo's shoulders to stop him from getting any closer. "Don't, Cairo."

Cairo backed away, his face suddenly grimacing as if a sharp pain had shot straight through him. "No," he said, shaking his head. "You're full of shit!" He pushed Jackson aside and headed for the tomb. Jackson didn't try to stop him a second time. Instead, he focused his eyes on mine as a soul-crushing howl came from Cairo's throat.

"No," I whispered. I walked toward them, feeling like I was about to be sick, forcing myself to look at the pale motionless arm dangling off the edge of the tomb. At the other end, I could see Angela's head, her black hair chopped off raggedly.

I tried to go to him, but Jackson caught my arm and warned me to stay back. Cairo lifted Angela's body over the small iron fence and dropped down on the step at the base of the monument marking the grave. He cradled his dead wife and wept.

The sun was rising. Soon people would arrive to open the cemetery. Cairo eventually wrapped Angela's naked body in his jacket and stood up, carrying her as we headed back to the front gates. Jackson shattered the lock and pushed them open.

Fuck the wall.

Jackson drove the Harley while Cairo sat in the back seat of my car, still cradling Angela's lifeless form, the hair he'd found in the Sapanths' lair gripped tightly in his hand. Among other things I couldn't bear to think about, they'd desecrated her body by attaching a note to her bare chest, sticking the pin through her skin. She'd been killed in retaliation for the four dead shifters we'd left behind in that tunnel, warning that three more would fall before the debt was paid—me, Jackson, and Cairo. An execution for an execution.

Not a single word came out of either of our mouths on our way back to Cairo's house. He seemed to be in another place, contemplating all the things a person suddenly had to think about when an unexpected death occurred. But I knew that look

I saw in my rearview mirror. Cairo was quietly planning his revenge.

The war was coming.

JACKSON STAYED at Cairo's to help with the arrangements. The passing of a Dimensional required a good bit of preparation before the funeral, so time was of the essence. Some kind of ritual, he'd explained. Custom required that it be done quickly, so they were already planning it for the next day. And although it was usually a private ceremony, Jackson and I were invited as witnesses. Whatever that meant. I didn't ask. I didn't care. Whatever Cairo needed he could have.

As soon as I walked inside my house, I spotted the light blinking on my phone. In the rush to get out the door, I'd forgotten it on the kitchen counter. Sugar had left me a message, wondering where I was since I wasn't at the shop. It wasn't even ten a.m. On Sundays the shop didn't open for another hour, but I was usually in by now and she was probably wondering why I was coming in late. Not ready to talk about what had happened, I decided to hold off on calling her back.

The other message was from Fin, and he sounded pissed.

I dialed his number. He answered on the first ring and immediately started barking at me.

"Mind telling me what the hell you three did inside that tunnel last night?"

I didn't know what he was talking about, and I wasn't in the mood for his attitude. "We flushed them out!" I barked back.

Not today, Fin.

Neither of us had talked to him since leaving Lillian's house with the map to the tunnels. I would have called him first thing this morning, but I'd been a little busy.

"And I guess blowing up half the cemetery was your way of doing that?"

"What are you talking about? We didn't blow up anything. Killed a few shifters, but we did that the old-fashioned way—with knives. The rest of them disappeared. Maybe they decided to come back and destroy their lair." I paused before delivering the tragic news. "They killed Angela. Dumped her body in the middle of Bonaventure on top of a tomb. Must have a thing for cemeteries," I added with a bitter snap.

He went silent for a few seconds, and I could hear his breath exhale. "Well, fuck."

"Yeah, real humanitarians. Cairo vowed to kill every last one of them, and I wouldn't doubt his ability to do it."

"I hope you're right, Miss Bishop, because we've got one hell of a mess in this town. Those bastards desecrated two-hundred-year-old graves on the south side of the cemetery when that tunnel imploded, and I just got a call from one of my connections down at the coroner's office. Three more bodies were found early this morning. They were eviscerated."

The war had begun.

2 6

I was a distracted mess from the moment I walked into the shop, recusing myself from working on Nick Peterson's black-panther tattoo. Looking at it reminded me of Kaleb and pissed me off every time I put the needle to his arm. Fortunately, he was also one of Mouse's clients, and she was free to step in when I told him I was feeling a little sick.

Sick like I wanted to scrub that damn ink right off his skin. *Don't do it, Nick! Panthers are murderous heathens!*

Before I had a chance to say something stupid in front of a client, Sugar came through the door. She walked up to the desk and folded her arms, nodding as she waited for an explanation.

I glanced at her with weary eyes, daring her to open her mouth.

"Well, I was gonna give you a little piece of my mind for ignoring me all morning, but I don't think you'd survive it." Her eyes walked all over me. "Baby, you look like hell."

"I feel like it," I grumbled. "Let's get out of here and get something to eat."

We walked across the street to Lou's and ordered a couple of burgers. The second we dropped our trays on the table and slid into the booth, the third degree began.

"I'm gonna warn you up front, Sugar. I'm not in the mood for a lecture."

This was usually the part where she ignored my warning and gave me one anyway, but something held her back. "Did you and Jackson get into a fight or something?"

"Angela is dead." I didn't see any reason to sugarcoat it.

She stopped chewing and stared at me. "Dead?"

"They killed her. We found her this morning. That's why I didn't call you back right away."

Sugar was rarely tongue-tied, but she just sat there with her burger dangling from her hand. "I thought Jackson was gonna give them all that money," she eventually said. "Wasn't it enough?"

"Things got a little out of hand last night after we delivered the money. Did you hear about the tunnel collapsing over at the cemetery?"

The wheels in her head started to turn as she put the pieces together. "Yeah. Why?"

"We found their hiding place. The tunnels under the cemetery. Killed a few shifters while we were down there."

She took another bite of her burger and gaped at me. "Well?"

"I guess they decided to come back later to blow it all up. Get rid of any traces that they'd been down there." I shoved a few fries in my mouth before continuing. Despite the tragedy, I was starving. "They killed her in retaliation. Pinned a note to her skin to let the three of us know that we were next."

Sugar's eyes flew wide as her burger hit the plate. "You shittin' me?"

I was about to inform her that I'd never "shit" about something that tragic when Jackson slid into the booth next to me.

"I'm fucking hungry," he growled, reaching for a french fry on my plate and popping it into his mouth.

"Baby, let me get you something to eat," Sugar said, getting up from the booth. "You want a burger?"

He reached for another fry. "I'm good."

"No, you're not." I cut my burger down the middle and handed him the other half. He wasted no time devouring it. I doubted he'd eaten in a while.

"I'm on my way back to Cairo's," he said. "I came by to grab some fresh clothes."

I'd gotten pretty good at reading his face, and the look on it right now told me he was avoiding telling me something.

"You might as well tell me. It's written all over your face."

He tossed his napkin on the table and sank into the booth. "I got a call from Kaleb about an hour ago. He wants to end this."

"This? You mean his murderous rampage through this town?"

"He wants to settle it personally," he replied. "A little hand-to-hand combat."

"With?"

"With me and Cairo."

Sugar's brow twisted curiously as she pursed her lips. "What exactly does that mean?"

I glanced at her, still trying to process what he'd said. "Yeah, Jackson, what *does* that mean? The asshole just killed Cairo's wife, and now he wants to have a little high school brawl outside the gymnasium? Winner wins and loser dies?"

"It means he plans to kill Cairo and take me back to Atlanta as Kara's slave. I think he'd like to include you in that package."

"Yeah, well, I'll probably be in jail for Christopher's murder by next week." I snorted, figuring the results of that DNA sample would come back in record time if Detective Ryan had anything to say about it. "Maybe Kaleb can spring me. He's good at that kind of thing, right?" His face went cool. I'd hit a nerve, reminding him of the past he wanted to forget. "I shouldn't have said that."

He ran his hand over my thigh, giving me a weak but

forgiving smile. "We're meeting them back at the oil terminals tonight. Ten o'clock. No clan. No pack except for one of his men, to make it a fair fight."

"You have to take me with you, Jackson. There'll be nothing out there to stop the dragon this time. No hostages, no walls ready to implode on top of us. Just an open sky. I'll stun them, you stake them."

A wicked grin slid up the side of his face. "Did I forget to mention that he specifically requested that you be there? Like I said, I think he plans to take you back to Atlanta too."

KALEB HAD no idea what he'd done. He'd sealed his fate by assuming I was just a has-been dragon equipped with a dangerous set of claws. But he was about to find out how wrong he was.

Emmaline had been kind enough to invite me over after I closed the shop, to pick up a little vial of fortification. She assured me that the blood I'd consumed the day before was potent enough to supercharge a dinosaur, but considering what we were up against, a little extra insurance was wise. We were planning to send those devils back to hell, and we wouldn't get a second chance.

I held the vial up to the light in my kitchen, allowing the thick crimson liquid to coat the sides of the glass. It was a small amount of blood. Maybe a tablespoon. Miniscule compared to the amount I drank straight from her vein at Lillian's house.

"Think of it as pomegranate syrup," Jackson said as he watched me anticipate drinking it.

"It tastes good actually. Like really expensive wine."

He arched his brow. "Maybe I should try it."

"No way. You'd be worse than a bull in a china shop."

A knock on my door made me shove the vial in my pocket. Cairo was standing on the other side when I opened it, stoic and calm as if it were just another Sunday night and his wife hadn't been murdered that morning.

I motioned him in and gave him a hug, careful not to ruin the moment with some blubbering comment about how sorry I was for his loss. God forbid I'd ask him something stupid like how he was doing.

How the hell would you be doing?

He walked inside and looked at the bottle of tequila on the counter, next to the bottle of scotch.

"I thought I'd put out some options," I said. "Help yourself."

Cairo grabbed two glasses and poured a shot of each. He drank the tequila first. "This one's for you, baby," he muttered before chasing it with the scotch. He wiped his mouth with the back of his hand and looked at Jackson. "Let's go kill some shifters."

KNOWING how potent Emmaline's blood was and how fast it could turn me into a raging beast, it was wise to hold off on drinking that vial until absolutely necessary. But make no mistake, I had no intention of letting that bastard get the upper hand.

We arrived at the same oil tanks where we'd exchanged the money the night before. As late as it was, the place was deserted.

"Kaleb!" Jackson called out.

No reply.

I glanced at Cairo from the corner of my eye. He looked like a junkie who'd just dropped his last fix down a storm drain. Jackson followed my eyes and noticed it too. Then he gave Cairo a look, some kind of silent bro language that seemed to take him down a notch.

Despite not hearing a single footstep, we looked up at a small army on top of the tanks. We were surrounded by cats, which explained their silent advance. Six mountain lions, a couple of cheetahs, the biggest damn lynx I'd ever seen, but not a black panther in sight.

And one spotted leopard.

"You bitch," Jackson sneered as the leopard shifted back into daddy's girl.

Kara cocked her head and gazed down at him. "You always know how to charm a girl, Jackson." She let out an exaggerated sigh, glancing at me before looking back at him. "I'll have to find a way to keep you in line when we get back to Atlanta. Can't have you running off again or sniffing around every dog that crosses your path. Maybe one of those electric cock rings will do the trick. I'll get one of those remote controls for it."

To hell with the vampire blood. My dragon was itching to break free, to end Kara once and for all. But I'd be damned if I'd turn my secret weapon loose before the guest of honor arrived. Then I'd kill them both.

Jackson glanced at the brigade of cats. "I should have known better than to trust a bunch of lying shifters. Where's daddy?"

That seemed to piss her off. "Tread very carefully, darling," she said with a warning look. I guess she didn't like to be labeled a daddy's girl, but then she shouldn't act like one.

"This wasn't the deal," Cairo muttered, that pound of flesh he was looking forward to quickly slipping out of reach.

"Yeah, no shit," I muttered back.

I shot Jackson a look, wondering if we should get on with it and hunt Kaleb down later. What else could we do? He shook his head discreetly, but Kara noticed it.

"Humph." She glared at me. "Your little dragon is outnumbered, Jackson."

A second later, she raised her hand into the air and brought it down with a swift chop. The army of cats jumped off the tanks with Kara sailing toward us right behind them, her skin shifting back to fur.

"Katie!" Jackson yelled, tossing me a big knife.

A repeat of the previous night wasn't what I had in mind, but a well-thought-out plan needed to be fluid. I caught the blade but sliced my palm in the process, sending a stream of blood running down my arm. My eyes went up in a blaze as the dragon responded.

Something hit me from the side, slamming my head against the ground like an angry linebacker. A deafening snarl filled my ears along with a blast of heat from its breath just before it bit the side of my face. I managed to blink the blood away from my eyes when it stopped for a second to lick its chops. It was one of the mountain lions.

An ocean of green light reflected off the metal tanks as my eyes went up in a blaze. My wings punched through my sides, sending the cat flying backward. It hit one of the tanks and let out a chilling howl that pierced the night air.

I lifted into the sky and took off toward the river, turning sharply once my wings had a chance to stretch. I spotted him as soon as I flew back over the tanks. A black panther stood on the highest one, crouching behind one of the ladders that extended over the top.

Jackson and Cairo were on the ground, fighting back-to-back to fend off their attackers. But the cats' attention turned to me. They paced back and forth between the tanks, with nowhere to run as I circled the yard. I opened my jaws and dove between two of the tanks where a group of cats cowered against the metal sides. I led the way with a river of fire, taking out everything in my path, sending them up in flames.

Cairo stood there frozen. Jackson grabbed him by a handful of his shirt and practically lifted him off the ground to get him moving. Once they were out of the line of fire and running toward the dock near the river, I turned and dove toward the Sapanths on the other side of the yard, lighting them up like torches and igniting one of the tanks in the process.

Kaleb was still in full shift on top of the other tank. He jumped off when I circled back around and flew straight for him. I caught him in midair in a tangle of deadly claws as he fought to escape my grip. He dug them deep into my thick skin, drawing blood. All it did was make me squeeze him tighter. Eventually he gave up and shifted back into human form before going limp in my talons. Maybe he thought I'd have more mercy for the man than the beast. He was wrong.

I circled the yard again, enjoying the feel of the wind under my wings with the satisfaction of knowing that the murderous shifter between my talons was about to be destroyed. A moan slipped from his mouth when I dug my talons deeper, igniting my own murderous thoughts. But Kaleb wasn't mine to kill.

With a sharp turn on the wind, I circled back to the dock where Cairo was standing. His eyes flew wide as I hovered and dropped Kaleb at his feet. A vicious growl snaked up my throat, warning Kaleb not to move. Then I landed a dozen yards away to watch Cairo get his vengeance.

He pulled Angela's severed hair from his pocket and held it up to Kaleb's face. "Take a good look at it," he ordered.

Kaleb opened his mouth to speak. With a swift thrust, Cairo jammed his knife into it, forcing it deep until it protruded out the back of Kaleb's neck. He pulled the knife back out and Kaleb gagged as blood filled his airway. Then he dropped to his knees and Cairo circled around to rip the shirt from his back. Kaleb began to shift, but the blade came down quickly between his shoulder blades, slicing dead center through the mark.

I closed my eyes as the dragon receded. By the time I reopened them, Cairo was walking to the other side of the dock with Kaleb dangling from his arms.

He reached the edge and dropped the body. "Let the fucking fish eat him," he said, kicking Kaleb over the side and into the river.

"You okay?" Jackson asked me, a wide grin edging up his face. "That was pretty impressive."

"I feel great." Actually, I felt fantastic. "I guess I'll be putting that vial of blood in the freezer for a rainy day."

My euphoria suddenly dulled. "You did take care of the others, right?" I asked, referring to the shifters I'd left charred and stunned in the yard before setting my sights on Kaleb.

"All staked and dead," he replied. "But what did you do with Kara?"

A sudden wave of fear jarred me. "What do you mean?"

Without waiting for a reply, I took off toward the burning tank with Jackson right behind me. I ran into the yard and started searching through the dead shifters. The smoke was so thick I could barely see, and the flames were beginning to spread across the yard toward the other tanks.

"What are you doing?"

"Where the hell is she?" I demanded, still sifting through the bodies.

He looked shell-shocked as he started to put the pieces together, realizing we'd missed someone.

"You win," I heard a female voice say to my right.

Kara was sitting on the ground about ten feet away with her back leaned against one of the tanks. She was holding the side of her waist where blood was leaking from a large wound.

Jackson looked at the woman who'd threatened to lead him around by his cock, the psycho bitch who seemed to think she owned him. He gave her a cold look and then turned to me and nodded. Then he started to walk away to let me finish her off.

"You're not going to let her kill me are you, baby?" she purred, her eyes turning doe-like and misty. "I'm down, Jackson. My father's gone and so is my pack. I'm not a threat to anyone anymore. Have a little mercy."

He stopped but didn't turn around. "I have about as much

mercy for you as you had for Angela." Then he continued back toward the dock where Cairo was still staring into the river.

As I watched him leave, a guttural snarl resonated through the yard. I turned back to Kara, who had already shifted. She lunged. The moment she made contact with my skin, my own claws came out. The razor-sharp tips of my wings burst through my ribs, spearing her through the side. She screamed and flailed backward, but she was impaled. With a forceful snap, I flicked my wings open and sent her catapulting into the air. Before she hit the ground, I flew up and snatched her just like I'd done to her father. Tighter and tighter I squeezed, shutting my eyes and flying blind as I felt the life start to leave her body and she shifted back into a human. Then I looked down and drove the tip of my talon into her back, driving it through the mark until she went lifeless under me. I circled back toward the dock where Jackson and Cairo were watching, dropping her corpse into the river so she could sink to the bottom next to her father.

Right, Cairo. Let the fucking fish eat them.

In the distance I could see the chaos of flashing lights. Fire engines.

I touched down on the dock and retracted my wings, pulling the dragon back inside. I could actually do that now, as easily as folding my arms to my sides. This was starting to feel good.

"Let's go," I said. "Those sirens are heading for us."

We hopped on the bikes and took off, passing the fire trucks on our way out.

Cairo raised his middle finger in the air and punched the gas. "Rot in hell, motherfuckers!"

27

I dug through my closet for the one dress I had that was appropriate for a funeral or memorial service. But the more I thought about who I was paying my respects to, the more I considered just grabbing my jeans off the chair.

With a heavy sigh, I opted for the navy sheath dress.

An obligatory knock came from the front door just before Sugar let herself in. She wasn't going with us to the service, having decided that she didn't really know Cairo that well and would feel more like an interloper than a guest paying her respects. *I ain't gonna be one of them funeral junkies*, she'd said, referring to people who crashed memorial services to siphon sympathy and eat free food. She was just stopping by for moral support.

"You need any help back there?" she yelled from the kitchen.

"I'm good. Thanks. Help yourself to those muffins on the counter."

I glanced at myself in the mirror, noting the brightness of my eyes and the glow of my skin. Ever since drinking Emmaline's blood, I'd been getting stronger and feeling more vibrant by the day. I'd been caught between the dragon and Katie Bishop all summer, struggling to maintain a comfortable balance between the woman and the dragon. Now I finally felt as if I'd found that sweet spot. I was the master, and the beast was happily purring on my back.

Sugar came down the hall and tapped her knuckles on the doorframe. "You decent, girl?"

I opened the door wider and invited her in. "Can you zip me, please?"

"You look real nice," she said. "Where's that man of yours?"

Jackson had gone home after breakfast to put on something appropriate for the service. I'd never seen him cleaned up in anything formal, and I was wishing I'd asked him what one was expected to wear to a Dimensional's funeral.

I was beginning to rethink the dress I had on.

"He's picking me up in a few minutes."

She zipped the dress and fiddled with my hair, twisting it into a neat spiral before laying it over my right shoulder. "Any luck finding that money yet?"

The four million was still missing. With the Sapanths dead— at least the ones in Savannah—it would stay hidden until either Jackson figured out where they'd stashed it or someone else stumbled across the find of a lifetime.

"Not yet, but it hasn't even been twenty-four hours. We need to get through today before thinking about that money."

We weren't going to the actual funeral. Jackson had explained that when a Dimensional passed, the body was covered with a white robe and burned on a pyre in the middle of the ocean. The service we were attending this afternoon was just the ritual. The handling of the remains was a private matter only attended by clan.

A motorcycle pulled into the driveway.

"That would be him," I said.

We walked into the kitchen as Jackson was coming through the front door. I know it's cliché, but my heart skipped a beat when I saw him. He was dressed in an elegant black suit with a charcoal-gray shirt. No tie. That, I figured, was where he drew the line at formality. His long black hair seemed to float over the fabric and blend in with it, making him look like an edgy runway model. The kind with all the right imperfections.

"Well, damn, Jackson," Sugar said. "You clean up real nice." She fanned herself dramatically with her hand. "I believe it's getting a little warm in here."

A brief grin appeared on his face as his hands slipped nervously into his pants pockets. "Thanks, Sugar."

I envisioned the sight of him gliding down the street on his Harley in that suit, and it occurred to me that he must have felt a little awkward, a fish out of water, wearing it. But then I remembered his background. He'd spent the first seventeen years of his life in clothes like that, choosing the right fork for his salad to avoid the wrath of his father. Jackson Hunter knew exactly how to wear a suit like that.

He turned his gaze on me, and for a brief second the solemn mood in the room disappeared as a wave of heat rippled through me.

"Ready?" he asked, breaking the spell. He glanced at my dress and heels. "I guess we should take the car."

Fin was attending the service with us. He liked Cairo and wanted to pay his respects to his departed wife.

"We're definitely taking a car," I replied. My phone rang as I finished my sentence. "And it just pulled up."

I answered the call and told Fin we'd be right out. Fin's Bentley was parked out front when we walked outside. Jackson took one look at the ostentatious car and groaned. Then he reluctantly climbed in, and we headed for Cairo's house.

THERE WERE motorcycles everywhere when we pulled up to Cairo's place, parked in front of the house and on the lawn in a neat row. There were cars too, but they were outnumbered by the bikes. I was beginning to wonder if we'd be the only people dressed in conservative mourning attire.

The Bentley stood out like a blue whale in a sea of minnows. Fin instructed his driver to drop us at the front door and take the rest of the afternoon off until he was called back. We had no idea how long the service would take, and Fin seemed to be thinking the same thing I was about that whale.

A woman with a strong resemblance to Angela met us at the front door. She greeted Jackson with a hug and then looked at me. "You must be Katie," she said. She turned to Fin for an introduction, glancing over his shoulder at the Bentley disappearing down the dirt driveway.

"Fin Cooper," he said, introducing himself.

She ignored his outstretched hand and invited us in. "I'm Evelyn," she finally said, leading us through the house toward the backyard. As soon as we walked outside, Jackson was greeted by Easter, his former dog. Angela had fallen in love with her and made it clear that Jackson wasn't getting her back. It seemed appropriate to honor that.

"Is Cairo in isolation?" Jackson asked.

She nodded and then headed back inside.

"Who is that?" I asked.

"Angela's sister. She lives in Charleston."

They looked like sisters, and I absently wondered if they'd badgered each other about the notorious rivalry between Charleston and Savannah.

I glanced at the people milling around the yard, relieved to see suits and conservative dresses mixed with blue jeans and T-shirts. It was an eclectic crowd.

"Well, I don't know about you two," Fin said, eyeing the bar set up on the patio, "but I'm a little thirsty. Can I get either of you a drink?"

It was late afternoon, and we had a meeting with Valerie Stephenson later that evening to discuss my possible indictment for the murder of Christopher Sullivan. The DNA results were due any day now, and I half expected a Chatham County patrol car to come flying up Cairo's driveway with its lights flashing.

"I think I'll pass," I said.

Jackson declined as well.

As soon as Fin returned with his bourbon, one of Cairo's clansmen rang a loud bell three times. Nobody but Fin and I seemed to question what that bell meant. Jackson took my hand and led me toward the chairs that were set up in the yard. It was eerily reminiscent of an outdoor wedding.

As soon as everyone was settled in their seat, a procession of clansmen came out of the house carrying Angela's body, which was wrapped in white gauze from the top of her neck down to the tips of her feet. Like a mummy.

Not a tear was shed as they continued down the center aisle between the rows of seats and laid her on a bed of evergreen fronds on the ground at the helm of the altar. Her severed hair had been meticulously woven back in place and fanned around her face as they positioned her on the greenery. The bell began to ring again. It tolled sixteen times, and Jackson leaned closer to explain that it was one for each year that Cairo and Angela had been together.

We sat in silence for a few more minutes before Cairo emerged from the house. He was clean-shaven, barefoot, and wearing a white robe. Another group of clansmen escorted him down the aisle to a small prayer rug in front of the body where he knelt. A small fire was started beside them.

A shiver ran through me. Jackson sensed my reaction and gripped my hand, reassuring me with a look that everything would be fine. He'd prepared me somewhat for what I was about to see, leaving out the details because it was considered disrespectful to speak of the esoteric ritual. All he'd said was that the death of a Dimensional's partner required a physical separation.

Evelyn got up from her seat in the front row and approached Cairo. "Show me the bond."

Still on his knees, Cairo repositioned himself to face the crowd. The witnesses. He slipped the robe over his shoulders and let it drop to the ground around his naked body. There was a mark on his skin, a raised brand near his heart in the shape of an elaborate knot.

"What is your intention, Cairo?" she continued.

He bowed his head. "To cut the bond." The words were spoken so quietly that I almost missed what he said. Then he sucked in a mighty breath and nodded once.

Evelyn stepped aside and handed a knife to one of his clansmen. The man stepped forward, and without a moment of hesitation, he dug the knife into the mark, working the blade swiftly around its edges. Cairo fought the pain, muffling a scream as the blood ran down his abdomen and stained the white robe at his knees.

My eyes shut as a quiet gasp slipped from my mouth. Jackson squeezed my hand tighter and whispered for me to open them. We weren't just there to pay our respects. We were there to witness the severing of Cairo and Angela's union.

I opened my eyes and watched the piece of flesh fall from his chest. Evelyn pulled the blood-soaked robe off the ground and laid it on top of Angela's body while his clansman took the severed knot and tossed it into the fire.

"Done," Evelyn announced. "You are both free."

We waited for the men to escort Cairo back into the house with Angela's body in tow right behind him. Just like that, it was over. You could easily tell who was clan and who was a guest. The clan disappeared from the property before the guests even got up from their seats.

We showed ourselves out, and Fin called his driver. Ten minutes later he drove up to the house. On the ride back to town, Jackson explained that Dimensionals are bonded with a unique brand at the heart chakra when they take their vows. The ritual of cutting it from Cairo's chest was to release him. To allow him the freedom to go on living and find a new mate. An act of love. The brand had been removed from Angela's chest in a private ritual before the service, to free her spirit and prevent her from attaching to Cairo for eternity. To prevent a haunting. Everything had to be done quickly to keep her spirit from trying to hold on. That's why they left immediately after the ritual. They were on their way to the sea, to set her adrift on a burning pyre.

"A Viking burial," Fin said.

Jackson smirked. "I think the clan would take exception to that."

I gazed out the window as we drove, thinking about how lost I'd be if something happened to Jackson. And we hadn't even been together for sixteen months, let alone sixteen years like Cairo and Angela. I think the closest we'd ever come to mutilation would be a matching pair of tattoos. Not likely though.

"Is Cairo going to be okay?" I asked.

Jackson smoothed his hand over my thigh. "He will be now."

It was almost six o'clock by the time we pulled into town. Valerie Stephenson was meeting us at six thirty, so we went straight to Lillian's house. That would give me plenty of time to have that drink I was reconsidering.

"How was the service?" Lillian asked when we walked through the front door.

Why do people always ask that? *How do you think? The woman's dead.*

"It was nice," I said, erring on the side of politeness. Like Jackson said, it would be disrespectful to discuss the ritual we'd witnessed. Let Fin have his bad karma if he decided to tell her about it.

Besides, I needed that drink.

"Mind if I..." I pointed toward the bar.

"Help yourself," Lillian said.

Valerie arrived fifteen minutes early and came waltzing through the front door with a cocky grin on her face. I couldn't tell if that was a good sign or if she was intrigued by the idea of going to trial.

She dropped her briefcase in one of the wing chairs and joined me at the bar. "You folks look like you've just come from a funeral," she said, pouring herself a drink.

I snorted but decided to let it go. Before I could bring up the tender subject of our meeting, Emmaline walked into the living room with Carmen Santos at her side.

"Emmaline," I said. "I'm... glad you're here." I glanced at Carmen with a little less love, wondering why they'd dropped by just in time for our meeting.

"Shall we?" Val said. "I'll save us all a lot of time and get straight to it. It's Monday, and I'm sure we'd all like to get out of here and go home."

"That would be preferable," Fin agreed. "It's been a trying day."

My heart sank into my feet at the prospect of hearing my fate.

"You're no longer a suspect, Miss Bishop," she said. "Chatham County found someone else to harass."

My eyes shot to Jackson and then back to Val. "What do you mean? What about the DNA?"

Emmaline couldn't contain the smile edging up her face, and Carmen looked downright guilty of something.

"Why exactly are you two here?" I asked them.

"Hold on," Val said, downing the rest of her drink before grabbing her briefcase. "As usual, this is my cue to leave."

I waited until she was out the front door and then looked at every face in the room. Jackson and Fin both pleaded innocent.

So did Lillian. That left Emmaline and Carmen to explain why my attorney just walked out of the house without telling me why I was suddenly cleared of murder charges.

Carmen took the wheel. "Your DNA didn't match the blood on that scarf."

"How do you even know about that?" I glared at Emmaline for an answer.

"I'm sorry," Emmaline said with a little bit of uncharacteristic mischief in her voice. "I had to tell her. So she could help," she added, wide-eyed.

I tentatively asked the next question, praying they hadn't done something I'd be digging myself out of in the morning. "What did Carmen do?"

"That bloody scarf in the evidence room," Emmaline explained. "We switched it with a scarf covered with my blood."

I nearly fell over. Emmaline was telling me that she just incriminated herself in a murder.

"Jesus! Are you crazy? What if they trace that blood back to you? And how did you even do it?"

"It was easy as pie," Emmaline said proudly. "I just walked in there and put a little spell on everyone. At first I was so nervous I didn't know if I could go through with it. But then I just did it. It only took a minute to make the switch. Can you imagine how confused they must have been when they tested my blood? I bet they'd never seen anything like vampire blood."

I had to admit I was relieved. I was no expert on vampire blood, but I suddenly realized that they'd probably never trace that kind of blood to anyone. It probably blew their minds when they looked at it under a microscope.

"What was Valerie talking about when she said they found someone new to harass?" Fin asked.

Emmaline continued with the details of their evidence tampering. "We also left a little something else in that evidence folder. I was a little uncomfortable about doing it at first, but that detective was never going to leave you alone, Katie." Her indignant expression was rare. "I wouldn't put it past him to try to frame you."

Carmen smirked. "We left a little semen sample in the evidence folder. Guess who that belongs to?"

Fin looked a little shocked. We all did.

"Who?" I demanded, my mind racing.

"Detective Ryan," Carmen said, looking at me like I was stupid or something. "We did a little digging on him. Apparently the detective isn't as squeaky-clean as he'd like people to think. He was accused of raping a woman a couple of years back when he was still driving a patrol car. The department took all kinds of samples to clear his name. Who knows, that DNA might still be in the system." She shrugged and laughed. "If it isn't, you never know when something might come up that requires another sample."

I still couldn't believe what she and Emmaline were telling me. I was free and clear of the murder. They'd tampered with evidence that could possibly frame Detective Ryan. For what? Having an affair with Christopher Sullivan and then killing him for some reason?

She saw the look on our faces and rolled her eyes. "Look, they'll probably never trace that sample back to Ryan, but it's our ace in the hole if he doesn't back off."

"How did you get your hands on Frank Ryan's... bodily fluids?" I asked, unable to say the word.

Jackson nearly choked on his drink when I asked the obvious question.

Then I remembered her comment when I ran into her at MacPherson's Friday night. *I just took one for the team*, she'd said to me.

You little slut. How was I ever going to repay *that*?

"Trust me, Katie," she said, grinning like a fool. "I don't think Detective Ryan will be bothering you anymore."

I quietly slipped out of bed so I wouldn't wake Jackson. We both needed sleep, but I had to get to MagicInk early to take care of those supply orders I kept putting off, and I had at least three bills past due because I hadn't had time to just sit down and pay them.

With the coffee started, I grabbed Jet's bowl. It was still full. He hadn't eaten any of the food I'd given him when we got home the night before. "Jet?" I called. Come to think of it, I didn't remember him greeting us at the door either, and we were too tired to notice.

"Oh no," I groaned, feeling guilty for not paying attention, and getting more alarmed by the second when he didn't come walking into the kitchen after I called his name. I searched the living room, under the couch, and on the bookcase where he liked to lounge.

There was no sign of Jet anywhere.

Just when I was about to have a full-blown panic attack and start searching the neighborhood, I heard a scratching sound coming from the patio door. He was outside looking in.

"How did you get outside?" I opened the door to let him in.

As I slid the door shut, I noticed the latch. The flimsy lever that locked the door had been replaced. In fact, the whole door was new.

"Jackson!" I yelled across the room.

He came running down the hall naked, half-asleep, and startled by the tone of my voice.

"Did you do this?" I asked, pointing at the door.

"Yeah," he replied in a gruff voice. "I had it installed while we were gone yesterday."

"You gave a complete stranger the key to my house to install that door?" It was a thoughtful gesture, but not at the expense of my belongings and my cat.

"Of course not," he said, heading for the coffeepot. "I know the guy, and Sugar was here. It was supposed to be a surprise."

It was a surprise all right. And now I felt like an ass. "You bought me a door?"

He nodded and poured us both a cup. "You were never gonna talk to that landlord of yours, so I took care of it."

I'd known women who'd gotten some pretty weird gifts from their husbands and boyfriends: lawn mowers, hedge trimmers. But a door was a first. I had to admit, his heart and head were in the right place.

I took the cup of coffee he offered me and gave him a kiss. "Thank you. But tell your guy he let my cat slip out. Jet slept outside last night. If anything had happened to him—" I didn't even want to think about it.

He glanced at Jet and his jaw tightened. "Yeah, I'll mention it to him."

"Well, don't kill the guy over it. Just... scold him."

I took a couple of sips of my coffee and headed for the shower. "Emmaline's expecting me in half an hour."

THE NIGHT BEFORE, Emmaline had invited me to stop by her place for breakfast. I couldn't pass up an offer to see what a vampire witch would whip up in her kitchen. Eggs? Bacon? Eye of newt with a little blood sausage on the side?

She was harvesting something from the side garden when I pulled up to her house. It was a quaint cottage on Lillian's large estate, complete with gardens on every side and a small pond that bordered the backyard.

"I love the smell of rosemary," she said, threading her fingers through it and smelling the oil it left on her skin.

"Yeah. It's one of my favorites too."

She handed the bundle of herbs to me and walked me into the house. "I hope you like french toast, but I have bagels for backup."

I liked French anything.

"I'll have both," I said, only half joking. I was ravenous enough to eat both.

She led me to the back patio where she'd set up our breakfast. It was the perfect late-summer morning for dining in the garden, and I felt more content in that moment than I had for weeks—which usually meant that trouble was on the horizon.

She lifted a dome off the platter of french toast and poured me a cup of coffee from the decanter. "This thing keeps it nice and warm."

We ate our breakfast and chatted about normal things. Not a single word about the business of keeping the city safe from demons or uninvited shifters.

When we were done, I reached into my bag and pulled out the unused vial of blood she'd given me to fortify the dragon. "I wanted to give this back," I said, holding it out to her. "Turns out my dragon didn't need it after all, and it doesn't feel right to keep it. Makes me feel like some kind of vampire-blood junkie." I snorted. "No offense."

She looked at the vial and then held her hand up to refuse it.

"No. You need to keep it. But it's nice that the dragon has finally found its place, and it does seem like it's growing stronger. I can feel it." Emmaline had spotted my dragon from a mile away the day I met her—before anyone told her about it. She had that gift. "There will be days when it needs a little boost," she continued. "We all do now and then."

She excused herself and went back inside the house. When she came back out, she was holding a small case. It looked like a vintage cigarette case, only a little bigger.

"I want you to have this." She sat back down and held it out to me with a nervous smile.

I took it from her hand and examined it. It was gold with a crimson-enameled cover. Looked pretty expensive. "This isn't real gold, is it?"

She nodded.

"What is it?" My curiosity won, and I lifted the lid before she could answer. Inside were six thin vials of blood—her blood. "Emmaline?" I cocked my head and waited for her to explain.

"The Crossroads Society needs you. Blackthorn Grove needs you. We all need you, Katie. I'd never forgive myself if you needed a little blood and I wasn't there to give it to you. Besides, I have plenty. Just make sure you keep it in the freezer so it stays potent."

Looking at the beautiful case and its contents, I supposed she had a point. I just needed to think of it as another tool in my arsenal. "I'll take the blood, but I can't accept this," I said, nodding toward the solid-gold case that had to be worth a small fortune.

"It's not just a fancy case," she replied, firming up her brow. "It's kind of like a miniature safe. You're the only person who can open it. Well, I can because I'm the donor and the one who put the wards on it. But no one else can."

Holding it up to the rising sun, I studied the glimmering case from a couple of different angles. "Humph. Fort Knox in a pretty little package."

"People will go to desperate lengths to get their hands on vampire blood," she warned. "I wouldn't mention to anyone that you have it in your freezer."

I was beginning to appreciate that new door now that I was about to have the equivalent of heroin stashed in my house.

"You're a good friend, Emmaline. A real badass," I added with a smirk.

She smiled brightly but quickly reverted back to the Gothic girl with the birdlike demeanor. "I'm no one, Katie."

I looked at her and shook my head. "You don't have a clue how special you are, do you?"

Her pale skin flushed from the compliment and then faded.

"Emmaline, you are a national treasure."

She flicked her eyes up to mine. "No, Katie. You're the treasure."

READ KATIE BISHOP'S BACKSTORY TODAY!

Want to know more about Katie? Read THE FITHEACH TRILOGY and find out where it all began.

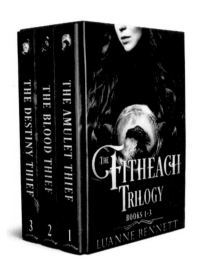

THANK YOU TO MY READERS

A book means nothing without someone to read it. Thank you for that. I hope you'll consider taking a few minutes to leave a brief review, even if it's just a sentence or two. Feedback is always appreciated and vital for authors.

ACKNOWLEDGMENTS

This book suffered a bit of an identity crisis before finally culminating into what it is today. A big thank you to my early readers who helped me see the way.

My deepest gratitude to David and Sharon and anyone else who has stuck with me since the beginning. Equal gratitude goes to my advance readers for their time and talent. I hope you all stick around for the next book.

Finally, a huge thank you to Anne Victory for squeezing me in for some great editing. Your feedback has been enlightening!

ABOUT THE AUTHOR

LUANNE BENNETT is an author of fantasy and the supernatural. Born in Chicago, she lives in Georgia these days where she writes full time and doesn't miss a thing about the cubicles and conference rooms of her old life. When she isn't writing or dreaming up new stories, she's usually cooking or tending a herd of felines.

I love to hear from readers. Contact me at:
www.luannebennett.com
books@luannebennett.com
facebook.com/LuanneBennettBooks

Made in United States
North Haven, CT
10 July 2022

21154117R20171